GREETINGS FROM JAMAICA,
WISH YOU WERE QUEER

MARI SANGIOVANNI

Bywater
BOOKS
Ann Arbor
2007

Acknowledgments

Despite the fact this book is not *A Tale of Two Cities* and more like *A Tale of Two Titties*, I nevertheless dedicate all the clean parts to my mom, dad, sister and two brothers. They inspired all the love and the fun, with absolutely none of the drama. Also, to my lovely sister-in-laws who found the astounding courage to marry into our family.

Thank you to Kelly Smith for her editing and advice: "Take the crazy Italian family on vacation, and let them run amok!" and to Marianne K. Martin for her encouragement.

Thank you also to the "Jamaica Girls" for letting Kim and I crash their party; and most importantly, thanks to Kim for my life.

Chapter One

Dead Relations & Relationships

I had high hopes of being traumatized when my parents announced they were getting a divorce. I was a frequently bored eleven-year-old, and since we three kids had lived within the cyclone of their marriage our entire lives, their news was not at all surprising. Because of this, my freshly fermenting hormones latched onto the impending event as a vehicle for adventure and self-pity, and, with any luck, perhaps even a dramatic lesson in survival tactics, if our family became as destitute as I planned. I finally had a reason to spend my saved allowance money on the dirty yellow military survival manual I been eyeballing in the thrift store.

What I never once imagined was how sadly mundane the outcome would be. I was too busy joyously festering over what would happen to my family financially, and quickly conjured up visions of Mom and us kids taking up residence in the rusted Pontiac in the field across from Margaret Sullivan's house. We would eventually have to wear clothes made from animal skins, or perhaps from the more readily available grocery store boxes, since squirrels were about the only animals around, and I would take a stand against hunting neighborhood pets, no matter how cold it got in that Pontiac. I pictured us cutting berries from thorny branches using Indian arrowheads we made from a broken slate countertop my older sister Lisa and I had found discarded in the woods. Our fatherless family would endure bitter cold nights but the field grass would be warm in the morning sun and we would spend our days crushing out grass nests by rolling and crawling in a circle, like dogs do. Of course, there would be no school for us since the bulk of the day would have to be spent chewing on hay just to get the bare minimum amount of nutrition we needed for survival.

I figured my mother would try sending us to school for the first week of the separation, since she was very big on school. (Mom insisted on the 3-B rule if you wanted to stay at home. She needed to see Blood, Bone, or Barf.) I figured her insistence wouldn't last long, however, since Riley Elementary School had a very strict policy about chewing in class, and I guessed within days of our separation from Dad, our newfound poverty would soon be the cause of amending the no-gum policy to also include no hay chewing. With chewing hay being banished from the classroom, this would leave only lunch and recess periods for chewing, which, I hoped, was not enough time to extract all of the vitamins needed for daily survival. It was hay, after all. So, I planned for the no-school thing to be the first enormous plus of the divorce.

I imagined that experimental first week of trying to stay in school would be very hard on us kids, taking the three of us hours to walk home on spindly legs which had become scrawny from lack of proper nutrition. We might soon get as bad as little Alex Fishburne, who, I heard a teacher once say, was born in a wheelchair. Why a mother would decide to give birth to her son directly into a wheelchair, I could never understand. Did she know in advance he would need it, I wondered, or was it the act of being born into a wheelchair that made him bent and crooked the way he was? Since I was expecting our own legs to wither away to bare twigs, I decided that a chair with wheels might end up being quite handy, so I would consider asking for one from Santa, if we were all still alive come Christmas.

Always in my dreams, I had to reduce my older sister Lisa to a younger sibling so the fantasy of me finally taking charge would seem somewhat realistic. Lisa was only two years older than me,

2

but such a dominant figure in my life that not only did I have to shrink her in size and age, but sometimes I would split her in two so that she was a set of twin toddlers. I named them the Two Lisas, or sometimes, Lisa and Theresa. I simply could not imagine all of her personality fitting into one shrunken body, smaller than my own. This seemed to work, and in all of my fantasies I took charge of the Two Lisas and our younger brother, Vince, as well. By the first Thursday of the separation (things always seemed to take until Thursday to really happen, didn't they?) I imagined the Two Lisas and Vince would grow so weak that they were forced to crawl like infants to school. I, however, being elevated to the oldest in my fantasy, was not only strong enough to walk, but also carried my withered-limbed siblings effortlessly on my back.

Mom and Dad had fought for as long as my sister, brother, and I could remember, and at thirteen, eleven, and seven, my siblings and I had already logged countless hours in secret meetings under our bed covers, analyzing why on earth they stayed together if they argued so much. My brother was the baby, so it scared him when Lisa and I talked about the inevitable divorce. But for my sister and me, it was our first taste of drama, and it was unfolding right under our own roof.

The separation caught me off guard me in only two ways: First was the realization that Mom had been the major money-earner in the family, and second, the realization that she had pretended for thirteen years (and very well, too) that she hadn't been. Maybe this was why Dad moved barely a thing when he packed up one Sunday afternoon while Mom distracted us by taking us to play at our cousin's house. I came back home just a few hours later, disappointed to find that Dad had cleared out, leaving barely a ripple of evidence of his desertion behind.

I combed the house, trying to find at least one devastating clue of him being torn from our lives. I had spent the entire drive back from my cousin's house imagining the gutted house he would leave us: wires dangling from the ceiling where the

3

fixtures once hung, the door from the refrigerator removed from its very hinges, the wallpaper roughly peeled from the bedroom walls ... the tiniest breadcrumb stolen from the fireplace like the Grinch had from the tiny mouse. However, going from room to undisturbed room only served to mount disappointment once again.

Until I saw it. There, in the corner of the living room next to my dad's chair (which apparently wasn't his, after all), was the evidence of a crushed ring on the carpet where Dad's reading lamp used to be. I tried a gasp, but since I had never actually heard someone gasp and only seen the word "gasp" written in books, I failed miserably at it and my Mom said, "Excuse you."

I then tried sinking to my knees, concentrating on not blinking so my eyes would sting enough to possibly get watery and cry (a trick I eventually perfected in my teen years in community theater) but still, nothing happened. I tried picturing myself from an aerial view: the Devastated Child crying on her knees as the six-inch vacant area of carpet grew and loomed like a circular grave in front of me ... My daddy was gone (although I never called him Daddy, not even once) ... Daddy ... Oh, Daddy ... Damn, I had blinked; the stinging in my eyes instantly soothed and hopes of any tears were dashed ... leaving me merely a Kneeling Child ... not quite the effect I was going for. So I casually crawled over to the television before anyone noticed me.

Lisa waited just long enough to make me think I had bailed on the dramatic scene in time before being discovered. "Are you done being an idiot?" she said, never looking away from the Brady Bunch. I didn't think I should answer her, since I had no idea if I was done.

Over the next few weeks I would try manufacturing different visuals. I imagined my dad in a tiny, four-wall prison-cell apartment, outfitted only with a filthy toilet (with no lid) directly in the center of the one room, and of course the dingy brass reading lamp (though it had been shiny at our house) as his only furniture. Unfortunately, I had to let that thought go when we went to visit him and found he had rented a rather comfortable apartment that came fully furnished, near the tool-making shop where he worked.

The toilet was where it should have been (and, I noticed, with a perfectly good lid) in a small but clean bathroom with a stand-up shower and a fancy dark green sink with faux marble wisps of white running through it. I made one last failed attempt to feel some sort of tragedy about the scene by clinging to the lamp as if it had been a long lost puppy, until Lisa spanked the back of my head to make me let go of it, which I did. Meanwhile, my brother Vince was happily playing in the room Dad had arranged for us, enthralled with the promise of future bunk beds if Dad got his expected pay raise that year.

I had begun to fear nothing about this separation or impending divorce would ever impress me, until one night over dinner Mom informed us that we would be selling the house, and for a moment I was elated by the idea that at last we were going desperately broke. Maybe the loss of the brass lamp had eventually taken its toll on our family finances and we were spiraling into a forever-widening fissure of debt ... But I couldn't trick myself into being afraid for very long, since we had lived to see Christmas and, in fact, the presents seemed more plentiful than usual, with no wheelchairs needed. It turned out that Mom's little "side accounting business" had been a little more than that, and we were doing just fine. But still, she was planning to sell the house ... that had to mean something, didn't it?

Dad started coming over for dinner just about every night to fix things around the house so it would sell at a higher price. Eventually, our house did get sold, but when it did, we all moved into the bigger house, including Dad. I continued to pretend the rusted Pontiac was just days away from becoming my bedroom; but when more months passed and everything went back to normal, I had to eventually accept that I would live no more of an extraordinary life than anyone else in my school. I still had two parents at home, Oreos, canned soup and saltines instead of hay in the cupboard, and a gray Buick in the driveway that had nary a rust spot.

I had noticed Dad's grumpiness about Mom's side business long before he had moved out, but it was Lisa who informed me it had been the main reason for their fighting. Lisa was convinced Dad resented Mom's business since she made more money than he did at his job, and he had begun pressuring her to sell it. When she wouldn't, he moved out, assuming that Mom would not last long on her own. Mom had done just fine, and added six new clients to make up for the drop in income. That meant Dad was faced with still paying for half of the old house plus an apartment he could barely afford.

Despite her show of strength, Mom couldn't admit her marriage might be falling apart. She had tried to keep Dad's moving out a secret from the rest of the Santora family for weeks, and when it finally leaked, they instantly called a family meeting to get all the details. Mom didn't cave. She insisted to all of them that Sal, her husband, was just being stubborn and would be back soon. She had been right and Dad slipped back into our lives as quietly as he left, lamp and all.

Things were different when Dad came back, and for a while Mom and Dad treated each other so kindly that it made me nervous; and it made Lisa angry. She said they looked utterly ridiculous being so polite to each other and kissing hello right in front of us kids. I had never heard the phrase "utterly ridiculous" before, and commenced using it liberally ("Why, I'm afraid this cartoon is utterly ridiculous"), until Lisa threw a brown Lego pirate ship at my head to make me stop saying it. Specifically, what got my attention was the doubloon-filled treasure chest, which broke apart from the starboard deck, as it made direct contact with my face.

Vince was happy Dad was back, and basked in the new, albeit short-lived, "Family TV Nights" and curled himself deeply between Mom and Dad like a stowaway puppy on a first date. I was happy for Vince, since he was the youngest and had been

6

worried about Dad moving out. Lisa was not as good at comforting him as I was and would yell at him to stop whining whenever he voiced his fears about our parents. It was the beginning of a lifelong protectiveness I felt for him that he didn't really require, but to my knowledge it was the only thing I was better at than Lisa, so I would not give it up. Mom and Dad's trials ingrained another pattern I carried into my adulthood as well; I thought, if Mom and Dad could keep a marriage together with their polar opposite personalities, anyone could, if only they made the slightest effort. And this was what kept me with Jessica for so much longer than I should have stayed.

As I learned from my parents, one of the major differences between a new relationship and an old one is the dwindling politeness. Over time, you stop asking if the person is all right every time you hear a thud come from the shower. Your years together cause you to assume that it's simply the soap slipping from their hands, and so you simply stop asking. Anyway, Jess and I had long since passed the soap-checking stage, so I ignored the second thud I heard and stood, arms crossed, waiting silently at the bathroom door.

"What took you so long?" I yelled, when I heard the water finally shut off.

Jess hissed back behind the door, "Give me a God-damned break."

"You knew I had to take a shower and be out of here by two," I said.

"Since when I have you been concerned about being on time for anything having to do with your grandmother?"

"Jess, for Christ sakes, it's her funeral!" I snapped back.

"So, she won't know the difference if you're late. Besides, wouldn't you rather go celebrate the occasion?"

Jessica is a bitch, but what I hate most about her is that she knows me too well. Your enemy should never know you that well.

7

"Excuse me," Jessica mumbled as she passed me in the doorway. It wasn't a polite "excuse me," it was the get-the-hell-out-of-my-way variety.

I vaguely noticed she was nude and thought how remarkable it was to look at her body and not feel anything except its separateness from me. Six years ago, I felt I knew her body better than my own, and I thought she would always stay beautiful to me. Now, as she walked away from me, all I could see was a line of familiar flesh shifting past, and felt I was not close enough to her to be entitled to such a personal sight. Most times these days Jess and I moved like a well-oiled machine, with gears pushing or pulling in the opposite direction of two people who didn't care to be, even accidentally, close to each other. It wasn't the loss of touching her that bothered me, but rather the extra veering of an elbow or shoulder as we passed each other to ensure there wouldn't be any contact. It wasn't even strange anymore that we didn't kiss hello after not seeing each other all day, but only strange if I noticed it.

Jessica was a beautiful woman. At rare times like this when I would stand back from the disaster that had become our relationship, and view her as a stranger, I could see a glimpse of the woman I had originally fallen in love with. Her striking physical beauty had wrongly convinced me that I would never be able to look at her and not love and want her, regardless of her faults, of which there were many. What an amazing thing it would be to have a mate who was so powerfully attractive, I had thought, and assumed it would wash over everything. I was wrong when I assumed I would be incapable of staying angry with someone so beautiful, and I would always be able to forgive her for anything she might do. Around the same time I discovered that forgiving was not my strong suit, I also found that honesty was not Jessica's.

Now I had to remind myself of her beauty. I was no more aware of her beauty than I was of the Tiffany lamp I yearned for so desperately, and now passed by without so much as a glance. The lamp had become merely a detail in the room. Buying a three-hundred-dollar lamp had not changed my life as I hoped it would ... Jessica had not changed it either.

The apathy I felt for my relationship had grown, along with her dishonesty, into disgust. I came to realize I was staying with Jessica only because I could not afford the condo on my own, nor weekly habits like Chinese take-out on Thursday nights. I don't know why she stayed with me, but I suspected it was for much the same reasons. My ego was not so bloated to think it was because she couldn't find anyone else. She literally could, as the saying goes, have anyone she wanted, and I knew she often did. I purposely took no notice of it after the first time I had caught her.

It was an unspoken and even exchange; in return for my disinterest in her trivial affairs (there was always a new "friend" calling the house), she ignored the fact I had displaced all my passion for her into something else ... although she didn't realize it was for writing. It was understandable for her to ignore my love for something so pie-in-the-sky, since I had decided one morning over coffee (alone) to give up my ridiculous childhood dream of becoming a novelist, and instead pursue something a bit more practical ... like screenplay writing. I secretly took a weekend screenwriting seminar in Boston, telling Jessica, and even my brother Vince, that it was a trip to visit an old Riley Elementary School friend. Jessica asked no questions, and I didn't ask her what she would be doing with her free weekend, since I already knew damn well what she would be doing.

The screenwriting course promised a lot for the steep two-day admission price, but I remained hopeful even after I found that the teacher's first order of business was to have his young, blond assistant set up a rickety card table in the front of the class to display the books, tapes and pens he had for sale. Everything, for a limited time of course, was available at a special seminar price. He was especially proud of the pens. Made in China and constructed of a metal so thin that pressing on it could dent the belly of the pen, they were emblazoned across the barrel, "LIGHTING

PEN." The instructor offered with much enthusiasm, "They have a light built right inside so you can jot a note down in the middle of the night if you wake up with a brilliant idea for a screenplay." So that's how it was done, I thought. There was a stampede to the card table. I elbowed past the skinny girl ahead of me and grabbed four of the batteries-not-included pens. I didn't regret buying four of them since it turned out to be the best thing I got out of the seminar, as the rest of his advice was limited to vaguely inspiring or impossible little nuggets like: "You need a clear beginning, middle and end," and "Think Positive." Best of all was his most critical piece of advice, "Move to California." Despite the useless class, Jessica had no idea that it was only the faintest sense of financial reality that kept me from doing just that.

I envied my grandmother tonight. She still had to attend the funeral, since it was her own, but she wouldn't have to mill about with the loved ones left behind, desperately trying to think of something good to say about her. Her role was easy ... she wouldn't have to pretend the family would be better off without her bitter personality thrown into the mix. She didn't even have to dress herself.

The highlight of Grandma's funeral was Aunt Aggie's failed attempt to do a triple gainer into Grandma's grave. Threatening to toss oneself into the grave of a loved one is the Italian way of paying your ultimate respect at a funeral. As I fantasized about holding up an 8.5 from the USA judge, the largest of our male relatives moved to restrain Aunt Aggie. There wasn't the slightest look of surprise on the funeral-goers' faces—after all, they knew it would happen; it was just a matter of when. My father stood in the background trying to make my brother Vince and me crack up by imitating fast shoveling motions. My father and his sister Aggie did not get along famously to say the least, and if he had access to a shovel, and she had landed in the hole, he may have used it.

Only after Aunt Aggie's flailing arms were pinned against her black housecoat, and her thick legs (with panty hose rolled like the skin of a sausage) were stalled at the very edge of Grandma's grave, did she dramatically give herself up. I wondered what would happen if her foot had gotten snagged or if she neglected to give the decibel-cracking warning wail before plunging forward. We were all fairly confident Aggie wasn't all that devastated, since before her mother died, she hadn't even spoken to her for over five years.

After a sufficient amount of woeful muttering had been displayed, the sea of black dispersed and people scattered off to their cars like a disorganized flock of crows to their nests, waving their arms as they talked (Italians really do talk with their hands). I watched Aggie being helped to her car. On public occasions such as this, she chose to move about with a walker, not because of arthritis as she claimed, but because of pasta. She ate too much, and was too heavy to walk more than a short distance unassisted. Everyone knew, however, she could have found the strength to hurdle Grandma's grave if an inheritance was on the other side. It was, in fact, the knowledge that she may never see a dime that may have encouraged her to attempt the jump.

"Marie ... hey, Mare!" It was my brother bounding to catch me, his long dark hair flying behind him.

"Hey, Vince. I was noticing you didn't cut your hair in honor of Grandma's funeral," I said, as he slipped his arm around my waist.

"And judging by those comfy shoes, you didn't go straight, so the Embarrass-Mom-Contest continues," he grinned. "So," he whispered as he leaned closer, "I guess Dad was wrong when he said his mom would outlive us all. Where's Jess?"

"Last I checked, at home. Who knows by now."

Vince frowned, his thick, dark eyebrows almost touching together.

"Uh-oh, I wasn't going to ask."

I noticed I didn't feel the slightest urge to defend her like I used

11

to. This was just as well, since Vince never let me get away with making excuses for her before.

"Being alone would be better than what you're doing," he said as he walked me to my car. "Why don't you leave her?"

"I don't know ... I guess because she's beautiful," I said stupidly. But as I said it, I realized I didn't believe even that anymore.

"What good is that when you hate each other? Actually, I was sort of hoping that she would come today. It's so much fun to watch all the guys try and hit on her," he said laughing, as he flipped the hair away from his face.

"It's never been quite as much fun for me, I assure you. Besides, I don't hate her. I just ... we don't love each other anymore."

"So why stay? The condo? You should never stay in a relationship for good closet space," he said, giving me a playful squeeze, "especially when you don't spend any time in the closet." He paused a moment and said, "I'm serious, though, Mare, you should leave her."

He was serious. I could tell because it was one of those rare moments when a smirking grin was absent from his face.

"You don't even care enough to hate her anymore," he said, as we reached my car.

Unfortunately, this was one of the not-so-rare moments when I felt junior to my younger brother. I never figured out what the hell I did with the four years I had over him when I should have been maturing. He caught up to me around age twenty, and the gap seemed to grow wider, with him pulling further in the lead each year.

"Well, let's go fulfill our duty as relatives to the deceased," Vince said as he opened the door for me.

"You mean eating sausage and pepper sandwiches till we puke?" I asked.

"Exactly," he said. He leaned against the door and muttered, "Who would have guessed there were this many Italians in friggin' Connecticut?" We both watched as the cars filed past.

"You know, Mare, you could come with me rather than taking separate cars ..." He winked at me, knowing my refusal to get in a car with him, especially on a short trip. Vince liked to amuse himself by seeing if he could get home without once touching the brake pedal. This was not a fun game from the passenger seat.

"Thanks anyway, Vince, but I'm not ready to join Gram just yet. Besides, I need a nice, boring ride before facing our relatives."

He faked an expression of concern as he poked his head through the window. "Looking back on the ceremony, I should never have told Aunt Aggie that Gram once threatened to be buried with all of her money ... maybe she wouldn't have tried to jump for it."

I laughed at him. "It's not going to be the same without Gram around to make the family events run less smoothly."

"You know Marie, I've always been more than a little jealous about how you and Gram used to get along ..."

"Yeah, I know. She always hated me best."

Chapter Two

Silly Stages, Suspicious Siblings & Stealing Scraps

Dad was leaning against the kitchen wall thoroughly enjoying what looked to be an egg and green bell pepper sandwich. He periodically nodded in annoyance to the people who interrupted his dinner to offer condolences about his mother.

"Mmm. Thanks," he grumbled, between dipping his sandwich first in a tiny tartar sauce cup filled with white vinegar, then in tomato sauce.

"Hi Dad, how's the food?" I asked.

"Mmm. Thanks," he said. "Can you believe they forgot the fucking meatballs?"

"It's good to see your appetite hasn't suffered through all of this," I said.

We both knew better than to giggle ... not out of respect for the deceased, but because Mom had warned us both not to embarrass her today. For Dad, that meant keeping the swearing to a minimum, and for me, it meant not bringing, or bringing up, Jessica.

"Vince should have cut his God-damned hair," Dad said, the eggs muffling his voice.

"His hair is exactly like mine," I said.

"Well, it looks fine on you, but it's ridiculous on him. For Christ sake, when will he grow out of his hippie stage?"

"People don't really use that word anymore, Dad."

"Stage?"

"No, Dad, 'hippie.'"

"Well whatever. Not growing out of stages seems to be a family trait." Dad didn't look at me when he said it, but I knew that one was for me. He managed to elbow me to make sure I got the joke while he effortlessly scooped a stray piece of egg off his plate with the last of his bread. This was Dad's way of handling my unconventional choice in lifestyle. It was "Don't Ask, Don't Tell," Italian style, more commonly known as: Busting Balls.

"Yeah, well I hear you still haven't grown out of your hippie stage of keeping those funny-looking plants in your garden."

Dad grew his own pot and justified it by saying, "How else could I be sure the stuff didn't have any 'bad' drugs in it?" He truly was the hippie he teased Vince about being. Dad may have cut, or more accurately, lost most of his hair, but the hippie gene in him still believed there was no harm in a little recreational marijuana. His favorite joke was, "Sure, I talk to my adult kids about drugs ... I say, hey kids, do you need any drugs?" Mom would slug him in the shoulder while he guffawed at his own comedic genius.

"Don't be disrespectful to your father while he's in mourning," Dad said.

"Don't talk with your mouth full," I answered.

This was how most of our conversations went, although sometimes they were just louder discussions of the same subjects. If Vince cut his hair and I got myself a husband, maybe visits home would be more peaceful, though a lot less entertaining. Vince and I decided long ago the trade-off wasn't worth it, so we opted to keep his long hair and my questionable lifestyle, while our sister Lisa had opted to simply live out of state.

While Dad often pretended not to notice my relationship, he was always polite to Jessica. Both Dad and Mom seemed to have an unspoken agreement with me, although I can't remember the day we actually sat down to agree on the terms.

"Hi Marie," Mom said from behind me, and I whirled around as if she had been reading my thoughts. "How are you two doing?

15

Marie, can I get you anything? Sal, how about you ... a Coke? Some wine? I just hope we have enough of everything ..." Mom was doing her imitation of a flight attendant again, which was usual when company was around. She didn't necessarily want to serve you anything; she just needed to ask.

"Marie ..." Mom asked, making an exaggerated puzzled look as she scanned the room, "Where's Jessica?"

Mom was laying on the "too bad she could not make it" sound in her voice just a little too thick, so I bit my lower lip to trap my sarcastic tongue. Mom was famous for this one. She had gone out of her way over the phone to say that the ceremony would be "family only" and "it would be very tight at the house" and a dozen other comments which clearly meant that Jessica was not welcome, not that Jess would have come anyway. Jess hadn't attended a family function in well over a year. I resisted the powerful urge to tell Mom that Jess was in the car changing into her black leather funeral outfit and would be in momentarily.

"She's at home, Mom."

"Oh, it's too bad she couldn't come ... we always have room for one more," she chirped, making it sound like Jess was missing out on a family trip to the beach.

"Nice dress, Mom," I said. I wasn't being sarcastic. Mom always looked nice. In some ways, she reminded me of Jess: attractive, polite, and very accommodating in a social setting ... if things were going according to her plan. I watched Mom studying Dad's sister Aggie from across the room. She would never mention it out loud, but I could see her calculating the fashion faux pas. She winced at Aggie's over-dyed black helmet of hair and outfit contrasting with the wide expanse of white flesh, dangling like pizza dough from her sleeveless housecoat. Aunt Aggie's paleness and pronounced dark circles under her eyes (Vince called them "Elvis's mom's eyes") were worse than I remembered, possibly due to age, or more likely, due to lack of sleep worrying about the division of her deceased mother's money. By contrast, Dad looked like he didn't have a care in the world.

"You should go over to say hello since it's been a while since you've seen your aunt Aggie. She looks good, don't you think?" Mom asked, not really expecting an answer.

Dad cleared his throat, a signal for me not to let Mom get away with that one.

"She looks a lot like Grandma," I said.

"Well, she was her mother," Mom answered.

"No, I meant she looks dead."

Dad sputtered a laugh until Mom silenced him with an icy glare. While growing up, Vince, Lisa, and I never needed spanking, because that look was enough to inspire fear from the very soles of our Keds.

"I just hope there's enough food," Mom said before walking away.

There was *always* enough food, and Dad had already filled his limp paper plate again. I watched as he piled three sausages on one side of the sauce-stained plate. As Dad sauntered off to get himself a drink, I watched the paper plate sag to the point of appearing like a death-defying magic trick. It *was* death defying, since Mom would kill him if he made a mess.

"Don't worry," Vince said coming up to me, "he won't drop anything. Old school Italians never waste food."

"He and Mom will never change," I laughed. "You know, not that it matters much anymore, but Mom still doesn't accept Jess. She's not even willing—"

"Ahhhhh! Speaking of wills ..." Vince whispered, "You were specifically asked to be there. You are going, I hope?"

"No way. I'd prefer not to be there when Grandma gets her parting words in. It would be just like her to start a fight I can't finish."

"Aren't you the least bit curious as to why, out of all of us grandkids, she specified that *you* be there?"

"More like uneasy," I said, sitting down. Vince plopped down next to me, smelling of Coors beer mixed with Brut.

Vince continued, "I think you're crazy ... she could be leaving

17

you all her loot. Especially since Aunt Aggie has as much of a chance of getting a penny as a snot surviving a sneeze."

"That's a pretty visual, Vince, but I think you're wrong. She may not have spoken to Aggie for years, but Dad's latest fight with Gram only lasted about six months, and that's a personal best for Dad. Mom said Grandma actually said hello to Dad when he visited her in the hospital last week. Besides, I know Grandma, and if she singled me out, it's only so she can embarrass me."

Vince leaned in closer. "Just you remember your little brother when Gram gets her revenge on Aggie and Dad by leaving everything to the black sheep of the Santora family."

"Don't worry, Vin. If that happens, you and Lisa will get a third of everything I do ... but remember, a third of nothing is nothing."

Jess had not left the porch light on for me, probably on purpose. I was mildly relieved when I rolled into the driveway and found only one car. This meant I would be spared standing there like an idiot while she introduced me to some new friend she invited over for dinner. Several months ago, she brought home an undernourished blond woman. She stood nodding and smiling in agreement as Jess did all the explaining, as if they had worked it all out beforehand so they would not step on each other's lines. Jessica claimed they were collaborating on a project for work as the woman nodded vigorously, attempting to smooth her disheveled hair.

"Let's not pretend I'm stupid in front of your friend, all right Jessica?"

"OK," Jess had answered, quietly defeated. The blond looked at Jessica, then back at me. Her smile had suddenly wavered, and now she looked upon me as a competitor. Realizing it was all out in the open, she seemed both threatened and a bit disappointed. I also picked up on a flint of anger directed towards Jess, who had no doubt told her I wouldn't be suspicious, and who now had been forced to treat me with a tiny shred of respect.

I decided I owed it to myself to ruin her evening, so I said, "The last two were much better looking, Jessica. The available crowd must be thinning." She hadn't dared to bring another one around since that night, but out of habit, I still looked for a second car each time I came home.

Jess was in the living room watching television as I came in.

"How did it go?" Jess asked without looking up.

I didn't answer since I knew better than to think she was interested.

"Mom asked for you," I finally said.

"I'll bet she did."

I went to my bedroom, which had become my sanctuary away from Jess on the rare evenings she stayed home. We probably would have had separate bedrooms a long time ago except the spare bedroom had been used as a dumping ground for books and clothes. When we finally cleared it out and made the separation of a corridor between us, the sadness I had dreaded feeling never came. My bedroom became a place I could go to be alone with my first serious writing project, and it was the privacy of the space that gave me the courage to finally write. I had kept the screenplay I was working on a secret from everyone, even Vince. I had completed the final stage of acting the third grade teacher who had it in for her worst student, seeking revenge with a red pen as I made my last edits. I had been ruthless with the editing, tweaking, and re-tweaking until I felt it read smoothly from scene to scene.

The first draft had finally been completed and I was fairly proud of the way it was shaping up, especially the sex scenes. I had actually written those scenes first (this is what happens when you haven't had sex ... specifically, with another person in the room, in over six months). Sadly, the storyline had not come together, quite literally, as easily as my main characters had. It took a long time to work out a plot which would allow an opportunity to accommodate so much sex, since I was reluctant to cut a single scene, but I finally was pleased with the work. I gave some of the credit to my LIGHTING PEN, which I kept by my

19

bedside table for those moments of inspiration my seminar teacher assured us would come while we slept. They hadn't come quite the way he had promised, but several times the LIGHTING PEN had meant I could jot down ideas born from insomnia without Jess witnessing the light flick on and off from across the hall.

The most difficult part of the whole project had been choosing the actress I wanted to play the lead character. The narrowing-down process had taken several months, since I was rather finicky about actresses. The wrong choice for the starring role had ruined many movies for me, and I was not about to have that be the downfall of my first movie. I had finally culled the list down to just three actresses when Vince caught me in the middle of a weekend movie marathon while Jess was out of town. I had celebrity magazines and printouts of Internet clippings spread out all over the living room floor, with a short stack of three photos remaining in the KEEP pile, consisting of Mimi Rogers, Kate Mulgrew and Lorn Elaine. At the moment my doorbell rang, Kate Mulgrew had just gotten knocked out of the running since I couldn't find any pictures of her in anything other than her Star Trek Voyager costume, and it was the repetition of the red and black jumpsuit with shiny Comlink badge that eventually kicked her to the curb. There were runner-up actresses torn from magazines and shreds of unwanted scraps and articles all over the carpet, and I made a half-hearted attempt to kick some of them into a spilled trash can. I had mistakenly thought Vince was the pizza guy, or I would have cleaned up the evidence better, but instead, I just stacked the remaining clippings into one pile, with Lorn Elaine placed on top, before answering the door.

When Vince scanned the mess on the floor he gave me a puzzled look as if he was unsure if he should laugh or call for help. He looked from the floor to the movie on the TV, both which prominently displayed Lorn Elaine. I panicked and blurted a fake confession rather than reveal my writing project to him: "So, I'm obsessed with an actress," I said, pretending to be embarrassed, which was easy, since I was. "It isn't a crime to be a fan," I said, and I was pretty sure it wasn't.

"No, in the beginning it never is," he said, and then threatened to tell our sister and Mom and Dad just for fun. It didn't matter that I was over thirty; siblings always revert back in time when there's an opportunity to have fun torturing each other.

Since I didn't want Lisa, and more so Mom and Dad, to think I was obsessed with an actress, I was forced to counter-threaten Vince. I told him I would tell about all the times he had stolen the neighbor's garbage when he was eleven. He had become convinced the crazy old lady next door was throwing money or jewelry away just to spite her grown children. She had often ranted about her non-visiting offspring: "They'll never get a cent from me, or my jewelry," she would mutter during every conversation, regardless of the subject at hand. You could be in the middle of a conversation with her, like trying to score a lawn cutting job, and she would find a way to turn it into a tirade about her ungrateful children.

While I had heard her say these things just as Vince had, I didn't immediately make the leap to steal her garbage, assuming there would be treasures buried inside. In Vince's defense, the lady was a bit indulgent with the way she packaged and displayed her trash, so it did make it a wee bit suspect ... still, if I were him, I would have done more research before committing to his scheme. Each week, there were always one or two boxes wrapped in pristine brown paper, creased sharply at the corners and tied neatly with white string, just as you would prepare a Christmas gift to be mailed to a distant relative. They were always very neatly balanced at the very top of the pile of garbage, like she was daring someone to take them, Vince had said ... and Vince did take them ... many times.

You might imagine that my brother would have only absconded with the mysterious well-wrapped boxes, but he had a theory that those could be the decoys, so he scurried off every

21

trash day before school with all of the lady's garbage. If the brown boxes were decoys, they were very good ones since each and every one always contained fish scraps; but Vince explained he was no quitter. He had sallied forth undetected for several weeks, until early one morning I caught him sneaking outside before anyone else was up. He came clean under my swift and thorough interrogation. I learned what he had been doing, and unfortunately for Vince, our neighbor must have gotten wise to the bizarre thievery as well. She began waiting until we had all left for school before she would put out her fish-scrap decoys and treasure-laden trash. However, this turn of events just further convinced my brother it was proof positive she had been discarding her cash and jewels.

Like any smart sibling, I blackmailed Vince for years with that one; so when he brought up the actress obsession again a week later, his concern that I would really reveal his garbage stealing made me suspect he already told at least Lisa about my obsession with an actress. The garbage threat had lessened in power over the years, as it had become a running joke that I kept alive with outrageous "fish gifts" to ensure the memory of his childhood stupidity stay alive. Last year I bought him one of those metal religious fish emblems to put on his car, but Vince upped the ante by buying a second one. He positioned one fish so that it was munching between the back tail fins of the other. Mom had made him remove them pronto by leaving a series of threatening phone messages on his voicemail. I knew Mom was really serious since she had broken her vow to never use voicemail, because, she said, "it's totally different than an answering machine, and I am not pressing numbers on my phone just because a machine on the other end tells me to." After all, she had just gotten used to the electronic intrusion of her first answering machine a scant four years ago.

When Vince finally left that evening, I returned to the pile of actress photos. I looked down to the floor and thought it fitting that Lorn Elaine was on the top of the pile; my selection had been made, however unconsciously. The practical side of me said I knew it would be easier to convince a television actress with slightly less exposure than the other more seasoned actresses to work on a movie project with an unknown writer. However, I also wondered if I picked her not just for her acting skills, but because I liked the sound of her name.

I began my nightly ritual, only with greater purpose this time since I had made my final selection. I pushed the DVD in, and didn't even consider skipping the credits, although I could recite them in order. Instead, I let them roll as I changed to get ready for bed, taking care to turn toward the television when the music came to a halting pitch because I always liked to see her name, now being able to imagine how it would look under the title of my movie.

I had watched this particular movie of Lorn's again and again, easily five times as often as I watch her other work, because it was a love story and most like my screenplay. As usual, I had to ignore Jess's nasty comments coming from the next room as the music from the opening scene of the movie began once again, and sighed with childish hope ... Lorn Elaine will be the one to bring my writing to life ... if I can somehow get my screenplay into her hands. Sending the screenplay off blindly just wouldn't do. I had read many stories about writers who waited for years for a studio or agent to respond to a script so I wanted to get it right into her hands, so she could fight to do the project. I started to drift off to sleep as one of the scenes on the DVD played out in my mind. Lorn, I'm going to make you a star, I thought, ignoring the pesky detail that she wasn't exactly an unknown celebrity ... but I could make her a bigger star, now couldn't I? She was wasting her time with small television roles when my screenplay could make her a movie star. How could she say no to an offer like that?

Chapter Three

Love Lessons from Romey and Juliet

Juliet taught me a lot of things, but the most important was that I was gay. This particular Juliet was not the Shakespeare version, but the Maine version, and there was a vast difference between the two. Mom and Dad were on their brief "Aren't we just a picture perfect family" kick after the (unannounced) cancellation of the divorce. This meant we rented a cottage up in Maine that summer, I guessed to properly celebrate the separation's failure. Dad had told us endless stories about his childhood summers in Maine, and Lisa and I speculated he thought spending a summer there would make our family more like the one he grew up in. Since we had spent a lot of time around his constantly feuding family, we could only hope he was wrong.

Our cottage was not "lakeside" and from the day our car pulled into the neighborhood, reeking of blue exhaust and my brother's ripe gerbil cage, we learned just what this entailed. The house which first caught our attention was the pristine log cabin house with a contradicting batch of grimy children playing in front of it.

"Too bad you're on the other side," one of the older boys yelled as our over-packed wagon rolled towards them. "You have no water rights and you can't use our path unless we say," the older girl yelled after her brother. Both children had red hair that looked matted in spots, hopefully from tree sap, but probably from grease, and the only way you could tell one was a girl was the filthy powder-blue pocketbook she had slung over her shoulder. It was worn less like a fashion accessory and more with the attitude of a soldier who had stolen an extra belt of bullets from his freshly killed enemy.

The girl strolled defiantly into the street right in front of the car with her arms crossed. Dad drove carefully and obediently around her, since he was used to accommodating all the females in his life by taking the path of least resistance (it was a path that was well worn and free of weeds). The girl stared back at me, making the exaggerated scowl that children, especially girls, use when they spot someone their own age. Or maybe it wasn't exaggerated at all, and so I was thankful for the car window that separated us. My mother must have had the same thought because she rolled her window up as if they might decide to spit at her, and it sealed off the sweet smell of pine I was sure belonged to the "Lakeside" of the street. I noticed before she stared me down that the delicate line of freckles across the bridge of this girl's well-shaped nose conflicted with her hardened attitude. With an attitude that sour, she should have been ugly, but she definitely was not. I guessed she might have even wished she were more ugly, just for the effect it might have on others.

Before Mom's window went up, I could smell the water, cool and musty like rotting September leaves, except that it was the beginning of summer. Despite the lack of warmth from our welcoming committee, the excited feeling in the pit of my stomach insisted that I would be swimming that day.

We turned away from the log cabin toward a funny-looking cream-colored house with faded brown vinyl trim. I thought perhaps the house had once been white, but now the little cottage was the exact color of whipped cream that had long since spoiled from exposure to the sun, and was outlined in wood painted the color of strips of stale chocolate that had suffered the opposite fate of freezer burn. It was overgrown with vines and spider webs so large they were clearly visible from the street. I wished silently as hard as I could, but our car turned and parked in front of this tiny, neglected cottage anyway.

Vince was the first to yell from the back seat, "Ooooh, I like it!" and he meant it, because he was still too young to know a dirty thing was generally not a good sign. "It's so cute!" he said, and I thought if cute meant small, he was right. Not small like Dad's Divorce Place, but merely a fraction of the house that sat across the street crawling with grimy kids—the same house that entirely blocked any view of the lake. Lisa ran inside the unlocked house to claim the best room for herself and I knew it was pointless to try to intervene, as my shoulder still stung from the punch I had earned when I placed my leg too far over to her side of the car seat. Like Dad, I was also used to taking that same accommodating path when it came to both Lisa and Mom.

The odd thing was, as I got out of the car and stood in front of the little cottage, I decided that I liked it too. It would be impossible not to feel almost protective and nurturing over something so terribly small and neglected. Of course, I was the same person who felt compassion for the yellow marshmallow chicken Peeps last Easter and rescued them all by hiding them in a shoebox so they could not be eaten. Mom eventually followed an orderly trail of ants to the back of my closet and the jig was up. So, surely I could love this helpless little house that appeared to be made of the most fragile of foods, so easily hurt by the sun and rain. It seemed what might be left of its sweetness was being swallowed by hungry vines and crawling bugs.

"Your house is dirty."

I turned to see it was the red-haired dirty pocketbook girl. Her words seemed ironic to me since she was so visually grubby. I was surprised I had not smelled a rancid odor from her standing so close. Stranger still was that I could smell her, and it was instead the barest hint of fresh strawberries wafting from the breeze that blew towards me. I was young enough to wonder if red hair naturally smelled of strawberries.

I fought the urge to answer, "So are you." But it wasn't a very

26

strong urge. I imagined her pocketbook filled with jagged Lakeside rocks propelling towards me and flattening my face on contact. I had dealt with her kind before ... or at least seen them on TV. I heard a clip from Lisa's favorite cop show, *CHiPs*, blare inside my head: "We'll proceed with caution," Eric Estrada advised.

"So, we'll clean it," I said over the pounding fear in my chest.

She made a face. "Your mother makes you clean?" And in that instant I knew she was the type of girl who could turn any phrase you handed her into whatever her whim. I could call for back up, I thought, but Lisa had disappeared into the cottage and even if there was only one bedroom to be had, she was probably erecting some sort of makeshift wall between our beds to further stake her claim.

"Sure, and I get paid for cleaning, too," I lied, but it did temporarily wipe the smirk off her dirt-mottled face.

"Name?" she demanded.

She sounded just like the mole-faced lady at town hall who gave my mother attitude over her lost car license plate, as if the cost of the warped piece of aluminum would come out of her very own pocket. I stared at her blankly, distracted by the realization that half of what I thought was freckles turned out to be mud. I opened my mouth to answer but she gave me a little shove and shouted, "Too late!" Her movement had loosened one of her dirt freckles and I watched it fall into anonymity onto her filthy shirt.

"I'm gonna call you Keds."

I continued my strategy of staring.

"Your shoes, dummy. Your name must be Keds—it says so on your stupid shoes."

"My name is Marie ..." I said weakly, wondering why my real name suddenly sounded more ridiculous than the name she had just bestowed on me.

"I like Keds better—so that's who you are for as long as you're on my street."

I believed her. After all, if I had been driving the car instead of my dad, I would have maneuvered it to carefully accommodate this grimy girl with her strawberry-smelling dirt freckles, too.

"Juliet!" One of her brother's called to her from across the street. "You have to come home now!"

Juliet stood her ground to let me know she didn't jump for anyone, least of all a dumb boy.

"Juliet! Mom says!"

Juliet's brother was teetering on the edge of his lawn as if the earth ended there.

"You're gonna get in trouble with Mom," he spat at her, too afraid to approach.

"Shut up Romey."

I wondered if this was short for Romeo and if she was kidding. I took a chance. "Do you also have a brother or sister named Macbeth, too?"

Juliet flinched in surprise as if I had slapped her with the words. "Of course not, that's a stupid name. Besides, smart ass, Romey and I have a baby sister and her name is just Beth." She tried to look indignant, but I could tell that she was bothered by my close guess. I had never been sworn at by a girl my own age who was also named after a Shakespeare character, and this impressed me. My heart pounded louder for no reason, especially since I was aware I was no longer as scared of her; although maybe I should have been.

"Juliet." A deep female voice cut across the street. Juliet's mother had appeared at their door, but her face was blurred through a cloud of cigarette smoke as thick and blue as my dad's car exhaust. "Leave the new people alone."

My mother startled, but recovered and twirled around to give a neighborly wave in her trademarked Queen Elizabeth flair, but had to retract her hand from the air in mid-wave, since Juliet's mother quickly moved from the slamming screen door, stepping back deeper into the blue cloud of smoke to avoid a hello. Mom hated bad manners worse than anything, so I knew this would seal her opinion of Juliet and her entire family before she had even met them. Juliet gave me one last stare through squinted eyes, before turning to march off to her yard where her brother still teetered timidly on its grass coast.

"Hey Juliet," I called out to her before she was halfway across the street. She turned around, surprised I would have the nerve to call out to her. No one was more surprised than I was. I pointed to her brother. "I was wondering ... if you have one of those doggie invisible fences that works on boys, I'd like to borrow it to use on my brother."

Juliet turned back to see her oblivious brother still balancing stupidly on the edge of the grass as he held the fence to keep his balance. She turned back to me, ignoring her brother, who was now asking her what I had just said.

"Very funny, Keds," she said with a scowl that I knew was barely hiding a smile. I had learned early on that girls could always bond over their hatred of boys, and this would be my angle.

I remained staring until Juliet entered the dissipating cigarette cloud at her doorway, and disappeared with her mother. I glimpsed the crisp blue lake though the trees behind Juliet's house and that excited and nervous feeling persisted anew ... but maybe it was from meeting Juliet.

We had adjusted well to our new home on our non-Lakeside address, and Mom seemed to be happy with all the distractions of the new environment. She did not, as I predicted, like Juliet one bit. However, her relief at me finding a "friend" seemed to outweigh the concern of the quality of that friend, since it got me out of the house. What Mom didn't know was that Juliet reminded me daily that she was not my friend. Instead, she was someone I instinctively knew I had to keep close, so she wouldn't become my enemy. She also completely mesmerized me, and in short time I found myself mimicking her speech, her hand gestures, and the gait of her walk. I even started carrying an old pocketbook I found in the attic of the cottage, until Lisa teased me mercilessly and so I had to give it up.

Juliet and I hadn't actually become friends. In fact, our more recent conversations were no warmer than our first, but she both fascinated and scared me, so I wanted to be around her. As for Juliet's interest in me, besides Lisa, I was the only girl around close to her age, so I believed she was just tired of hanging around with stupid boys. Lisa was closer to her age than I was, but since Lisa instantly hated and ignored her, Juliet was stuck with the youngest sister, me. Two lions cannot co-exist peacefully on the same street, even if it's only for a summer. Lisa might have known she'd met her match in Juliet, and took the teenage-girl solution of getting the upper hand: she acted too stuck-up to acknowledge her.

Within the first few days of our arrival to her neighborhood, Juliet had announced several things I must accomplish during my stay. I needed:

1. To learn how to throw rocks with extreme accuracy (especially at boys and garage windows, because parents expected both things to be hit or broken).
2. To back a car secretly a few feet down the driveway without getting caught.
3. To leap from the highest branch that overhung the lake in her backyard.
4. To stop paying such "girlie attention" to the fact that my bare feet bled from the pine needles (which felt more like hypodermic needles) as they pierced my city-soft feet.

Most important of all was number five on her list:

5. To view a real penis.

That summer, I found out Juliet was right about many things, too:

1. That I would get a kick out of doing each of these things.
2. That the feeling of out-smarting the adults far out-weighed the risk of getting caught.
3. That my feet would eventually toughen up and not bleed if I didn't give in to wearing shoes.
4. I was suddenly embarrassed to never have seen a penis.

I figured, since she had been right about so many things, how could she be wrong about my severe lack of penis-viewing and how it may affect my future social status? It really wasn't just my curiosity that made me agree to something that felt pretty wrong. Juliet had decided it was downright embarrassing that I had not seen a "real penis" yet. A "real penis" was deemed one that did not belong to a family member, and she was prepared to take care of my problem so she wouldn't be embarrassed to hang around with me. By the time Juliet was through taunting me, I really did feel embarrassed about my incompetence in the penis-viewing department, and besides, I hadn't chickened out of any other challenge she had placed before me. Was I going to let a dumb boy's penis be the one dare that I chickened out of? I thought not.

Romey acted dumb about the whole plan, but Juliet explained to me that while boys acted dumb about most things, they were the masters of dumb when it came to matters of the penis. Again, she proved to be right. When Romey found out what we were plotting, he became very arrogant about it. He acted as if he had something we needed from him, and while in a way it was true, Juliet informed me there would be "a swift and terrible attitude adjustment" and we both had no reason to doubt her.

Romey had overheard Juliet and I talking about how the tree fort would be a safe place for the viewing, and all she had to do was figure out how to get her twin brother to go into the fort and drop his swimsuit while I peered through a hole in the wall, undetected. Even if Romey was as dumb as Juliet claimed, Juliet decided even he wouldn't fall for my plan. My plan was to tell Romey that when I had gone into the tree fort earlier, my shorts and underwear fell accidentally down, and suddenly pieces of candy had started showering into the fort. Then I would tell him that Juliet had done the same, just to see if I was lying, and when she pulled her own shorts and underwear down, pieces of candy rained into the fort onto her head, too. My idea was when Romey went in, Juliet could hurl candy into the roofless fort to distract him from pulling up his shorts too quickly. It seemed foolproof to me, but in the end Juliet opted for her tried-and-true method of psychological torture to get him to agree quite humbly to her Plan B, which was: Do as he was told, or else. Besides, she reasoned, if we had money for that much candy, we would have already bought it and eaten it.

When doing as he was told or else did not get the desired result, Juliet informed her brother that since he was fourteen, it was downright embarrassing that no girl had ever seen his penis, and that if word "accidentally" got out to all his friends, Romey could end up being the joke of the street and the entire school come September. For a minute or two, Romey wavered between disbelief and fear that she might be right. He foolishly decided to call her bluff.

"You're lying," Romey said, but the fear in his voice was evident and Juliet pounced.

"Fine," she said, so casually, that even I thought for a moment she was going to drop the whole idea. But then the real torture began.

Juliet announced to him, "You can be the kid they all call a faggot-momma's-boy-fairy-fucker." She placed her hands on her forehead to show that she was very worried and said, "How embarrassing it's going to be for me to have a fag for a brother ... Come on Keds, we'll find a real boy to do it. I won't have you tortured the way they are gonna torture him ... Of course, it's *way* worse for boys—the things they do to them ... you know ... down there ..." Juliet managed a subtle shiver before tugging my arm to leave Romey standing there with widening eyes.

"I know it's a trick," he said weakly as we walked away. Then he shouted, "What things?"

"Forget it Romey. We'll ask someone else." And we kept walking.

"What things?" he asked, desperately. Juliet spun around.

"Things with broom handles and pencils to test if you're a queer. I saw a boy after he had that done, and every time he sat down in math class he would cry from the pain. He would beg the teachers not to make him sit, but when they asked him why, he wouldn't tell them. He would just sit and cry—which of course made even the other boys who didn't know what happened to him call him a big queer baby."

I gulped in horror, and began to protest to Juliet, until she grabbed my arm very hard to shut me up. It worked.

"I'll do it." Romey blurted out. "We should do it today," he said, self-consciously and protectively hovering his hand in front of the crotch of his shorts. I had no idea what she was hinting "they" did with the pencils and broomsticks, but I figured it wasn't good and I guess Romey had figured the same.

I felt bad for Romey, but honestly, his stupidity was starting to annoy me, as Juliet had warned me it would. Juliet could be a monster, but it was hard not to respect her talent for getting the job done. Romey was in the awkward position of being the weaker twin, and it clearly bothered him. They looked exactly alike, Juliet being not quite as feminine as she should, and Romey, probably only in comparison to his sister, not being as masculine as he should. Both had beautiful red hair with pale hazel eyes and physical builds and voices that met in the exact middle ground of male and female. This seemed to work nicely for Juliet, but for Romey ... it just seemed to invoke pity in the eyes of the viewer who, while noticing his soft and somewhat feminine features, had to figure he was in for a rough ride in the world. I noticed they would both be even better looking if they could somehow switch genders. Of the two, Juliet carried off her masculine femaleness much better than Romey's feminine maleness, and this was something Juliet exploited to scare him into believing there would be an inevitable gang-attack upon his manhood if he didn't do exactly as she commanded.

Awkward as the whole plan was, I had no fear of being ratted out by Romey since his justified fear of Juliet was far stronger than any worries I had of an adult discovering our penis-viewing plans. Juliet set the viewing for the following day at the tree fort, with its newly installed sliding lock.

On "Penis-viewing Day," I found it hard to get dressed in the morning. (What does one wear to her first real penis-viewing? Despite my late-night investigation, *Tiger Beat* magazine held no clues.) I arrived at the tree fort to find an angry Juliet waiting by the door.

"You're late. Don't you think that I might have better things to do than help you out with your pathetic problems?" Juliet said.

My problems? I wanted to say, "Not that late," but knew better.

"Romey is already inside, and he's already tried to leave once, but I climbed the tree and kicked the door closed on him. I'll wait over by the bushes and blow this whistle if anyone comes by, just like we planned. And don't forget to lock the fucking door."

We planned? *We* had not actually planned a thing. If it had been up to me, I would have been able to view the thing without Romey even knowing, all for the cost of some candy rain. I had learned that second-guessing her schemes was not appreciated, so, just as I grew used to being called by a new first name that wasn't mine, I also grew used to when Juliet decided something, my only role was to wait for it to take place exactly as she planned. Although no one ever "comes by" in this area of the woods, I agreed that it didn't make sense to be reckless during a penis-viewing, so I thanked her for standing guard and climbed the ladder to the fort.

When I entered the fort, I found Romey obediently standing in the very center of the floor. He must have re-positioned himself several times, because he was in the exact center of the room. He was nervously fidgeting with the front of his swimming trunks as if they were irritating his crotch.

We stared at each other for a moment and suddenly I wondered if I would have to instruct him, since I had never witnessed him do anything without Juliet telling him exactly what to do. I was relieved when he quickly dropped his swim shorts onto his bare feet and stared at the wall as if it were suddenly fascinating to him.

Perhaps it was because he was staring at the wall with such interest, or perhaps it was simply spending so much time with Juliet, but I was not at all self-conscious about staring at Romey's small and trembling penis.

"Lock the fucking door!" Juliet's voice came in a stage whisper from below.

I backed up to lock the door, not wanting to look away. There it was ... It hung from his hairless body like an armless rubber doll that was deathly afraid of heights ... just dangling there like a chubby displaced finger with no bones. Romey's face was blushing as red as his hair and I noticed when I turned back from locking the door that he still would not look at me.

"It's no big deal, Romey. No offense of course," I said, rather diplomatically.

He relaxed a little, and when he did, I noticed his penis seemed to have gotten a little bigger and was now, bizarrely, pointing right at me looking more like an accusing finger ... only now it was even chubbier, like a thumb. Or maybe I had imagined it, I thought. But I hadn't, because now it changed again, and looked as if it was pointing at something just over my head.

Would it turn into a big snake right in front of my eyes, I wondered? I was both horrified and intrigued. I had seen a dirty magazine photo once that a boy had snuck into school, and the man's penis was surrounded by a thick cloud of wiry hair that look like the dust around the Peanuts character, Pigpen. Romey's did not have the dust cloud of hair so it was not as scary, but since the darned thing was changing by the second, who knew what it was going to look like in another few minutes?

"Um ... it's growing," I said to alert him.

"It's the wind," he answered.

"The wind?" I asked. Boys are strange fucking creatures, I thought. Since I had been hanging around Juliet, I had starting swearing inside my head.

"Plus you're looking at it. When you look at it, it sometimes grows."

I noticed he called it an "it," like it was not a part of him. When you look at it, it grows? But now, as I had a better look, it seemed more like a pink blushing mouse that was not recently dead, stiff and hairless. It was ugly but kind of interesting too; much in the same way a dead mouse would be if a dead thing wasn't sad and didn't smell bad.

"Why is it standing up like that now?" I asked, "And it seems to be turning a different color." I thought he should know.

"I have to put it away before it—does something," he said, and Romey quickly snapped his swim shorts over his penis, which made a funny little tent underneath. He looked down at his crotch as his face reddened deeper. "Don't tell Juliet," he said looking back up at me in total terror, and I was going to ask why until I noticed he had wet the front of his shorts. He dashed by me, smacking into the door that he forgot was locked. I was concerned he may have hurt the stiff little mouse in his pants.

I reminded myself to tell Juliet that I now understood why boys are so dumb. It must be a ridiculous distraction to have a stiff little mouse in your pants all day that gets bigger every time the fucking wind blows or someone looks at it. I also noted to myself that while it was interesting, this was definitely not something I cared to get to near, since he obviously had no control over when it would decide to pee.

Days later, Juliet and I were sitting in the blue spruce as her brothers played professional wrestling in the yard beneath us. Every once in a while I saw Romey shoot a worried glance treeward, probably wondering if I would tell his sister about the mouse-growing and peeing incident, which of course I already had. Juliet's influence may have rubbed off on me because I was enjoying the power of his fear more than a little bit.

Although I pitied the torture that Juliet put him through, the fact remained that Romey was a quite obnoxious boy. Just two days after I had met him he had informed me that I had a fat chest. "They're breasts, you fucking idiot," Juliet snapped at him before I could even react. It was the first nice thing she had ever said in my defense.

Naturally, Juliet had wanted to know everything that had happened in the tree fort. She badgered me for details until I finally told her I had seen it grow. Her eyes widen into perfect circles. Her reaction made me wonder if perhaps she had never really seen a penis before, but I didn't dare insult her. I wondered fleetingly if she was a great deal more innocent than she acted, as my mother had predicted. I was feeling quite superior at the moment, as if the mouse had matured me somehow. Once again, Juliet had been right.

"Next, I'm gonna show you two people fucking." My fleeting moment of superiority vanished. I knew (sure as shit, as Juliet would say) she would in fact show me two people fucking.

My only visual of the act of copulation had been when my sister Lisa and I had witnessed the neighborhood dogs go at it. That was the only live viewing, but there had been a much earlier time when I stumbled upon a nature show on TV that featured two chimpanzees doing it; which propelled me into an instant addiction of animal shows at six years old. It was the first time I could remember feeling that strong ache between my legs, which got more frequent with each school grade. It was both exciting and uncomfortable, and often led me to go outside and run up and down our street six or seven times to get rid of my energy, until my mother yelled at me to stop, threatening that I would throw up. The running helped a little, but the heartbeat in my crotch took a long, long time to go away. For a while I was obsessed with every nature show I could find until my dad became convinced that I was going to be a zoologist. How could he know I was just watching to catch the next chimp-fucking scene?

Juliet came through on her promise to show me two people fucking. We squatted behind some bushes, as we spied on two teenagers in the woods groping each other on a tattered yellow blanket. Juliet had seen them come through the woods before and this time we followed them. I don't think even Juliet antici-pated we would catch them going all the way, because when the boy started taking off the girl's underwear, we clasped our hands over each other's mouth to muffle our giggles. We watched, com-pletely fascinated. Then I felt Juliet reach over without looking at me, and carefully snake her hand up the leg of my shorts. I froze as her hand inched its way up to my crotch and began stroking my soft area over my underwear with the back of her fingers. My heart was pounding so loud I feared the teenagers might hear it. I did not stop her and mulled over the reasons why:

1. Because it felt very, very good.
2. Because it was the only time she'd ever been really nice to me.
3. Because I had been having thoughts of kissing her.
4. Because, like her twin brother had been during the penis-viewing, she was not looking directly at me.

We both continued to watch them fuck as she stroked me. I became embarrassed that I didn't have the courage to touch her underwear too, plus I was worried that she might soon feel my underwear getting wet as it did when my heartbeat moved down to my crotch, so I slowly closed my legs to make her stop. I wondered if this is what had happened to Romey's mouse in the fort. The throbbing down below was unbearable, especially since the teenage boy was grunting just like a chimp, his naked ass pumping on top of the girl. By contrast, the girl appeared quite uncomfortable beneath him, and more than just a little bored.

"He's coming now," Juliet said in a clinical whisper, seemingly unconcerned that I had stopped her hand from touching me. I turned around quickly to look behind us. Who's coming? I wondered. There was nobody around but the boy still pumping away on top of the girl. I finally got it when the boy started groaning. He was "ending" and his naked behind was bouncing wildly, just like the tiger's hips I once saw on PBS. I felt a chilled breeze against the wetness of my shorts; I had stopped Juliet just in time, since I didn't want her to know that occasionally I wet my underwear when I thought of sex, just not as much as Romey did, apparently.

I couldn't hang around Juliet anymore after that day, and when Lisa asked me why, I caved under some pressure and told her everything that had happened. I explained how, although it felt really, really good what she had done, I was not going to burn in hell for being a queer. She looked stunned (or that was how I interpreted her look) and for a moment I feared she would tell Mom. Instead, Lisa marched across the street and promptly began a steamy summer romance with Juliet. I spent the rest of the summer spying on them, worrying my sister would burn in hell, and also wishing I had not let Juliet go so easily.

Chapter Four

Revenge of the Dead Grandmother

Vince was calling me on my cell phone as I pulled into the driveway.

"Marie, you are not going to *believe this*!" he yelled over the traffic noise.

"What's going on?" I asked, only mildly interested since Vince frequently sounded wound up, and it often amounted to nothing.

"I'm calling from outside the lawyer's office—I had to be the first to tell you—I was so afraid that someone would call and tell you before me. No one beat me to it right?" He was out of breath.

"What the hell happened, did you win the lottery?"

Vince laughed, "Not quite, but you are *so close*."

I was getting aggravated now. "Vince. Just tell me."

I heard him take a deep breath before he blurted, "I'm at the lawyer's office—Mare—you got all the fucking loot!"

It took me a few seconds to realize what he was saying, but I didn't believe it enough to respond. He said, "Did you hear me? Gram fucking left you everything! The lawyer has documents for you. You have to come and get them, now!" he screamed in my ear.

I knew right away he wasn't kidding. His voice was pitched high like this only one other time in our lives. It was the summer after Lakeside with Juliet, and Vince came running home screaming that two dogs were doing something bad on the street near the school. I had asked if they were fighting and I could tell by his description that I had a live nature show on my hands. I sent him away (because he was too young) and I watched the dogs for ten minutes, as I waited for Vince to return with Dad's binoculars so I could have a better look without scaring the dogs away. Just like Dian Fossey, I had thought. The male was a poodle and his ass was pumping just like the teenage boy in the woods, only much faster, and with the bonus of a vibrating pom-pom tail. Vince's voice had screeched the news very high, just like today.

He was yelling into the phone that Gram had left me everything ... I thought, it had to be a trick of some kind ...

"When we were leaving, I saw a stack of papers for you with a letter on top; it was addressed to you in Gram's handwriting. They wouldn't give me the letter to give to you; you have to come get it from the lawyer and sign for it. It's all very official-looking and sealed with some gooey barf-colored stuff."

"That's wax, Vince," I said, because it was the only thing I knew for sure at the moment. "Two things: Where the hell is this lawyer's office, and this better not be a fucking joke."

"No joke! Aunt Aggie was so pissed and Dad just sat there laughing his head off ... and Mom looked like she was going to faint, but then recovered enough to start yelling at Dad for laughing about what his mother had done ... it was so surreal! And they don't even know there is a letter to you!"

I told myself this didn't mean anything. Gram and I had a mutual dislike, probably due to my "unnatural lifestyle," and my whole family knew it because information of this type was meant to be shared among an Italian family. More likely, this was some sort of cruel trick. Perhaps the real will was this mysterious letter, which would leave everything to Dad, his already wealthy brother Tony, and possibly Aunt Aggie, despite the decade-long feud. But that didn't make sense, because I could tear up the letter since the will had already been read ... Grandma was much too smart for that. My head spun with the possibilities as I pulled out of the driveway and drove according to the directions Vince had shouted into the phone as if I needed a hearing aid.

Did Vince say I got everything, or something? Maybe I misunderstood him, I thought, as I plowed through the traffic at an unsafe speed. When I arrived at the office Vince jumped at me from the top of the stairs like a diver springing from a board, grabbed my arm and pulled me into the office. The lawyer handed me the letter while issuing a warning totally devoid of all emotion: "You are under no legal obligation to follow the instructions in this letter. The binding will has been read and witnessed. As I already explained to a few of your family members, repeatedly, Mrs. Wallingford's assets are all in a living trust, which you now control. It's totally up to you what you do with the money that was left to you, Ms. Santora. I'm sure your brother informed you of the will's contents, but here is your copy. You can call and set up a time to sign everything during my regular business hours."

I nodded and took the letter from him. He excused us with another nod as he began gathering his papers into his briefcase. It was five o'clock on the dot as he closed and locked the door behind us.

"Open it, open it!" Vince chanted the second the door was closed. "Fuck, I can't believe this, Mare!"

I turned the letter over in my hands as if to glean some sort of hint of what was inside.

"*Open it!*" Vince yelled again with an impatient hop.

"Christ, Vince, you're acting like a lunatic," I answered, but I was just as nervous as him. I just didn't want to look like I had fallen for Gram's trick. Later, when this turned out to be a cruel joke, I wanted to claim I never really believed it.

I bent the envelope until the seal crumbled and released leaving a dye-stained flap from the wax. It was rather unsightly with the dirty smear left behind, and I took it as a sign that this could be what was happening inside the envelope as well. It was two pages, handwritten with the old crow-quill pen Gram had on her desk, and, I guessed, the antique bottle of sepia ink I always assumed was just for decoration. The paper smelled faintly of lavender, dust, and tomato sauce, just like her house had always smelled. It reminded me of childhood days spent running down creaky stairs, and sneaking up on scary old dolls dressed in yellowed doily dresses in the attic, and whining screen doors that slammed in the summer wind. And food, always lots of food.

Vince was chanting, "What does it say? What does it say!"

I ignored him and read the letter silently:

Dearest Marie, (I braced myself already, as Gram never called me dearest.)

As you have already learned, I have bequeathed my entire estate to you. It would not surprise me if you had to learn of this second hand, since I am assuming you did not attend the reading. I realize that any requests I make of you are at your mercy as to whether or not they are carried out. I will tell you in all honesty, that this is the only existing copy of this letter, so I am relying on your good conscience to carry out these few instructions. As you can see, it has been notarized for its authenticity, while my lawyer tells me the living trust is the only legally binding legal document. (If that crook could have figured out a way to charge me for holding this letter for you, I am sure he would have not hesitated, the beast. He's an Irish lawyer and I believe he takes a stiff drink with his lunch and at the end of every day.)

Although our relationship was stormy at best, you have always been an honest young woman, and I feel confident that you will do as I request, regardless of my motivations, which I will not pretend to elevate to something other than what they are.

My requests are as follows:

It is my wish that my daughter, Agatha Santora Bellatoro, inherit my house and all of its contents. It is my wish that my son, your father, Salvatore Santora, inherit full ownership and control of the land upon which it rests. My eldest son, Anthony Santora is a wealthy man and so I trust he would not require a thing from my estate, as all he has ever desired was his dearly departed wife and I am afraid I cannot give him that. However, on the extremely remote chance that we end up in the same place at my death, I will look after his wife for him. I am sure she could use some mentoring on the ways of making the most of her after life, but I suspect I will have a different view from my room, as she was such a ridiculously good-natured woman.

The money, my dear, is yours. I will not insult your intelligence by claiming it's because of our unrequited love and devotion for each other. I will say only that at least what we felt for each other was honest and my reasons for the other decisions are purely of a spiteful nature. (As you see, you are not the only Santora with the ability to be brutally honest.) It would be my wish that your siblings, Vincent and Lisa Santora, each receive a substantial portion of the money; this I leave for you to decide, because frankly, since I am dead, I could not care any less. However, it is my strongest wish that my daughter Agatha and your father receive none of the money; you know why.

My final request is that you not inform or bequeath my house or land to my daughter or son for at least six months after my death. This should bring a smile to your face, Marie, but make no mistake;

44

Aggie and your mother will make your life a living hell trying to make sure the other does not get their hands on the money.

Please allow no one to read this letter. In you, I place my trust.

                              Gabriella Santora Wallingford

That was the letter, complete with an embossed notary stamp. I immediately ignored Grandma's last request and read Vince the highlights. He sat down on the steps of the office with his mouth open in shock. When I finished, Vince finally spoke.

"Why?" was all he said.

"Why, which part?" I asked.

"Why, all of it? Why leave the money to you, the house to Aggie and the land to Dad ... and why wait six months?"

I sank down to the steps beside him. "It's actually pretty clever the way she divided the house and the land. Dad and Aggie can't get along in the best of times, but now neither can make a move without the other being in agreement. Aggie can't sell the house without the land, and vice versa. The six-month wait is simply to make Aggie and Mom squirm ... as for the money," I said shaking my head, "she undoubtedly wanted the joy of denying it to them."

"God, Mare, I guess I shouldn't have pretended to like her a little. Who would have guessed ...?"

Suddenly, Vince thumped me in the side with his elbow.

"Remember I asked you not to forget your little brother when you got all the loot?" He was grinning and shaking his head in disbelief along with me, "Mare, you're *fucking rich!*"

I didn't know how to respond to this. In her later years, Grandma had re-married an older, very wealthy man after her first husband, my grandfather, had died, and she had inherited twenty-one million dollars when her second husband died just a few years later.

"I guess so," I said foolishly.

45

"You guess so?" Vince was getting excited again. "Do you have *any idea* what kind of money we're talking about?"

"Looks like over twenty-one million," I said, finding it bizarre to say the words.

"That's without the house and land ... Holy shit! Mare, you're *fucking rich*!"

It crossed my mind for the briefest moment to inform Vince I probably should not accept anything from that woman ... until the thought struck and ultimately stayed with me: *I was free*. The money would free me to finally leave Jess ... and to move to California to pursue my screenwriting career ... to convince Lorn Elaine that she had to be a part of my movie. It was only the reality of my financial situation that kept me from doing it before.

It was ironic that my grandmother, who had taunted me all the time I was growing up because I would not put up with her bitter attitude towards me as gracefully as Lisa and Vince had all those years ... had now saved me from my current stagnant life, to pursue a dream she would have split a gut laughing at; but I would never have shared my dream with her.

Jessica was stunned. Not because of the money, or the fact that I was planning to jet off to California. She was stunned because I told her *I* was leaving *her*. She couldn't believe I'd actually beaten her to the punch. She was equally furious and insulted that I'd leave her "just as our ship had come in." She told me that it was completely out of my character to do something this crazy, and actually, she was right.

Although I would be leaving Jessica, right now my reasons for leaving the state had more to do with preserving my sanity than ditching a cheating girlfriend or finding an actress to read my screenplay. One week after the will was read, I was forced to have my answering machine take all of my calls. My mother became obsessed with my day-to-day activities, wondering where I was since I was not answering the phone. She left a series of eight phone calls, each reminding me in a different manner that she was an accountant by trade, in case I had forgotten what my mother did for the last thirty years. She kept asking me to come over for dinner so she could help me plan my finances to "make the money work for me," and to please bring Jessica, since it seemed like forever since she'd seen her. It was ironic that the money had purchased my acceptance, since I was no longer in the market for it. Apparently, money made a pair of dykes much more palatable. My aunt Aggie, who never felt the need to phone me before, was now checking on me daily, so I suspected she had gotten wind of Mom's canvassing for a new accounting client.

The only one who wasn't calling more than usual was Vince, and when I didn't hear from him for nearly a week, I grilled him to see what was up. He finally confessed he didn't want me to think my new fortune was making him a suck-up brother, and so he had become paranoid about calling too much. I promptly yelled at him that he had *always* called too much and to knock it the fuck off.

After the initial shock that I was planning to leave, Jess went into total denial of my announcement that we were over, and actually began making plans for our future. First, we were going to buy a home in Florida, since, she informed me, there was no need for either of us to continue working. Second, we'd buy a boat to entertain our friends on. She apparently forgot I inherited my dad's DNA, which made me violently sick just standing near a dock. Jess also forgot that she had fucked all of our friends, so a sailing trip involving any mutual friends might be a bit awkward for me.

The biggest change in Jess came in the form of her new non-existent social life. There hadn't been one call from a new friend of hers since Grandma had made me wealthy. It seemed such a strange coincidence that, I'm ashamed to admit, I wondered if there was a connection. The young voices of a half a dozen women had been conspicuously barred from calling our home ... such a shame, since we had the answering machine poised to dutifully record all incoming calls. To be fair to Jess, maybe they couldn't

47

get through, due to the constant calling of Aggie, Mom, and other stray relations (some of whom I could barely formulate a picture in my mind) who wanted to "touch base" with me just to see how I was adjusting to all that money. The relatives were in a bidding war for my phone time.

It was probably the remainder of Jessica's pride which was the only thing that kept us from fighting about the inevitable end of our relationship. I felt tempted to thank her for that, since I still had some major packing to do. My plans were taking on a life of their own, and Vince and I had to prepare for a family meeting before I could take my trip to California to jump-start my new life. There would also be the two "Hell Weeks" to get through when I got back from California.

Vince had been a lifesaver. He helped with the moving plans, and offered to store things in the basement of his apartment that I didn't want to sell or take with me. But I was most grateful for his (albeit smirking) support of my reasons for moving. "I know why you're going out there," he had said one night as we dined at our favorite Mexican place. "You're going out there to see if you can finally meet that actress."

After catching me at my actress-selection-movie-marathon-magazine-clipping-weekend, he naturally assumed I had gone over the deep end for Lorn Elaine. He also was going to make fun of me again for it; who wouldn't? Since I could not bring myself to fess up the real reason I was interested in this actress, I had to simply take his teasing while I drank my margarita in silence. He took this the wrong way and stopped dead in his tracks.

"Wow ... you've got it bad for this woman, huh?" he said gently, and then he let the subject go ... at least with me. I wondered again if he had told Lisa, or even Dad and Mom, that he'd discovered I was head over heals in love with someone I'd never met. Somehow letting them think I was lovesick over some actress seemed a less crazy option than confessing I was planning to move across the country to chase a dream of becoming a Hollywood screenplay writer.

That is, it seemed a better option until my mother caught me answering the phone one night (I thought it was Vince calling back) to tell me about a friend who was helped so much by a therapist who specialized in obsessive behavior. She masterfully worked it into our conversation, as only Mom could. While on the phone, I hadn't questioned why she even mentioned this woman's pathetic chasing of a married man, but I thought about it later. Even my dad called me, but, thankfully, had been too embarrassed to reveal the reason for his call. Later, I knew what his stammering had been about. I grilled Vince and found out he had opened his yap about my "obsession" to all of them but assured me he hadn't told Jess a thing.

At first I wanted to kill Vince but he convinced me he had spilled the beans to my family out of concern, and not because he had a weakness to share a great story, which we both knew was often the case. I had told him many times he gossiped like a gay man, and while he appeared to be straight, he had that one gay gene in him. I attempted to hold a grudge and didn't speak with him for a few days, but I missed the little shit. Besides, I told myself, I was the one who allowed him think I had gone a little nuts just to spare my ego if I failed.

Now, at yet another dinner with Vince, I picked at my enchiladas with the corner of a tortilla chip as if checking underneath for bugs. I suddenly had lost my appetite.

"I have to go out there and give it a try," I finally said.

Vince put down his top shelf margarita. A grand gesture for him; this was going to be serious. "To be honest, Mare, I won't pretend it isn't a little crazy." But when he saw the wounded look in my eyes, he softened up, as I hoped he would. "But maybe you need to do something crazy right now … it would probably be more nuts to stay with Jess." He looked at me with sympathy, but still with the inescapable veneration a younger sibling has for an older one … but I was certainly testing his limits. He finally said, "I think you are a saint to put up with Jess for so long."

"Maybe a fool," I answered. "A saint would have warned Jess

she shouldn't make plans to live the life of a millionaire's girl-friend, or sign a loan for a new boat. I decided to let her think what she wants for a while, and see how much damage she can do to her own life, instead of other people's for a change. Not exactly the work of a saint."

Vince smiled and raised his margarita glass, which I clinked with a frozen thud.

"I'll miss ya," he said quietly.

"Good. That means you'll visit me," I said. I took a large swallow of my drink, but it didn't clear the lump from my throat.

Quitting my own job had been surprisingly easy. I had very few friends at work, which was Vince's fault, and I can prove it. He had made a CD of one of our favorite bands and I had brought it in to work. While I had left to go to the ladies' room, a co-worker decided to be adventurous and play the CD over the speaker system so it would be playing all through the loudspeakers when I came out. I came out, all right. Interrupting the first song was my brother's voice, "Attention, attention, Marie Santora is a lesbian! Marie Santora is a lesbian! This has been a public service announcement! Thank you very much." I remember thinking: at least he was polite and didn't use a potty mouth. It could have been much, much worse.

I had been in bathroom stall number three when I heard my brother's voice blaring over the speakers, which ran through the office, as well as the entire factory. After finally coming to grips with the fact that there wasn't an exit window in the bathroom, or an available noose, I had to go back to my desk. I wasn't exactly "out" at work, but only because I had been there about a year and had not felt close to enough to anyone to share my personal story. That, and because the office was filled with an extraordinary amount of conservative republicans that frequently made off-color remarks about anyone not white, straight, or male.

"That was my brother ..." I stupidly tried to explain, "he always does things like this ..."

As the stunned office staff stared at me I began to laugh, both at the awkward and deafening silence, and at the fact that they were staring like I had been exposed as a serial killer. I was the exact same person I had been for the last year. But instantly I had turned into the person most avoided in the office. I found myself having coffee alone most mornings and made a practice of leaving the building at lunch to give everyone an opportunity to freely talk about me without suffering the inconvenience of having to whisper. So, as it turned out, Vince actually did me a favor by making it really easy to pack up my personal things (South Park figurines, several fuzzy sheep, and various photos of dead pets—of course, alive at the time the pictures were taken) and leave my job since I no longer had a need for a paycheck.

On the night before my preliminary trip to California that would precede the actual move, I was struggling to smartly pack just one large suitcase. If it were this hard to plan a temporary trip out there, how difficult would the actual move be? After I paced the room for ten minutes without packing anything else, I concluded I was finished.

I had ignored Jessica's many attempts to have a heart-to-heart talk, and this evening she was admitting defeat by sulking in front of the TV downstairs. I think she still held hope that when I returned from my initial trip, I would decide to not go back to California. Actually, I wondered that myself. Either way, I could now leave Jessica and buy a place of my own for the first time in my life.

I slipped into bed exhausted, but knowing I would not be able to sleep. My stomach felt poised at the highest rail of a roller coaster ... at that very point when you wonder why you've put yourself in a position you cannot get out of, just before plummeting straight down. I was crazy; Vince was right about that, just not quite as crazy as he thought. My current rationale was that since I knew it was a little crazy, this probably made it OK. Real nut jobs have no idea they are doing crazy things, right? Besides,

I thought, as I tried settling into bed, it had to be the right thing to do, since I felt tremendous relief about deciding to finally leave Jess. Long overdue ... maybe I would even meet someone out there.

Ever since I bought my plane tickets, the relief regarding Jess had helped to mask the irrational part of what I was doing. I was finally done with all the hurt and it felt good to make plans to let it all go. I adjusted my pillow and tried to get comfortable, and then, although I had not planned to, I began crying into it, thinking about how much I would miss my bed. The mattress was still nice and firm, and the headboard a beautiful solid oak that would cost more to ship across the country than to buy a new one. I sobbed soundlessly into my pillow. I would miss my pillow so much, too. Maybe I shouldn't go ... but then, I thought, as the tears continued to pool around me, I could certainly find room to pack my pillow. And, fuck it, I could ship the bed if I wanted to ... I was fucking rich. Shipping costs be damned! This at least stopped the stupid crying. There's no crying in baseball, I reminded myself; change for the better is not always easy.

Chapter Five

Avoiding Beanbags While Redecorating

Having so much money made what should have been very difficult a little too easy, and the result was that setting myself up took
much less time than I had planned. I purchased a small house
tucked up in the hills, just twenty minutes away from Flashmen
Studios, where Lorn Elaine's series was being filmed. It was a
decision I made with only half of my brain; the half that was
insane.

My logic was that it made no sense to pay high California rent
when I could instead be making an "investment" and simply buy
something. It almost sounded rational when I thought of it that
way ... but I knew it was just a way to make it more difficult to
tuck my tail between my untanned legs and run back home to
Connecticut. I did like the house, though, and I couldn't wait
for Vince and Lisa to see LA. If we didn't have the two Hell
Weeks coming up, I'd have them come out and stay with me,
but Vince especially had a lot of planning to do for me back
home.

I had found a cozy two-bedroom house with a beautiful stone
fireplace and semi-outdoor pool out back, encased in a sweet
little sunroom. The owner was motivated to sell so I talked the
realtor into working into the deal a way to keep the massive
tropical plants, which seemed to be searching with outstretched
arms against the glass skylights for a portal to escape. The best
part of the house was that, even with a pool, it still managed to be

tucked high into a private hillside, and, on a (very rare) clear day, I could actually see Lorn Elaine's studio building from the back bedroom window, which I took as a good sign. The house's sole contents thus far: the tropical plants (which, I realized later, the owners could not have possibly removed out of that room without first removing the entire sunroom roof); a new DVD player (the one I had back home belonged to Jess); a large television; a comfortable couch; a small writing desk; and my iMac laptop so I could continue to re-write the screenplay. I rented a car and decided adding a fridge and stove could wait until I got back. What had sealed the deal was the agreement of the seller to let me pay exorbitant fees to close immediately, since I was paying for the house in cash and didn't need to wait for a mortgage. Money seemed to make no problem insurmountable, but that had its downside.

For the first week in LA I was absorbed with finding a house, and the second week I spent settling into the house and shopping for necessities (who knew there were so many brands of DVD players on the market?). By my third week, my wealth had made things too easy for me and I was running out of things to do. I found out that when people with a lot of money run out of things to do, they invent things to do that will cost them money.

Since I was starting to have a strange love for the quirky little house in the hills of California, I tried to think of ways I would like to improve it. I liked the rush of independence I felt every time I walked in the door of a house I owned alone. I loved the strange and intoxicating smell of fresh lilies in the loft bedroom, even though there were no flowers. (I was convinced this was a mystical sign for me to stay in the house, until I finally found the source: on the top of the shelf in the closet was a dusty Airwick air freshener, still valiantly fighting to do its job.)

The climate was another good reason to love it here. I reminded myself that back home it would begin to get a chill in the air as early as September and the winter could stretch well into April, leaving a ridiculously short summer season. I liked this reason best, since it was such a normal reason to relocate your entire life across the country. I wondered if there would be a way to build out from the house to make more use of the pool area and the small plot of land overlooking the town below.

A big redecoration project would surely eat up a huge chunk of my time, and it would give me a job to do when I returned to stay. The only problem with redecorating was quite obvious: I'm not a gay man. Worse still, I am a gay woman, with all the handicaps this entails. While a gay man is born with the Pantone color swatch matching system programmed into his DNA, a lesbian might, in contrast, think the following: If I found one in a really cute color, a beanbag chair would be fun to have in this room. While a gay man might shop at West Elm, a lesbian would cut down the elm in the west corner of the yard to make it into a table and paint it to complement the beanbag.

Thankfully, I came to my senses and remembered that I could afford to *not* decorate my house. Now I was thinking like a real wealthy person. I did my civic duty and consulted the Pink Pages to find a dyke decorator (hell, there had to be some exceptions to the decorating DNA–deprived dykes I knew back east). I found several companies listed, and made an appointment with the only woman who answered her phone herself, instead of tumbling me into a barrage of annoying automated voice menus. Her name was Erica, "as in *All My Children*," she said in that helpful, California way. I had noticed the people out here gave *Entertainment Tonight* clues with their names and street directions. I wondered if they could even conceive that a person wasn't familiar with every TV show or movie, to understand the reference. Last week when I had asked for directions at a gas station, the friendly old man told me despite the embroidered name on his shirt, which read William, he liked to be called "Will, as in Smith." Another guy waiting tables proudly announced that he had the same name as Tom Cruise's first manager; before he got *Top Gun*, he added, with obvious regret. The waiter walked away from the conversation believing he had indirectly, but clearly, told me his name. Tom Cruise's *first* manager? What other details should I know to live here effectively?

So here was this decorator doing the very same thing, but I thought, oh fuck it, and made the appointment with Erica As In All My Children, anyway. Her voice sounded a little young, but she sounded very enthusiastic, and claimed to have references from many of the stars from *Beverly Hills 90210*. (More California-style key information, which meant she was a skilled decorator?) I proudly let her know I understood she wasn't referring to an actual address where a bunch of her clients lived, but rather a TV show. "Um ... of course," was her answer, like there would ever be any other possible use for the number 90210. I told her I lived on 852 Channing Drive, as in Carol, but she said, "Who?"

She agreed to come see me that afternoon for a consultation, which sounded a little like I was the one auditioning for her time. Indeed, moments later, I caught myself preparing the house as if a friend was coming to lunch. I had to admit to myself that I was lonely for human companionship. I had even considered inviting Will Smith to dinner when I saw him for another fill-up and we chatted about the non-existent weather.

Erica As In All My Children arrived in a very non-decorator type Jeep Wrangler, Safari Edition. While I judged instantly that the girl had capable shoulders, I had to concentrate vigorously to ignore the young sound in her voice that might be a bit too valley girl to get the job done. The fact that she was a whiz with her expandable measuring tape helped a little. She wielded it like a sword and I started to wonder if she was whipping it about to impress me. Then I realized that she was whipping it about to take measurements. She looked to be about twenty-eight or so, and she appeared to know exactly what she was doing. She also appeared to be flirting in that way young dykes do when they want older women to notice them, but have no intention of noticing them back. I had fun pretending to not notice her feline-like movements as she crawled up the counter, like Spiderman with a vagina, to inspect the highest cupboards.

What Erica didn't realize was that I was never impressed by anyone younger than me. It was sort of my cut-off point to make sure I didn't end up with someone less mature than I was. In fact, I had a slight contempt for anyone younger than me, especially girls with valley girl voices and soap opera names. It just wasn't fair that you had your best body at a young age, but your best mind at an older age. Still, it was difficult not to notice that she did have a kick-ass body in addition to being dressed quite nice for someone under thirty. This girl was smart enough to know that her body would be noticed, even if she didn't wear Girls Gone Wild belly shirts or distracting piercings.

She squatted a bit too close to me as she flung the tape across the kitchen floor. I took two steps back and she said coyly, "Don't worry; I don't bite ... at least not my clients."

"I wasn't worried," I said, deciding not to hire her. She was a little too cocky for my taste.

"I have some fabulous ideas for this place, using stone and some antique wood I found at an auction last month. And since you have such a great view out back overlooking the city, you really need a much bigger deck with an enclosed porch overhanging the valley to take advantage of your pool area. You game?"

I hired her. I liked her confidence in asking outright for the job before showing me any references or photos. I later wondered if I hired her simply because she agreed to start right after I returned from Hell Weeks, or maybe because she had suggested adding a porch overlooking the studio where Lorn Elaine worked every day. Anyway, Erica As In All My Children did eventually leave some impressive photos of her work as well as references (none of which I bothered to call, of course). If I made a mistake, I could always fire her and pay all her expenses, and this was the greatest luxury of being wealthy. You could make impulsive decisions, and buy your way out of them later if they turned out to be mistakes.

Chapter Six

H.I.L.S. (Homesick-Italian-Lesbian-Stalker)
Seeks Actress

My plan was to stake out Flashmen Studios and try to grab one small victory towards making contact to prevent heading back to New England without some small taste of victory.

I planned to begin early the following day, around 4:30 a.m., because I had read all the studios had early calls. I would have to pack and park my rental car carefully, since I would be spending most of the day in it.

My list of supplies was as follows:

> 1 small cooler stocked with light foods and drinks (I went light on the drinks to avoid needing pit stops);
> 1 extra cushion for the car seat;
> 2 copies of the screenplay;
> 1 pair of binoculars;
> 2 steno notebooks to record times and details;
> a digital camera (that I almost didn't buy because of the expense, until I remembered I was rich).

The most embarrassing items:

> A wide-brimmed hat, a pair of sunglasses, and a scarf to hide my face, if necessary.

The studio had four entrances, so I would alternate between parking in front of each of them, figuring she would probably arrive and leave work from the same entrance each day—I just had to figure out which one. My one fear was that if she used different entrances and exits I could quite possibly spend forever missing her at each exit. I only had a few days before I had to head back home, but would continue this routine when I returned, if I had no luck.

Surprisingly, the first day passed quickly, despite the fact that I wouldn't allow myself to read to pass the time or even look away from the entrance for more than 20 seconds. I had timed it, and this was how long it took a person to walk from the door to the parking lot at the south entrance. (I adjusted this by five and ten seconds for entrances east and west respectively.) I followed my plan: to sit in the car, happily munching on peanut butter sand-wiches, Fig Newtons, and diet soda; and I did this rather well. It seemed that just as time would start to drag, a car would pull into the parking lot and I would strain through the binoculars to see if it was her. I even double-checked a few African-American men with the binoculars just to be on the safe side. After all, the entrance to the parking lot was across the street, and at four-thirty in the morning the light was a bit dim. It was a little like playing a slot machine, with the suspense keeping me going.

In between verifying six-foot black men for their likeness to a five-and-a-half-foot auburn-haired white woman, I tried desper-ately to repress the insistent thought that I had become a stalker. I countered with rationalizations that stalkers were nut-jobs with plans to hurt or kill their subjects; and I was merely planning to have my subject star in my movie. Still, the fact that I had just referred to her as a "subject" gave me pause ... until I got interrupted to double-check a teenage boy on a skateboard with my binoculars before he whizzed on past. Not her.

I had no luck that day or the next when I watched a different entrance, but I had found something: an extra couple of pounds from the peanut butter, even despite the fact that I had decided to forgo the extra crunchy so I could eat more quietly. Or maybe the pounds came from the two bags of Fig Newtons (which I had learned from Potsie on *Happy Days* were the best cookies to take on a secret mission because they made no sound when you chewed them).

Since it had been many, many hours dedicated to the task without so much as one clue to jot down in my steno book (I had even brought one of my light-up pens in case I had to write in the dark), I decided I would quit early on the third day to try a different tack. I called the studio and succeeded in getting the phone number of Lorn Elaine's agent, by pretending I was an inexperienced reporter from *Us* magazine. Sure it was another embarrassing moment, but I was running out of time and I wanted to go back to Connecticut with one tiny shred of success under my gradually tightening belt. Before calling the agent's office, I tried to anticipate everything that could go wrong so I'd have smoothly rehearsed answers to any questions that might be asked. Then I found a public phone, so I would not be traced of course, and felt finding one was an accomplishment, since pay-phones are rapidly growing extinct, especially in LA, the home of the beginning of the cell-phone craze. I stood happily with the untraceable phone in my hand, despite the fact that my hat and scarf were causing me to swelter in the booth. I felt I had enough brilliantly deceptive notes jotted down to make the call, and I was actually feeling well prepared and slightly cocky, thinking if someday I happened to lose all my money and needed a job again, I might consider being a private detective.

I called at 1:15, when I thought I had the best chance of her agent being out to lunch. (Californians took their tofu fries a bit later than they did back home.) I practiced a few words to see if I could pull off sounding rushed and in a slight panic, and when I felt I finally had it nailed, it took several attempts to dial the number with my sweaty fingertips sliding off the smooth metal buttons. When the secretary answered, I opened the booth door slightly and spoke with my mouth far enough from the receiver to allow the traffic to be heard in the background.

"Yes, can you put me through to Gretchen, please," I said.

I had already decided that if she put me through, I would have to hang up and try something else.

"I'm sorry, Gretchen is taking a lunch meeting, may I take a message for her?"

"Oh, no ... I *must* speak with her," I lamented. This was one tricky bit of acting, since I was relieved her agent was out, but had to appear to sound upset.

"May I ask who's calling please?"

"Certainly, my name is Julie Adams. Gretchen scheduled me for an interview with Ms. Elaine later this afternoon. I think I have the right street address, but I'm afraid I may be in the entirely the wrong town since I can't find the house. It doesn't end in an 'e', does it?" I said, blowing my entire load of *Wheel of Fortune* knowledge on this one critical moment ... my strategic thinking: Many words ended in the letter "e."

"I'm sorry, but even if I had access to the address, we aren't allowed to give out that information. You have Ms. Elaine's phone number, I assume?"

I hesitated, wanting to get it, but decided not to push my luck.

"Yes, of course, but to be honest, I just didn't want to call and tell her I was lost and sound like a total idiot," I said with a loud, very fake laugh. "So I thought I would call Gretchen instead."

"Well, I'm sorry, I really wish I could help," I heard clacking computer keys and held out for a stroke of luck ... maybe she would take pity on me. "I'm really not supposed to do this ... what did you say your name was again?" she asked.

"Julie. Julie Andrews," I said.

"Did you say Julie ... Andrews?" the woman asked, this time with a certain *tone* in her voice. The tone made me hang up the phone quicker than you can say supercalifragilisticexpialidocious. So maybe I was wasn't as prepared as I thought.

I made a mental note that once Lorn was working on my

movie, I would suggest she change agents. She shouldn't be represented by a careless agency that would even consider giving up her home address over the phone to a stranger ... it simply wasn't safe.

That night, one of the last I would have in California for several weeks, I watched Lorn Elaine on TV on her show *Razor Falls* as a feeling of dread swept over me. What if Vince and Jess were right? *What if I had gone a little nuts?* I debated once again which was more crazy, chasing an actress to read your screenplay, or chasing an actress for love; and decided it was a damned toss up. But as I watched her show, my doubts slowly melted away. I had to have her in my movie ... she was the only one that would be right for the part. Seeing her now, against the cold glass television screen, I thought, I have come to take you out of there ... and put you on the *big screen*. Besides, I was rich now, and when rich people did something crazy weren't they simply called eccentric? Maybe it would have been crazy to think screenwriting was a suitable career move before Gram had kicked it ... but now I could afford to be eccentric.

I almost died the first time I saw her. I'm not exaggerating; I just missed hitting a tree with my car. I had miscalculated my liquid intake and was exiting my parking spot early to find a public restroom, when I spotted her. She was in the back seat of a dark blue Lexus with her window rolled down halfway. Her driver, I supposed, was in the front seat. I didn't want to stop my car when I glanced right at her, so I rolled slowly past as I looked. The color of her hair had caught my attention and I was so engrossed in watching the car, that when the driver got out to open the rear door, I only got a quick glimpse before I had to pay closer attention to the tree I was careening towards. Later, I made a notation in my notebook that she looked quite beautiful in person, but I actually got a better look at the tree; a nice wide redwood, I believe. What the hell was next? Tailing her? I needed a better plan, and I needed it quick, or I would be leaving

California no closer to getting the script to her than I had been before I had arrived. Tailing her car just seemed so ... desperate.

By that afternoon, I decided I was desperate. I gathered up all of my notebooks, my pages of research, and every photo or piece of information I had gathered off the Internet about her, and tossed it into a tall metal trash can and carried it outside to my small deck overlooking Flashmen studios. I lit one of the notebooks on fire and laid it carefully in the bottom of the can to ignite the rest. In moments it was all gone, and I felt a little better, having burned the stalking evidence. I watched until the last wisp of smelly black smoke had faded. I felt bad that I'd ruined a brand new fifteen-dollar trashcan, when I remembered I was rich and shouldn't care about such things. It was time to sever my plans from steno notebooks and do something to actually meet her.

I drove back to a street two blocks away from Flashmen Studios and waited. I checked my watch and for the tenth time felt for my script in the passenger seat of my car. I opened and closed my window several times, not being able to tell if my sweating was from being hot or from nerves. I wiped my sweaty hands on the seat of my car, while I reminded myself, I must do everything *perfectly*. I could not let a stray rational thought convince me how crazy this was because I had not been able to think of a Plan B. I kept telling myself, someday, this would be the stuff of Hollywood legend ... if it all went smoothly.

Perhaps there was a better way to meet her, but I was here now ... and I was too impatient to coordinate a "chance" meeting at one of her frequented places, mainly because I had no idea what those places were. Besides, a chance meeting would be a one-shot deal ... not so with this solution. I was about to make a move that might allow for several meetings, even though so much could go wrong.

It was nearly six when I saw Lorn come out of the studio. While she was waiting for her car I moved mine into position. The dark blue Lexus finally appeared in my rearview mirror. I was ready, with my steering wheel already turned. Slowly ... go slowly, if you pull out too soon, nothing will happen ... if you pull out too late—you can't pull out too late! Easy ... her driver will have to slow down at the corner before the turn ... there, just like that ... he's stopped ... Now! I commanded myself, move now! I pressed my toe against the pedal, as gently as I had rehearsed before leaving my house, and in perfect slow motion, I was rolling ever so gently towards the back of the Lexus. Wait! What the hell am I doing?

A split second before I could change my mind, my front bumper gently kissed the rear end of the Lexus. An image ran through my mind: me in a mental institution ... where even the jackets are straight. What have I done? ... And now it was too late. I had done it ... and I had decided not to, just one second after the deed had been done. But at least it had been done perfectly ... or, at least as perfectly as one car can hit another. There wasn't even a noise; Lorn's car had simply rocked gently like a skiff on a pond. The thought struck me: Maybe I hadn't hit it at all? Maybe I had stopped too soon! Suddenly, all my concerns rotated on their axis until they were the complete opposite. You idiot! You stopped too soon ... you didn't hit the car!

When the driver got out, I realized I had hit the car. I had hit Lorn Elaine's car! What an idiot I am ... I started to panic. I rolled down my window and the driver leaned down to me with a concerned smile. "You all right?" he asked. I was staring at the back door of the Lexus, waiting for Lorn to get out. I knew exactly what I would say to her when she got out ...

"Miss?" he asked.

I looked at him blankly. He was smirking and shaking his head now. "You all right? Don't worry, honey, you barely tapped me."

I was drawing a blank ... what was I supposed to do now? I was sweating profusely and I felt a little sick to my stomach ... and Lorn Elaine was *not* getting out of the car. I reached over and touched the script on the passenger seat ...

"Miss, are you OK? Did you bump your head or something?" He was starting to sound concerned for me.

I finally remembered what I was supposed to do next. I reached into my pocket and handed him a piece of paper with my rental car insurance information already written out on it with my personal information. He looked at the paper a little baffled.

"This happens to you a lot? You're very prepared," he said.

Christ ... he hadn't asked for the insurance info yet! Why the fuck did I hand him that? Outside, I heard the whir of a power window and snapped my attention back to the rear door of the blue car. Lorn had lowered the window halfway, but I still couldn't see her.

"I'll get the owner's insurance information, but I wouldn't worry about it. It's really minor ... probably not worth the trouble fixing, but you never know with these expensive imports. But I don't think the studio will need to report it. I'll be right back." With that, he left me, and walked over to the window and spoke to her. He reached in and pulled out an insurance card. When he came back to my car he said, "Don't worry, I'm sure the studio will take care of the cost, they own the car, we just need to swap info."

He handed me the paper. It appeared Lorn had copied down the insurance information as well as the license number of the Lexus. There was no personal information on the paper at all. I stared at it in disbelief, but ran my finger absently across the writing. No number to call to apologize to her ... no nothing. Just the insurance company name and license plate number.

"You sure you're all right now?" he asked once more.

"I'm all right," I said. Just insane and stupid, I thought, as he finally walked away. I saw the rear window slowly close as he got into the car. A moment later he had driven her away from me. What had I thought would come of this, I wondered? The plan seemed much more logical before it had actually happened. Lorn would have gotten out of the car ... maybe I could have told her I was a fan of her work ... maybe I could have told her I had written a screenplay and was actually trying to get a meeting at the studio ... maybe I could have handed it to her, telling her it was an extra copy and I would value her opinion ... maybe she would have read it and thought the project was perfect for her ... or maybe, at the very least, I would have gotten her contact number to send her some sort of gift as an apology ... maybe I should have counted all the maybes before hitting her fucking car.

I got a call later from the police department who asked me a few questions before saying the insurance companies would haggle it out, but they required a record of the accident in case some of the facts got more creative once the insurance companies were involved. Great. They would be keeping a record of it. My stalking career would have to come to an abrupt end, and after it had been going so well.

"The main problem with lesbians has always been this U-Haul thing," Vince gloated as we hugged at the Hartford airport, "... but Mare, you have taken this to a whole new level. You moved even before you even *had* the first fucking date! This has to be a new record. Shouldn't you contact your people about this? There must be a T-shirt or award or something ... maybe a golden U-Haul?"

"You fucker," I laughed, as I gave him our traditional loud Italian slaps on the back, like two brothers. He took pride in the fact that he could swat me hard, so I took it like a dyke and spanked him harder. It was so good to see him. "Thanks for holding up the 'Lesbian Sister' sign, or I never would have spotted you."

He laughed, quite proud of himself, as he grabbed my small carry-on suitcase. "You can grab the big one, since, of course, you never will."

"You've got a million of them, don't you Vince?"

"Well my sister has been away, and I have some catching up to do. Dyke jokes tend to pile up ... you know how it is. We straight guys are obsessed about the subject after all, we can't help it." He took the big suitcase out of my hands. "Gimme that suitcase; I really just wanted to use the 'big one' line."

"Of course you did."

As we headed to his car, Vince asked, "So are you ready for the big family drama—I mean, meeting? Hope you got a lot of rest out there, you'll need it for the clean-up afterwards."

"The clean-up?" I asked, already exhausted at the thought.

"Yup. Well, you know what they are expecting, Mare. Anything you give 'em will never be enough. There will be drama ... oh yes ..." he said, shaking his head.

"I think what we've decided to do is quite a nice gesture, actually. Have you taken care of the rest of the details while I was gone?" I asked him.

"All set. But I am just saying ... it's great and all, but it's not what they will be expecting."

"Oh, I know that ... but it is all they're getting right now, until I have a chance to see how they act towards each other. How has Aunt Aggie been with Dad?" I asked, afraid to hear the answer.

"She and Mom are both driving him crazy. You know Dad doesn't give a fuck about that house or the land, but Aggie's obsessed with it. She has Dad on speed-dial and Dad refuses to talk on the phone with her," he said. "Of course Uncle Freddie and Uncle Tony are both fine and are staying out of it."

"I don't suppose she realizes that Dad has always refused to talk on the phone?"

"Nope. Mom is hounding him to *address* the situation, which of course is code for: Get our share of the money from your kids before your sister does. Dad insists he doesn't want to go against his mother's last wishes ... even if Gram's last wish was only to piss off her children."

"Uncle Tony is coming too," he said, "but I had to go over to tell him in person since his hearing has gotten ridiculous. He still refuses to get a hearing aid. What a spitfire, though—he said he wouldn't miss being in a room with Mom, Dad, Aunt Aggie and

67

Uncle Freddie when there's money up for grabs ... just for the show, you know. He said he could give two shits about the will, since he planned to be dead in a few years, but wouldn't miss the drama for anything."

"He doesn't seem much better, does he?"

"No," Vince said in an unusually serious tone. "He doesn't seem like he is clinically depressed anymore, but I still get the feeling it's because he is just too tired to suffer anymore about Auntie Celia. His sense of humor is back with a vengeance though. He wants to start a betting pool that Aggie will end up belting someone before this is finally settled. And he's betting it will be Mom that Aunt Aggie attempts to belt."

Our uncle Tony kept up a front of his old fun-loving spirit as four years passed since his wife's death. He resigned himself to living a life alone and tried to fill it with activities and friendships, but those who knew him well could see the profound change in him. No one would ever be able to replace Auntie Celia in his heart, but his love of life and memories of all they had shared seemed to keep him going.

"What a good time we are going to have, all together at last," I said, rolling my eyes. "Is Lisa going to make it in from Maine?"

"Yes, can you believe she's coming? I had to tell her everything already, since she was coming the farthest," he said.

Lisa had been the first to do the unthinkable; not only had she come bursting out of the closet at the ripe old age of fourteen, but by eighteen she had moved out of our parents' house and up to Ogunquit, Maine. She lived alone except for her miniature pinscher and about 800 tons of limestone. Lisa was an artist, a stone sculptor, who eked out a living by selling her sculptures and renting space in the large log cabin home she had built herself to other artists during tourist season. As soon as the summer wound to an end, as she so eloquently puts it each year, "Then it's time to kick the Earthy-Crunchies the fuck out."

Lisa also supplemented her income in the winter by inviting

68

her neighbors for Sunday dinner, and charging them eight dollars a head. The weird part was, they came in droves and often had to wait two lines deep in a makeshift lobby in her garage to be seated. She had no license to serve food or wine so the transactions were strictly cash, or she bartered in labor for something she needed fixed around the cabin. Lisa, amongst her varied other talents, was a fabulous Italian cook. A fabulous cook with balls of brass and language so foul it was amazing people trusted her with the food she served.

Vince and I didn't know how to break it to Lisa that she was a bit Earthy-Crunchy herself. She was under the mistaken impression that since she shaved her armpits and didn't can preserves from the berries that grew behind the quarry in her backyard, she was somehow set apart as a "City Girl." A City Girl, with a quarry of limestone to sculpt, a living room of diners to feed, and a micro-sized Doberman always at her heals, since she was allergic to cats.

Lisa thought that dykes who were allergic to cats but had one or several of them anyway should be the calling card for their elimination from the planet. She also felt that cats were too much of a dyke stereotype, so she would have refused to have one even if they didn't make her wheeze. Of course, she considered the New England Patriots jersey that was perpetually in her clothing rotation, and her Red Sox baseball cap, fine garb for a dinner out on the town, since she didn't see a stereotype there at all. Lisa was one of the most confident creatures on the face of the earth, and Vince and I had the fortune of being her younger siblings, since, apparently, we had so very much to learn from her.

"I'm glad she decided to come. I wasn't sure she would since the last message she left on my machine mentioned something about accusing me of being a closet suck-ass to her favorite dead grandmother," I said.

"Nahhh, she was just checking in as usual," Vince replied. "She says she's looking forward to it."

"So when you said you told her everything, this was because she was coming the farthest? You only meant about the two Hell Weeks, right?" I asked, probing him. I had a feeling there was more to this story ...

He opened the back trunk of his car. "I might have mentioned something about your situation ..."

"Vince!"

Chapter Seven

A Battle of Wills

The family meeting began simply enough. Up until the threat of arson and the slight concussion, I had hoped it might go well. Lisa was helpful enough to tell me later that my first mistake was telling the family about the additional letter from Gram, since I was under no legal obligation to do so. This, she explained, was just adding tinder to the (not so) proverbial fire. Lisa was always helpful in pointing out what should have been done, after the fact, and although she had continued this practice since the days of our births, clearly her job was not yet done.

Apparently, my second mistake was not agreeing to share the letter, after telling everyone there was one, which Lisa explained was the match to the tinder. Some of what I remember, although the details are foggy (for reasons that will become obvious), is the following:

> Mom: "A LETTER? A LETTER! What letter?"
> Aunt Aggie: "A LETTER? A LETTER! What letter?"
> Dad (quietly): "Oh boy ..."
> Aunt Aggie and Mom: "What letter!"
> Vince: "Oh fuck ..."
> Lisa: "Marie, you really shouldn't have told—"
> Aunt Aggie (to Mom): "She said there was a letter!"
> Mom: "Marie—What letter? Why did you keep this from
> me?"

Aunt Aggie (to Mom): "You mean why did she keep it from all of us!"

Vince: "Actually, I've known since—"

Me: "VINCE!"

Lisa: "Vince knew something before I did? Well, I think you should've—"

Aunt Aggie: "MARIE, I DEMAND TO SEE THAT LETTER!"

Mom: "She may have a point, Marie, it was her mother after all ..."

Vince: "I think I'll wait outside ..."

Dad: "Me too—"

Me, Mom, Aunt Aggie: "Oh no, you won't!"

Lisa: "Dad you should really be here for this—"

Dad: "I just came for the food, there's food, right?"

Me: "Can we just all settle down? Why is everyone standing up?—OK, I'll stand then ..."

Lisa: "We really should all sit."

Vince (to me): "Should I just get the letter?"

Me: "Vince!"

Aunt Aggie: "The letter is here?"

Vince: "I was just trying to—"

Lisa: "You know, Vince, you really should just stay quiet."

Aunt Aggie (to me): "You will go get my mother's letter this instant, young lady!"

Lisa: "Hey, you shouldn't talk to her that way, Aunt Aggie, you aren't her mother—"

Mom: "Well I am! Get the letter for your aunt ... now!"

Dad: "So there isn't any food?"

Aunt Aggie: "I will burn this entire house down if you don't hand me that letter!" (She began rustling in her pocket book, probably for matches or a lighter, but apparently forgetting she had quit smoking almost twenty years ago.)

Mom: "Now, Aggie, that's a little extreme—"

Lisa: "A little? Mom, you shouldn't have egged her on, adding tinder to the—"

Vince (laughing): "Holy shit ..."

Me, Mom, Lisa: "It's not funny, Vince!"

Dad: "Are there meatballs? 'Cause I thought I smelled meatballs when I—"

Me: "Can I just have everyone's attention!"

Lisa: "Marie, you really shouldn't stand on that chair—"

Vince: "Marie and Lisa and I are taking you all to the Caribbean for two weeks ... on us, of course!"

Me: "Vince!"

Vince (whispering to me): "Well, things were going so badly, I just thought—"

Aunt Aggie: "What does he mean, *US?* Did he and Lisa get money from my mother—"

Lisa: "No, we got money from OUR sister ... well, I haven't decided if I want mine yet since money is the root of all—"

Me: "Can I please have the floor—"

Lisa: "Marie, you shouldn't be standing on that. What you need to do is—"

Aunt Aggie: "What she needs to do is get that fucking letter!"

Dad: "I was thinking she should get the fucking meatballs ..."

Me: "Can I just have the floor, please?"

I got the floor all right. That was all I remember, but Vince and Lisa filled me in on the rest, after I got the floor ... in my face. The chair had tipped and apparently, I did a face plant into Mom's Rambling Rose-colored carpet, but I really don't remember much about that part since I apparently blacked out for a moment. Lisa said later this helped to settle Aunt Aggie and Mom right the hell down, so in the end it wasn't really a bad move. In my fog, I could hear Dad still concerned about how this might further delay the meatballs; but at least he voiced his concerns for my head as he picked me up off the floor. Vince was unavailable to help since he had already run out to the car to get the Jamaica resort brochure and missed my entire move.

After I got my bearings, we all sat around the table and it was actually Aunt Aggie who served me from Mom's thick, ceramic soup tureen with the scripted words "Chicken Soup" followed by what looked like a dancing chicken shitting tiny white flecks of paint that were supposed to be eggs, hand painted on the side. She filled a miniature soup bowl version of the tureen, without the shitting chicken, with three giant meatballs so heavily sprinkled with parmesan cheese it appeared as if the top had fallen off the shaker, but of course there was no shaker. It was freshly grated parmesan cheese, since no one before our generation would have dared to buy that standard green foil cardboard parmesan cheese shaker with pre-grated cheese from the supermarket. Lisa still refused to buy it, and always kept hard chunks of cheese in bowls on each of her dinner tables in her cabin, each with individual graters. The food revived me, and I wondered if Aunt Aggie would have fed the meatballs to me if I had let her.

When Lisa, Vince and I were kids we loved to visit Aggie's house because she loved to feed us. And it wasn't just authentic Italian cooking. She stashed away odd treats like orange sugar-crusted jelly slices and coffee nips. The nips were a hard, then gradually chewy, candy that lasted for hours and tasted like coffee, which we hated but ate because we thought it was "adult-only" candy. Lisa said coffee nips were probably illegal for children to have, so they quickly became our favorite. Aunt Aggie was diabetic and shouldn't have had any sweets around the house, but she claimed she kept them around for us children. She most often kept her candy in a cubbyhole of her roll-top desk, and this was a secret she shared with only us kids. When Dad would eventually scout out her stash, she would secretly move it again and only tell us where it was. Dad would watch our every move to see if we would lead him to where it was hidden. She had other things around her house that fascinated us too, like a marble statue of two baby twin brothers who were raised by a wolf; but to us they were two pudgy, naked babies that freakily suckled milk from the underside of a wolf's boobies. I thought it was very dirty, kind of like a sculpted version of one of those nature shows, so I would sneak away to the sitting room with the plastic-covered armchairs and study it for hours. Sometimes I even touched the wolf's nipples with the nail on my pinky finger if I was lucky enough to be alone in the room. This was a favorite activity until Lisa discovered that if you trapped and crushed a Cheeto under the clear plastic sleeves on the armchairs, it made a fabulous orange splat design between the tapestry and the plastic. This activity did not last long, and we got into big trouble for defacing three of Aunt Aggie's armchairs (six arms total). We had thought it blended in well with the floral design and nobody would notice and Lisa had me convinced the chairs actually looked better with the Cheetos, so I had gone a little wild with the crushing after that and probably this was how we got caught.

Aunt Aggie was always very spirited, like all the Santoras, but as she got older she got very crotchety and difficult to be around. She really obsessed about money after Uncle Freddie retired, and now Gram's death had made her strangely possessive. As we kids got older, we only saw our more elderly relatives at weddings and more often lately, funerals, so the distance grew between us. Funny though, I really enjoyed her serving me that bowl of meatballs, and after I finished, when Aggie whispered in my ear, "I'll bet you need something sweet," I didn't think for a moment it was not genuine. She reached into her housecoat pocket and slipped me an unwrapped dark caramel. It had lint on it, but I tossed it in my mouth anyway, partly because she was watching, but mostly because I inherited my aunt's sweet tooth. As it melted in my mouth, for a few moments there seemed to be no will, no letter, and no money as Aunt Aggie gave me a satisfied smile as if she herself had eaten the sugar.

Everyone was behaving for the moment, but I wasn't fool enough to think it would last. Vince was the first to try to restart the conversation. "Just in time for my mom's big birthday, when she will be turning the unmentionable decade that follows fifty, we're taking you all to a fabulous all-inclusive resort in Jamaica for two weeks! It has four beaches, three restaurants and five bars ... and everything is paid for in advance. If you want something to eat or drink, you just simply ask for it or take it. Even tipping is strictly forbidden."

Vince had read the brochure more than a few times, and he was doing his best to sound enthusiastic for the crowd.

"Count me in!" Dad said, with his mouth full of meatball and bread.

"Me too!" Lisa said.

"What the hell does an old lady need to go to Jamaica for?" Aunt Aggie grumbled, but at least she was smiling, sort of. "Aren't there a lot of ... of ... those Anglican Americans down there?"

Lisa said, "I think you mean African Americans; and no there probably aren't many of those. They're Jamaicans, Aunt Aggie, they aren't Americans."

"Whatever they are," she grumbled, sounding more like herself, "I don't want any part of it. They smoke that funny tobacco down there, and they tie their hair in those strange little dreaded knots!"

Her husband, Uncle Freddie, spoke up for the first time, "What do hairdos have to do with anything? They won't tie your hair in any knots, Aggie." Then I saw him turn to whisper to Lisa, "Will they?"

"Shut up and eat, Freddie," Aggie said.

Dad said, "Hey, you think they really have a lot of that Jamaican weed down there? I wouldn't mind paying extra for it if it isn't included ..."

"Sal, don't say that in front of the children," Mom said.

"Mom, we are all in our thirties," Lisa said.

76

"Speak for yourself, you old fart!" Vince said patting his chest. "Twenty-eight, bitch ..."

"I am just not going, and that's final," Aunt Aggie said, but she didn't sound final at all.

"It's sweet of you to remember my birthday, kids, but I can't imagine going either, I'm not good with humidity," Mom said. But then she paused and said, "Of course, if you really want us to go ..." Although she hadn't said it, I could hear the "to get the money" part of the sentence loud and clear. Odd, that while they protested, both Mom and Aggie looked happier than I had seen them both in a long time. It was one of the few times I saw them in agreement with each other, agreeing to disagree, aside from both demanding I produce Gram's letter. Thankfully, my face-plant and the Jamaica trip had distracted them for now. Aggie was still concerned about the possibility of "dreaded" locks, and was stroking her black helmet of hair protectively.

"You're all welcome to think about it, but the tickets are non-refundable so you'll be wasting a lot of Grandma's money if you decide not to come," I said.

If you want to get an older Italian to do something, tell them they'll be wasting money if they don't. I continued, "If a vacation in the Caribbean sounds like something you can muddle through, you have three days to pack; and don't forget to bring your birth certificate or passport. Here are your tickets." I laid them down on the table like a casino dealer. "See you all Saturday morning bright and early at the airport. Remember to show up two hours before the flight." I started to clear my empty bowl in the silence. "Oh, and there is only one rule: No talking about Gram's will while we are away, we can always continue arguing when we get back."

Of course, I would be in California by then, but I saw no need to mention that now ...

I drove back to my house for the first time in about six weeks. I found that I had missed my neighborhood, and the old Victorian houses that lined the quaint New England streets. It made me

77

appreciate New England, in comparison to California, which had a random, more forced style in the ornamentation of its architecture. I reached my street corner, and slowed down for a jogger. I would have let him cross the street in front of me if he hadn't been wearing a fanny pack around his waist. Fanny packs are the pinnacle of American fashion faux pas, so I felt someone had to take a stand against them. If not me, who? I pretended I did not see him and drove on while he waited at the crosswalk.

Unfortunately, fanny packs are very popular with lesbians, especially with the vacationing, or mommy-variety lesbian. I just couldn't see anything so necessary to carry to warrant the "kangaroo laden with joey" look. And the attempts to adapt the fanny packs with the current trends in fashion ... a shudder went down my back in anticipation of seeing the first leopard skin fanny pack. I had shunned the jogger in an effort to do my part to leave the neighborhood better than I found it ... maybe next time he might just think twice before cinching a shiny black parachute pouch over the tiny nylon running shorts he clearly stole off the wardrobe rack from the *Vision Quest* movie set.

Jessica was at the door waiting dutifully for me when I got home. In fact she was in exactly the same spot as when I last saw her. I wondered if the money had kept her waiting at the door for the last six weeks. Had she sat down at all? How did she take her meals with her nose so close to the screen door, waiting for her rich girlfriend to come home? God knows I had eaten enough meals standing there when she was too busy with a new friend to come home, or even call. We talked only once during my trip, but when it threatened to turn into a "discussion," I made up an excuse and hung up the phone and did not call back. Damn, I had to admit she looked good, though. I hadn't missed her ... but I realized I might have missed looking at her. I heard my sister's voice inside my head: "Keep it in your pants, Mare." Damned good advice, I thought.

Jess opened the door for me as I came up the steps. Since it was the first time she'd ever done this, I misunderstood her action and stepped aside, assuming she was heading out the door.

"Marie, I have missed you," she said, leaning in to kiss me. I did the quick cheek turn usually reserved for sloppy relatives or lecherous men, or both. She hesitated before giving in to kiss me there. I made a dramatic point of leaning to check the number on the house, in case there had been a mistake and her friendly twin had moved next door.

"Hmmm ... appears to be the right house ..."

"I guess nothing changed while you were away," she said, peeved at my joke.

A lot changed, I thought, as I brushed by her. I had bought a house, stalked an actress and crashed a car, planned a surprise trip to Jamaica, and topped it off with a face-plant cherry on top. My jaw was still hurting from the fall ... or maybe it was from Aggie's stale caramel. I carried my small bag to my room, deciding to deal with the big suitcase tomorrow. Jess would be a big enough headache for my first night back. As if to get a jump on this notion, she followed me dutifully to my room.

"We need to talk after you get settled," she said.

"About?"

"Us."

"So a short discussion then," I said.

She sat down on my bed and launched right in. "How can you be so sure about throwing away everything we have?"

"You mean the lies, the cheating, and all the cruel, deceitful ways you've treated me over the last two years?" I said. "I guess I am finally willing to give that all up ... call me fucking crazy."

"Oh, don't worry, people are calling you that," she snapped back at me.

"I don't care what you and your stupid friends think of me," I spat back. "You're not the prize you appear to be, and someday, when they're all drunk at the same bar, they'll begin to compare notes about what a joke it was that they all had you."

"It's not my friends I was talking about," she said, getting up from the bed, "I was talking about your own family. They wonder if you have gone nuts, Marie, and I don't know what to tell them. Chasing an actress you don't even know across the country— people just don't leave everything they have to do that!"

I froze for a minute and could not answer, so she took the opportunity to continue.

"I told your mother and father I think this might be a cry for help ... maybe you need to talk to a professional. Marie, I also said if you wanted to work on things, I would go with you, since I know this is partially my fault."

I was furious. "Well that had to be the longest conversation you've ever had with anyone in my family! You never bothered to make an effort to talk to them before I inherited money ... now, suddenly, you feel the need to check my temperature with them and reveal every detail of my personal life? A personal life that you have no claim to anymore, I might add."

Jess got up from the bed and slowly walked to the door. I knew her well enough to see the wind up, and here came the pitch, "Marie ... they called me," she said, and I knew this was one time she wasn't lying.

Hours later, I was alone lying on my bed, taking inventory of how I had made a mess of everything. It wasn't just that I had bought a house on the other side of the country to pursue a career that hinged on a person I didn't know from a hole in the wall—although that would have been a sufficient mess. Now I had insisted on taking my entire family, who were probably all convinced by now that I had lost my mind, on a two-week-long vacation. To make matters worse, my parents (who were challenged enough to get along with each other) didn't get along with my aunt Aggie on a good day; and now they actually had multi-millions of reasons why they should fight. Add free booze into the mix, and things were sure to get ugly. I found myself listening to a phrase that had permanently taken up residence in my head:

"Bad luck, get the fuck behind me ... and quit pushing!"

Chapter Eight

The Accidental Tourist

"Dad, don't you dare," I warned him as I watched him observe a woman on the plane, sporting a very ample ass, bending over to adjust her luggage in the aisle. Lisa and Vince spotted the woman as well, and their eyes simultaneously locked on Dad ... waiting for the inevitable.

"Brrraaaap!" It was one of Dad's better faux-farts. His additional talent, as if he needed to be blessed with more, was that he could do it without changing the expression on his face.

We all dove our heads into our laps while rows 11 through 20 of the airplane gawked at the bent lady and chuckled. The ample-assed lady was none too pleased when she straightened up, but too embarrassed to make a scene. This was, unfortunately, not a rare occurrence with Dad. I accused Vince of being an accomplice, since he always egged him on by laughing so hard he'd cry.

I heard a stinging slap and I knew Mom had swatted Dad on the arm, which made him laugh harder, and now we were laughing from the sound of Dad getting a slap, which is much funnier when you only hear it. Once, when we were all at a Halloween party, Dad got wind that some people were complaining about all the noise coming from our table, since we were the rowdiest group in attendance. Dad circled their table as casual as a shark while Vince and Lisa and I watched, not knowing what he was about to do. With the grace of a dancer, just as he sauntered near the barrier of a pole, he unleashed an entire bucket of candy corn from under his Japanese kimono, to rain down on their table, hitting the entire group, and walked away completely undetected. Who would suspect a middle-aged man of doing such a thing? He never even cracked a smile the whole walk back to our table, while the men stood up shaking corn from their hair and scanned the crowd to see whose ass they needed to kick. They never found the ass. It was masterful, and even Mom had marveled at his skills once I convinced her we could not get arrested from a candy corn assault.

"Are we there yet?" a drunk man yelled from the back of the plane and everyone laughed again. "Where are the margaritas? You call this service?" His friends cheered him on. Dad whipped his head around longingly in an effort to locate his estranged soul mates, tragically separated from him and sitting at the rear of the plane. He raised a thumbs up to encourage them, as it was all Mom would let him do.

I saw Aunt Aggie swing her head around to look from the first row of the economy seats. She had cut ahead with the young couples carrying infants and the older folks, professing to need a little extra time to board. However, she was eventually moved from her precious exit row with the extra belly room, but not before the flight attendants had to painfully explain several times that you couldn't board early claiming mobility issues, and then sit where you are expected to assist in the event of an accident. The two flight attendants, who tag-teamed their explanations to her, earned their wings several times that day. Uncle Freddie fidgeted in his seat next to her, as if we'd already been on the plane twelve hours, while Uncle Tony was in the row directly behind them, already sound asleep. I guessed he was snoring because his mouth was wide open and facing the overhead reading light, like he was about to have some major dental work done.

"I'm so excited," Vince whispered to me. "Thanks, Mare, for doing this."

"Remember, you and Lisa paid for it too, out of your shares," I said.

"Yeah, from money you gave us, so you still paid for it all. Have you tried talking to Lisa again about taking the rest of her share?"

"I don't want it," she bellowed from the next row. "Money corrupts people," she mumbled over her *People* magazine. "I like my life just as it is, thank you. Let the old folks mud wrestle for it. I'll bet the farm on Mom."

The flight was only about four hours since it was direct to Jamaica. After we landed, Aunt Aggie made a small scene at customs when a lady with two small children cut in front of her. Uncle Freddy begged her to ignore it, but it simply wasn't in her power to do so.

"I have to use the restroom and she shouldn't have cut us just because she has children. Does she think she is doing God's work, and so this entitles her to special privileges?"

One of the children started crying then as if on cue, and a guard moved the mom and the children to the front of the line to see the next available agent. "She probably pinched that kid to make it cry so she could move up the line ... I know her type!" Aggie yelled after her. Uncle Freddy just smiled apologetically to the woman, when she turned around, horrified. I wondered how many apologetic smiles he had logged over the years.

"This could be two very long weeks," I whispered to Lisa without moving my lips. She answered with a helpful suggestion: "Maybe you should've sent them to one hotel, and us to another. Or better yet, us to Jamaica, and them to Aruba."

"It's done now," I said. "You'll love the hotel, though. It's got laid-back quiet areas and hard-core party spots too ... and although Jamaica isn't known to be 'gay friendly,' this resort advertises in some of the gay magazines, so you never know. It also has a nude beach if you are so inclined."

"Dear God, can we make a pact to hide that last bit of information from Dad, shall we?" Vince said. We sealed our promise with thumbs poised in the thumb-wrestling position we used since kids to seal all major sibling pacts.

The resort was only a fifteen-minute shuttle-bus drive from

the airport, but that didn't stop Aunt Aggie and Mom from muttering, "Oh dear," about a hundred times, while looking out the window of the creaky bus as it gunned its way along the bumpy dirt road. They didn't miss pointing out one makeshift house or Jerk Shack, assembled from metal orange Crush signs and rusted roofing tin with odd American logos on them. When a barefoot child of about eight years was spotted alone walking a donkey on the side of the road, Aunt Aggie gasped as if she had witnessed a murder. I knew my mother was thinking her usual driving advice to beware of the other idiots on the road, "Watch out for the *cavones*!" didn't apply here. In this case, we were the *cavones*, and we were speeding along a road that didn't appear fit for travel.

The resort was called Sunset Hideaway Resort and Spa, and it was as picturesque as the brochure had promised. It was on a gorgeous peninsula which jutted into Montego Bay and carved the beach into two perfect turquoise inlets. "Like two perfect, teal-colored tits," Lisa offered, as if we had all been thinking it, which we of course hadn't. Mom and Aggie took places in line to check in, while the rest of us cut across the open-air lobby to steal a peak at the view. Lisa was right about the water's color. It was an electrified, vibrant teal, and it took my breath away. Although I had been three times before to the Caribbean, each time it had struck me with the same awesome thrill upon arrival as it did the very first time. This was, however, my first trip to Jamaica, and everyone else's as well.

Vince, Lisa and I all got separate rooms so we wouldn't have to share a bathroom. It was the first time I had ever had my own room on a vacation. At thirty-two, I still had the funny "ain't I a big grown-up" feeling as I explored my own private room, which the resort called a bungalow. Immediately there was a knock on my door. Dad had already scored a tray filled with frozen drinks for us to pick from.

"Ha, ha! I told the young fellow to give me one of each, and he did! And, I walked away without paying a dime! Can you beat that? I even tried to tip him a couple of quarters but he wouldn't take it," he said as he slurped a green drink, made a sour face, then switched to a red one, cautiously sipped and smiled with pride as if he had made it himself.

"People living in this century tip in dollars now, Dad. Maybe the guy didn't know what to do with a quarter since they don't appear to have gumball machines here," I said. Dad ignored my comment and pushed the tray towards me, offering the drinks.

"I'll take whichever one hasn't already had its straw violated," I said, laughing. As if on cue, my brother appeared from the next room to select his, and then my sister, who grabbed the last red one from Vince's hand, before he could take his first sip. Grabbing drinks out of her brother's hands was one of Lisa's favorite pastimes, and she had been doing it from the Kool-Aid years all through the tequila years, and I could easily picture her stealing his liquefied dinner one day when they were both old and gray.

"Next round, I'll get a whole tray of red ones so there will be no fighting!" Dad said. "Free drinks ... I felt kind of guilty taking them, but I love it."

"Don't worry Dad, they were definitely paid for," Lisa said.

"The view is unbelievable from here. I think I like being wealthy!" Vince gushed, giving me a squeeze as we peered out the balcony window.

"Shhh, Auntie will hear you," I laughed. But we all toasted his sentiment with the dull thud of plastic All-Inclusive glasses. Mine was a perfect margarita, tart and laced strong with tequila. I was suddenly gleefully happy we were all there together. Maybe this trip was exactly what our family needed. When else in our lives would Vince, Lisa and I all be single and free to enjoy this time together? I cursed myself for having thought the worst about this trip.

I'd heard it was smart to make reservations for the entire week at the restaurants as soon as you arrived or they could get filled, dooming you to a vacation of buffet dinners. So I went back to the lobby as everyone else headed off to the buffet for an early dinner since we had not thought ahead to reserve dinner at one of the restaurants for our first night. Aunt Aggie and Uncle Freddie insisted it must have been the time change that made them so hungry (although there was no change) so I told them to start without me, and that I would catch up.

Jamie, the concierge, was a tall and gorgeous Jamaican man, with a brilliant, flirting smile and warm handshake. He had clearly been chosen for the job for his ability to charm the ladies. *All* the ladies, I guessed, even me. I endured his playful, yet relentless, questions about where my boyfriend or husband was. It was only after I told him I'd left them both at home that he finally let me attempt to make my dinner reservations. I immediately hit a snag trying to imagine my aunt Aggie and Freddie at a French or Japanese restaurant, but couldn't manage it. I guessed we would not be able to pry them away from eating Italian or from the buffet every night. Aggie and Uncle Freddie insisted eating "Oriental Food" was like buying a foreign car, it costs America jobs. Hearing their voices bickering in my head, I gave up the idea of pre-planning our dinners.

I looked through the excursion brochures and picked a few out to pass on to Vince and Lisa. Vince wanted to go to Jimmy Buffet's Margaritaville one night, and since it was only a few minutes away from our hotel, we'd secretly planned this might be a night for us sibs to escape from the old folks. By the end of the first week, I anticipated us craving some distance even this spacious resort couldn't offer.

"Whenever you decide, I can arrange any trip for you my beautiful lady, no problem," Jamie said, taking my hand one more time. "Remember, my name is Jamie, mon, and I'm completely at your service. Anything my beautiful lady desires ... *anything,* and I mean that," he winked. Subtlety was a skill Jamie could stand to improve upon as he gently pulled me closer to him and I braced myself for a frank proposition as he whispered into my ear. Turned out I was thinking sex while he was thinking marijuana.

After thanking him for the kind offer and telling him to expect my dad to come around for that offer, we parted ways, with him acting as if I shattered his heart, or his enterprise, I really couldn't tell.

I walked away to cross the lobby, enjoying the chance to observe people milling about, and could instantly tell the people who had been here a few days from those of us who had just arrived. It wasn't just the difference in the tans, vast as it was. It was mostly a difference in speed. I made an effort to slow my pace since I was still walking like a tourist in an airport, or worse yet, still part of the working world, rushing to keep to a schedule. The folks who had been at the resort a while moved very differently. They lazily held their drinks and even turned their heads slower, looking for places to hang out around the lobby area and pool. Some couples took advantage of the mini beds in the lobby, which substituted for couches, to lie down among the crowds to nap or just to drink and watch the uptight new arrivals walk by. I vowed that from this point on, one of the uptight arrivals would not be me.

I easily found my family's table at the buffet restaurant called the "Banana Hammock." (Apparently in Jamaica, the term "banana hammock" was not used to describe a man's unfortunate choice of wearing a Speedo bathing suit ... or maybe it was?) Aunt Aggie and Uncle Freddie were diving into their plates of food, making faces at each other to silently rate each bite, as only people who had been married so long can do. Mom was chatting with Uncle Tony, and she was actually starting to look like she might relax in the next week or so. She waved at me to signal where the buffet was like an air traffic controller, on the chance I had missed the 80-foot-long line of tables stocked with food. I couldn't find Vince, so I grabbed an empty plate and walked over to Dad, who was standing near what appeared like a huge metal trough of meatballs. He sampled a meatball from his plate before filling it up, as I thought: only my father could score meatballs in Jamaica.

"Hey, these aren't bad ... 'Jerk Meatballs' ... kind of spicy, but in a good way. The sauce could be improved, but not bad at all, more like barbecue sauce than Italian gravy, though," he said, stuffing a second bite into his mouth. "Here, try one," he said. "I watched the guy with the bin and these just came out from the kitchen, hot, hot, hot." He jammed his fork into a steaming ball and plopped it on my plate, as if he had given me a great gift. An Italian parent simply cannot stand to see an empty plate in their child's hands and must immediately christen it with food.

I wanted to tell him it wasn't appropriate for him to sample food while in the buffet line and I also wanted to tell him I usually try to avoid eating meat while outside of the United States, but I decided to test my new resolution to relax. Especially since there were tourists discreetly smoking joints right at their dinner table, so, I accepted the meatball. "Thanks Dad. Where's Vince?"

"Still talking to your friend," he said behind another mouthful of meatball.

"You mean the concierge?" I wondered if Jamie had decided to work a new angle.

"No," he said, pointing across the restaurant with a meatball neatly secured on his fork, "your new ... friend." He had an odd smirk on his face.

I turned to look across the room at Vince. The woman he was talking with looked very familiar, even from behind. I knew that hair color ... and there, in the heat of the Caribbean, I completely froze.

"Vince had no idea you'd invited her ... why didn't you tell us you had a ... girlfriend coming?"

Something wet and steaming hot hit my foot and seemed to explode against it, and I yelped an extended high-pitched scream. This, of course, turned every head in the restaurant toward me. My meatball had rolled off my plate and impaled itself on the top of my foot, the steaming lump of burst meat now wedged tightly between the thong of my flip-flop, scorching my skin. I hadn't

88

realized it was the meatball at first. The pain was so sharp I thought something had blasted a hole at the top of my foot, and the red and meaty pulp was my exploded skin. Another wave of scorching pain climbed from my foot to my mouth, and I yelped again, though shorter this time, since half way into the second scream, I identified it was a meatball and not my own foot exploding. I tried to kick it off, but it held fast, bursting wider, and I yelped a third time as another wave of burning pain struck. I looked up at Vince, who was now waving and pointing to me across the room as the beautiful, auburn-haired woman turned slowly around. She was probably the only one in the place who hadn't yet turned to stare at the yelping fool at the buffet.

I knew it was her, even before she turned completely around to see whom Vince was pointing at. I vaguely heard Dad say, "Are you all right? Hey, I think that's my meatball ..." as he sadly pointed to my foot with his fork.

I was struck dumb as Dad said, "I think Vince said her name was Lorna Doone, or something? Your actress ... friend, right?"

I finally closed my mouth, which had dropped open some time ago, and frantically limped from the restaurant with the meatball still securely nestled in the thong webbing of my sandal, continuing to scald me with each new hop as it broke open further against my foot. I ignored Vince calling after me, as I hobbled quickly out of the restaurant, and with the help of a bartender, I stumbled into the first-aid station around the corner before anyone could catch up with me.

Chapter Nine

The Stalker, the Actress, & the Meatball

Eventually, the throbbing became less intrusive than my humiliation, and I was bandaged with Jamaican-brand "No Problem Mon, Burn Cream" and outfitted with a pair of well-worn crutches, so I could hobble back to my room unassisted. The man at the first-aid station explained that accidents, although usually of the alcohol and non-meatball variety, happened here often. Only when I reached my room did allow myself a mini panic attack. *Christ ... Lorn Elaine was here ...* I suddenly felt dizzy, and as I pitched slowly backwards, I had a vague thought that I should be grateful I was so close to the bed.

I woke up to a pounding that I first assumed was my foot. Instead it was Vince at my door. It took me a while to get my head together and hobble to the door to let him in.

"Are you all right? What the hell happened?"

"I ... Dad ... there was this meatball ... Christ, I think I fainted."

"From eating a meatball? What the fuck was in it?"

I opened the door wider and he saw my bandaged foot.

"What the ..." Then Vince launched into his favorite *Jaws* quote, *"This was no boating accident!"*

"Shut it Vince! It's just a burn ... never mind that ... it was *her*, wasn't it?" *Or am I seeing visions as well as being your basic crazy person?* I thought.

Vince answered, "Why didn't you tell me you invited her?

You've been keeping things from me!" He slugged my shoulder and nearly knocked me off balance.

"Vince, I didn't invite her! I've never even met her! What on earth did you say to her?"

"I … I naturally assumed you had invited her … so when I saw her …"

"TELL ME EVERYTHING YOU SAID TO HER!" *Oh God …*

Vince looked like he wanted to run. I even saw him quickly eyeball the exit before looking back at me, a deer in the headlights.

"TALK!" I said, as I closed the door behind him.

"I'm sorry Mare, when I saw her I thought it was a surprise … that you were actually, you know, together, or something …"

"What on earth did you say to her?"

"I said, 'What a surprise,'" Vince said sheepishly. "Then I said, 'I'm Vince, Marie's brother.'"

"Oh, Christ."

"When she said she didn't know who I was, I said, 'Oh I'll kill her for not even mentioning me.' And then I introduced her to Dad, who had made a beeline over when he saw me talking to a pretty woman … and then she looked even more confused …"

"I need to sit down," I said, feeling faint again. I sat on the bed with my face in my hands.

"Luckily, Dad barely knew who she was, and got distracted by the buffet and wandered away. So … I don't get it; if you didn't invite her …"

"It's a coincidence Vince! I can't fucking *believe* this." Although I did not want to know, I forced myself to ask, "What else did you say to her?"

"She said she didn't know you and that I must have her mixed up with someone else, but I thought she was just being a paranoid celebrity, so I kind of joked with her by saying, 'Don't worry, my sister tells me everything.'"

"Dear God."

"Right after that, you yelled, and I pointed out who you were,

91

which for obvious reasons now, did not clear things up at all, since she still swore she didn't know you."

"That's because she doesn't!"

"Well, she sort of does now ..."

"She probably thinks I followed her here ... that I'm some crazy fan ..." I stopped myself, for obvious reasons. "You have to find her and tell her—tell her you thought she was someone else, or ... tell her you got her mixed up with—"

"Another actress you're in love with?"

"Vince! I'm serious! I need you to *un*-fuck this up for me!"

"Have you even thought that it may not be a total coincidence? Not about you being here, but that out of all the hotels in Jamaica, she also picked the only one that advertises it's gay-friendly? That's good, right? Maybe she's a lesbian! That'd be half the battle, wouldn't it?" He tried to sell the idea to me with everything he had. Although he was transparent, I had to admit, it was something.

There was a knock at the door.

"OH MY GOD!" I said, grabbing Vince's arm.

"Mare, I didn't give her your room number. Not yet, anyway," Vince winked, walking to the door. It was Dad.

"I just came by to see if Marie was okay, and I figured, as long as I was passing by the bar ... I thought these might help." He revealed another tray filled with drinks, all red, as promised. "How's the foot after the attack of the Jamaican meatball?"

"I'm fine," I said, so shell-shocked I'd forgotten my foot was still throbbing from the burn. Lorn Elaine was here ... in Jamaica ... I couldn't believe it. I had gone all the way to California to find her, to run into her here ... with my ENTIRE FAMILY in tow.

"A margarita is just the thing for a nasty burn ... and the ocean will be good too. They both have plenty of salt," he said triumphantly. "You'll be better in no time. Mom said to tell you to elevate it for the first hour so it doesn't swell. Oh, I see we're a little late for that ..." He inspected the swelling welt creeping around the bandage.

"Hmm ... Did you pack boots? 'Cuz in an hour or so, people might mistake it for a manatee stranded on the beach."

Right then, I did something I haven't done since I was five years old. I stupidly started to cry in front of my dad.

"Oh, honey, I was just trying to make you laugh ... it looks fine ... really!" he said awkwardly patting my head. "There aren't even any manatees around here ... maybe if you were in Florida you'd have to worry about that sort of thing." He pinched my cheek both teasingly and affectionately. I wanted to punch him.

"Dad, you're really not helping," Vince said, taking the tray of drinks from him and, like a bouncer, leading him out of the room.

"Honey, I'm sorry for teasing you ... are you going to come back down for dinner?"

"Thanks, but no." I said getting a hold of myself. "I had a meatball to go, remember?"

"That's the spirit, honey, just laugh it off!" Dad said as Vince shut the door behind him. "You'll be better in no time," he cheerfully called out from behind the door. We heard him whistling as he scampered back down the hallway, probably in search of a replacement tray of drinks.

"I'll find her, don't worry. I'll tell her it was a case of mistaken identity, and straighten it all out," Vince promised as he sat beside me on the bed. I wasn't comforted by the thought of him trying to fix things, but what choice did I have? "Hey, you know, she's a really good-looking woman in person."

I stopped sniffing. "I saw," I admitted, but I was thinking screenplay and Vince was thinking hook-up. With some measure of comfort, I remembered my fear of my family finding out about my new dream of becoming a screenplay writer had stopped me from daring to pack a copy.

Before I had decided to, I found myself asking him, "So ... was she alone?"

"No, but she was with a much older lady. Looked like it may have been her mother. Sort of an older version of her ... she was damned good-looking for her age, too."

"Pig," I said.

He gave my leg a pat as we both watched my foot grow.

Later that night, my foot felt better and the swelling had gone down quite a bit, so I decided it was time to emerge from my room. Vince had come back earlier to tell me he found Lorn again, and that he covered for his earlier mistake by telling her she looked just like someone his sister used to know. He said she was the spitting image of my favorite college teacher whom our family kept a photo of her at our parents' house, so he could explain why Dad had assumed she knew me too. He said Lorn bought it hook, line and sinker. I wasn't so sure, until Vince said Lorn had even introduced him to her mother, Katherine. Vince reported that were both very friendly about the whole misunderstanding. This information, plus my own foolproof plan, gave me the courage to contemplate leaving the room.

My foolproof plan? Avoid her at all cost. This shouldn't be hard, since it had been so difficult to find her the first time; NOT finding her had to be much less of a challenge, especially at a large resort. Besides, I conceded to Vince, as much as I might want to, I couldn't hide in my room for the entire two weeks.

The evening was delightfully warm compared with the chilly evenings in Connecticut, and I breathed in extra deep as I hobbled down the stairs. By the time I had navigated my crutches, and changed clothes a few times, it was almost 8:00 on our first evening in Jamaica.

I made my way to the outdoor café to watch the sunset with my family. I tripped over my crutches several times, looking for signs of Lorn's auburn hair. I passed the pool and one of four white beaches on my way to the outdoor café, and, thankfully, she was nowhere to be seen. I took in another long breath of tropical air with relief. As much as I desperately wanted to meet her, avoiding her now was for the best. Getting to know her and trying to pitch my script with my entire family held hostage on an island would certainly mean a quick pruning of any budding career plans. Especially since there was a good chance my entire family may be convinced I had gone completely nuts for this woman.

I noticed she was not at the small bar I passed and I laughed at the thought that now it seemed I *had* become obsessed with her. I tried to relax a little, or as much as you can relax while hobbling on rickety crutches over slippery pool tiles. I finally saw Vince at the next bar with Uncle Tony, so I made my way over.

"There she is! *Mia Maria!*" Uncle Tony bellowed. Since he lost some of his hearing, he never used an indoor voice, anywhere, but he was especially loud outside. Apparently, the distant sound of the ocean made him assume that we couldn't hear him at all. He rushed over to awkwardly hold up my right armpit as I struggled to maintain both my balance and now his.

"How's my Marie?" he shouted into my right ear as if I had the impairment. "Come over here and we'll set you up with a nice orange juice."

"You seem better," my brother said, not bothering to whisper. He'd spent enough time with him to judge that Uncle Tony's audio levels were way out of whack.

"I am. Thanks for taking care of things, Vince."

"I just fixed what I almost screwed up."

Uncle Tony misunderstood and shouted, "So get her a darned screwdriver instead of the orange juice, Vince! I don't give a rodent's behind if you kids drink alcohol ... you're all adults now!" He started laughing for no reason, so we did too.

Several heads at the bar turned to check what the commotion was. They smiled at the sight of Uncle Tony trying to assist me in his blue dress pants, brown dress shoes, and head topped off with a cloth fisherman's hat, which only he could make look somewhat dapper. "The other girls are still taking naps!" he said. "Probably resting up for all that hot Jamaican action," he winked, as several of the onlookers chuckled. Uncle Tony was nearly deaf, but he knew when he had an audience in the palm of his hands. A friendly couple nearby toasted to his sentiment of finding "hot Jamaican action."

95

"Where's Dad?" I asked Vince, as a sudden, unexplainable feeling of dread swept over me. I tried to ignore it, and took a long swallow of the vodka and orange juice, which had appeared in front of me. It was strong for an All-Inclusive drink. I heard familiar voices laughing in the distance and before I could place them, Dad rounded the corner with the now-permanent tray of frozen drinks in one hand, and something quite different in the other: Lorn Elaine's mother's hand ... with Lorn linking his arm on the other side. It was Lorn I'd heard laughing; and, like a piece of familiar music, I would have known that sound anywhere.

"I'm going to give you a piece of advice, Mare," Vince said quietly to me, observing the approaching entourage.

"Drop my crutches and run?" I mumbled, as they seemed to be moving toward us in slow motion.

He tipped my drink to my mouth. "Drink!"

I did. So much for the "Avoid Her At All Cost" plan. Dad spotted us and sauntered over with the two women as if he was giving both away down a wedding aisle.

"Who's *la donna bella* woman in the pretty yellow hat? So beautiful!" Uncle Tony appeared struck by lightning. His eyes were transfixed on Lorn's mother.

"Her name is Katherine," Vince said. "She's a very nice lady. Don't swear in front of her."

"I wouldn't dream of it," he said gently, suddenly with perfect hearing. He drifted over to greet Dad halfway to the bar. I wished I'd inherited his confidence, since I was fighting the urge to shrink back to my room. Had it not been for the crutches, I might have attempted a run for it. Vince and I watched Uncle Tony elegantly bow and gently press one of Katherine's hands within both of his in a warm hello. He greeted her in Italian. We saw Dad then introduce Lorn, but Uncle Tony seemed unable to take his eyes off of her mother. I thought I saw Lorn glance over Uncle Tony's shoulder at me.

"You'll be fine," Vince said, as I gulped the rest of my screwdriver. "Remember, she's just a person, so just be normal around her. No offense, but it's not like she's as stunning as Jess ..."

Actually, he was wrong about that. She was a magnificent-looking woman. I had found her very attractive when I'd watched her films, but in person, she had that certain something that clearly contributed to her success as an actress; a star quality which could hold people's attention. I'd waited a long time to meet her; and now she was heading right for me. I cursed that she had to be so damned attractive when this would be plenty difficult enough ...

The group walked toward us. Uncle Tony was escorting Katherine in the old-fashioned way of wrapping a woman's arm inside his own, which only folks from his generation could pull off with a complete stranger without looking lecherous. Instead, he looked gallant and gentlemanly. Lorn's eyes were on me first as they approached, then she recognized Vince and said hello to him, remembering his name. I noticed that, like her attractiveness, the sound of her voice was even more striking in person ... but then, it could have been downing a strong, extra tall drink within a matter of seconds that made everything seem so amplified. Either way, it was downright eerie to hear a voice I knew so well, on someone I'd never met.

Dad started to speak first, but thankfully, Vince interrupted him to introduce me. "Ms. Elaine, this is my sister Marie. She's the one I spoke about earlier. Mare, doesn't she look so much like that teacher friend of yours?" If my imaginary teacher friend was fucking gorgeous, I thought, I would have been her worst student ... and what kind of teacher would keep in touch with a loser like that? Her reddish-brown hair seemed ablaze in the setting Caribbean sun and I noticed she had a trace of delicate freckles across the bridge of her nose ... how had I missed that before? Those Hollywood make-up people should be shot for hiding those.

"What friend does she look like?" Dad asked, but Vince ignored him and I was too paralyzed to think quickly. When nobody answered, Lorn put her hand towards me and finally I snapped out of my screwdriver-induced daze and jammed my hand into hers, hoping she didn't notice the delay. "Nice to meet you," she said. Her hand was soft, but she gave a confident shake. When she smiled more brilliantly than my Jamaican concierge, wild and naughty thoughts rushed through my head ... followed by: Screenplay ... ? What screenplay?

"This is my mother, Katherine," Lorn said, turning towards nobody, since her mother had already been swept away by Uncle Tony. He was leading her towards the peninsula under the palms for the best view of the sunset, as if he'd been giving tours there for years. He waved his hand gracefully across the expanse of coastline like an older, Italian male version of Vanna White, if Vanna wore fisherman's hats with tiny fly-ties on them.

"Well, Marie, I guess you'll have to wait to meet my mother since she appears to be otherwise engaged," she said, laughing.

Hearing her speak my name got my attention and I melted, just a little, but again, it could have been the drink. Nice laugh, great smile ... I had seen this smile so many times on DVD, but this one had been for me. That distant voice was still telling me to run, but now the voice was growing weaker.

Dad assured Lorn, "I promise, my older brother is quite harmless. He can't hear worth a lick and is the worst driver, but completely harmless, especially on an island. As long as we keep him away from the rental cars and golf carts, we should all be safe."

"Thanks, but I am not worried. My mother's a very strong lady and doesn't need me to be her keeper. This I know, because she tells me *all the time*."

I tried to think of something clever to say. Lorn seemed so comfortable, and it wasn't fair since I was under tremendous pressure to impress her. I finally thought of something to say.

"Did you just arrive today as well?" I choked, in a forced, casual voice that sounded both forced and casual. I sounded like an idiot, and although I knew better than to look at him, I knew

Vince would be working hard to keep a straight face, seeing me struggle. Besides, her eyes were back on mine and I wondered if it was a coincidence that the sunset grew more intense around us. My focus was blurred a little too, as if a camera was shooting her through a gauze lens, omitting any human imperfections; I gave some credit to the vodka, but swore she didn't have an imperfection to be found. I was also distracted by the music that was now swelling inside my head, until I realized with great relief that a band had started playing outside the café.

"Yesterday, actually," she answered, "but we were so tired from the trip that I barely remember anything. So, I'm counting today as our first day."

And our first day, I thought, like a complete idiot, as the music grew louder. She smiled warmly at me again. Better than I remembered, I thought ... keep it in your pants, I warned myself for the second time in a week.

"How many Santora family members are here?" she asked.

I was pretty sure I knew the answer to that question, so I dared to reply. "You've met Dad, Uncle Tony, and Vince, and there is also my mother, my sister Lisa, my other uncle Freddie, and his wife Aggie, who is my father's sister. Seven." There. I'd done it.

"And you," she said.

"Eight," I said. "I guess I forgot I was here; I swear I haven't even touched the rum."

"How's your foot?" she asked.

What an odd question ... then I remembered the meatball and burn, and the bandage and the crutches digging under my armpits, which had all strangely vanished from my mind. "Much better," I said. "I feel stupid about the whole thing, even if it's all my father's fault."

Dad said, "Sure was. I had mistakenly assumed my daughter had long since mastered the art of holding a flat plate under a round meatball." We all laughed, and I thought, it all seemed so normal. Dad even seemed normal ... maybe this was going to be just fine. After all, my family was nothing if not entertaining, and

Lorn seemed to be enjoying our company. Once again, I resolved to relax and simply let things happen, or not, whichever way it was to go, until a voice bellowed behind us.

"Well, someone needs to introduce me to this beautiful actress I've been hearing so much about!"

It was Lisa, wearing her favorite baggy camouflage military shorts. She had already punched her room key with a makeshift hole, so she could dangle it from her belt loop with a coiled blue cord attached to a mountain clip, which now swung out in front of her crotch like a sex toy. As striking as this image was, the best part was she was wearing a shirt that was screen-printed in huge letters that could be read clearly from across the resort: "I LIE TO GIRLS."

Oh, Christ.

"Here comes Lisa, our sister." Vince said, dramatically lowering his voice, "We aren't sure, but we suspect she may be leaning ever so slightly towards a life of lesbianism."

Lorn wasn't thrown at all, and chuckled at Vince's remark as she bravely took a step towards Lisa. As Lorn greeted her with that same confident handshake, Lisa said, "Ms. Elaine, you have the most beautiful hair. The color is fabulous. Oh, and I've enjoyed your work for years." Lisa paused a moment to turn away from Lorn so she could raise her eyebrows in her oh-so-subtle hubba-hubba way at me. Lorn thanked her graciously, since only Vince and I knew Lisa was lying and had never seen her work at all.

Back off, dyke, I wanted to growl. Why hadn't I said something about her work? Now, if I did, it would look like I'd been forced to say it. This was all a disaster, again. Why does the younger sibling always feel like they've lived their life trying to catch up with their older sister?

Uncle Tony and Katherine rejoined our group to finish watching the sunset. "I've decided we must all have dinner together tomorrow evening," Uncle Tony announced. Katherine smiled pleasantly by his side, as if they'd been married for years and he always made all their social announcements. I looked at Lorn, and since she seemed pleased, how could I fault my uncle for making our first dinner date?

When I got back to my room, my message light was blinking; it was from Jess, saying it was important I call home. I hadn't left our hotel information, so I had no idea how she'd found the hotel. Her purposely vague message left me no choice but to call, in case it was a real emergency.

"Hello?" She had answered on the first ring.

"How did you get this number?" I asked.

"Does that really matter? You take off without a word to me about where you are going and you leave the friggin' country?"

"Jess, I'm not in Guam, I'm in Jamaica, but I guess you know that. But in case you haven't pieced it all together just yet, we're finished, so I don't owe you any other explanation."

"Suddenly you're very clear over the phone, Marie. Your lawyer's letter notifying me about selling the condo was very clear as well. So why the fuck did you let me quit my job if you had no intention of us trying again? And now I have to buy out your half of the condo with no job!"

"You quit your job, Jess, I had nothing to do with that. Be honest, we both know you're more upset about losing the money than with losing me. You left this relationship years ago," I said, "I'm just making it official."

"From Jamaica," she said.

"What difference does it make?" I asked. "How did you know where I was?"

"It wasn't easy. Before I tried calling your mother, I assumed you had run off to California to chase that actress again."

"I don't have to chase her. She's here with us," I snapped. Had I given it a half a thought, I would've chosen not to tell her that ... but it sure felt good.

"What?"

"Goodbye Jess."

101

Chapter Ten

Staying Awake To Find It

I was having dinner with Lorn tonight. Me and my entire, imposing family ... I shuddered to imagine what Lorn and Katherine would think of Aunt Aggie and Uncle Freddie's table manners (in the old country, it is perfectly acceptable to talk with your mouth filled with food), and also tried to put out of my mind what T-shirt Lisa might show up wearing. I had to focus on what I'd say to Lorn ... how I would get to know her among this crowd, in which I was, by far, the least outgoing. After Jess's phone call, I hadn't been able to sleep soundly so I got up early and put on a bathing suit and shorts, to take a long walk down the deserted beach. My foot seemed to have healed a great deal overnight, so I took the bandage off, figuring Dad's margarita theory might hold some truth and the salty ocean water might do it some good. After all, I would have to find a way to wear shoes tonight.

The sun was brand new and the ocean took on a brilliant sparkle at the surface of the teal water, brighter than the most unrealistic painting; it appeared as if it were a cartoon. The light within looked as if it were shining up from below the sand. I noticed the paler areas were the precise shade of green as Lorn's eyes. This was something that had never been captured on film properly ... that, and the freckles. What other discoveries might tonight bring? I wondered ... until I reminded myself of the business at hand. I could not complicate things by letting this woman get under my skin ... or me all over hers. I hoped it was the contact with the ocean water that suddenly switched my headlights on at that thought, although the water was not even cool.

The warmth of the water was so pleasurable that I tried to enjoy just living in the moment and to put the thoughts of Lorn's arrival in Jamaica and my family aside. The sea was the exact same temperature as the air, and I reveled in the sensation of only feeling the texture of the water, and absolutely no temperature change from the air at all. The burn stung a bit, but I told myself it was a cleansing sting, and briskly walked it off until it dulled to a pleasant tingle, and then, until I no longer noticed it. The morning air was tepid but comfortable and I took long breaths as I walked more quickly. I felt overwhelmingly good about being here. I even laughed at how I kept going back and forth from believing this trip was exactly what was needed, and then in the next second, convincing myself it was a prelude to a disaster. My experience with my family would have had me betting on the latter, but just as often they surprised me.

One advantage of the evening was that it wouldn't be all upon me to keep the conversation going. I'd have a cast of characters to derail any uncomfortable silences; in fact, I couldn't remember a time it was ever silent around a Santora dinner table. Uncomfortable silences were unheard of in an Italian family's home. If something arose that was uncomfortable, it was simply raised high on a flagpole for the entire family to pledge its allegiance to, and usually during dinner.

My only concern was keeping Lisa and Vince in line about revealing too much. Before coming back to my room, and Jess's call, I'd spent part of last night in their rooms, reminding them that they had to forget what they knew of my previous link to Lorn. If Mom and Dad knew very little about my "obsession," I would like to leave it at that. Simply put, I told them they were to shut their cake holes if there was any doubt about what they should or shouldn't say.

With the others it was a bit trickier. I'd have to leave that to chance, since I knew if I came clean and gave them a list of things they couldn't talk about, it would be like placing the subjects right at the tip of my father's tongue, and he wouldn't be able to resist. As for my two uncles and Aunt Aggie, the less said, the better. They all knew about Lisa and me, but our "lifestyle," as it was (rarely) referred to, was the one subject that wasn't easily raised up the flagpole for discussion ... at least not when we were around. I think they didn't know what to make of Lisa and me, since their generation was not openly exposed to homosexuals. Gays were often portrayed as insane and tortured creatures back in their day. Re-educating my family was not the hill I cared to die on, at least not here in Jamaica.

For the sake of the screenplay, it would certainly help if Lorn were a dyke, I thought as I walked, but I wished I could tuck her away back in California where she belonged, safely away from my entire family. Maybe then I could just send her a postcard: "Greetings From Jamaica, Wish You Were Queer ... Oh, by the way, wanna be in my movie?"

"Good morning."

I turned around, startled. It was Lorn. She apparently had been walking behind me.

"Oh, good morning. I didn't see you." I tried to sound calm, but felt the panic rising.

She was in a bathing suit and a pair of straight girl shorts (a little too short, a little too cute, and no sport logos), and although I tried not to focus on that fact, it was already too late. I concentrated on not glancing downward, where she had more delicately freckled skin ... and instead locked on to her green eyes, finding them mesmerizing enough. With eyes like those, perhaps staring at her chest would have been the safer thing to do ...

"I didn't recognize you at first without your crutches. You seemed very deep in thought; I hope I didn't disturb you."

"No, no," I said, wishing I'd taken the time to throw a little mascara on.

"I was walking a little faster and was afraid I would sneak up on you."

Sneaking around behind someone was my job, I thought.

"Would you rather be alone?" she asked.

Of course she had no idea what she was asking me. No, I don't want to be alone ... I want you and I to become instant friends so I can feel comfortable enough to pitch my screenplay to you ... then we can make a movie that will make you a household name, and me too, of course. And then, when the business part of our relationship is squared away, well, you just never know ...

"Not at all," I said, and so we continued to walk together.

My mind raced as I tried to look peaceful; this was not easy. Did it mean something that she was here in Jamaica? If I had tried to make this happen, it would have taken years to work out the details. Just as recently as the plane ride here, I had mapped out alternative scenarios that might result in our meeting since the car accident had failed miserably ... and now she was here. And it left me with no time to plan, or craft or devise ... but just to react. And then it struck me as funny that this was how life is supposed to be. In any case, I didn't care for it; too unpredictable for my taste. Like right now ... I had no idea what to say. We were just meeting, but in my head I had fast-forwarded to making a friendship, making our movie, making some drinks ... and (as I snuck a peek at the front of her) maybe some mind-blowing sex ... Focus, Marie, I warned. Keep it in your shorts, Lisa and now Vince said again, only this time in unison in my head ...

"You're wincing. Is your foot bothering you in the water?" she asked.

"No, I'm fine. It is probably doing it some good to cool it off." I should sit in the fucking water, I thought.

"Are you the only early riser in your family?" she asked.

"Today I am. I didn't really sleep well last night."

"Because it was a strange bed?"

"I'm not sure," I said.

"My mother would say, if you can't sleep, it means you're

missing something in your life and you're staying awake to find it. People who sleep peacefully aren't looking for anything."

I smiled. "I would say that your mother is a smart lady." She was polite enough not to ask what I was looking for, but I couldn't resist. "So ... you're up early."

Lorn laughed. "I admit, she was making that observation about me. Right now, I'm pretending it's the jet lag. Work with me on this?" she said.

"You got it, that jet lag can be a bitch," I said.

We walked along not speaking for a while, and it seemed strangely all right. I fought the urge to make small talk, fearing that I would say something stupid, and because of this, the walk evolved into an intimate stroll. I felt as if the salt of the ocean and the gentle massage of the sugary sand sliding under my feet were intoxicating me as we moved along the coast.

"It's unbelievably beautiful here," she finally said, but I was feeling so ridiculously happy that I couldn't find a way to respond.

Finally I said, "I don't feel like I could be looking for anything missing here."

She turned, gave me that stunning smile and just when I thought we might be gearing up for some sort of moment, she said in the voice of a cheerleader, "That's the attitude. So, maybe you'll be able to sleep tonight."

I thought, if dirty dreams about this woman didn't wake me, she might just be right.

Lorn and I parted ways so she could go meet her mother, and I met my family for breakfast at the Banana Hammock as planned. They had been there for a while because as soon as Auntie Aggie saw me, she released Uncle Freddie like a retired greyhound from the gate to go fill their dishes. I had obviously been holding up the show. Vince jumped up to greet me.

"Where were you?" he asked, "We thought maybe you over-slept so Mom made me call your room."

"I was just walking on the beach."

He could tell by my ridiculous smile that something had happened. "You were with her!"

"Shhh! Yes, we ran into each other on the beach ... it was ... very nice."

"Nice? You're kidding, right?" He stopped me from walking over to table.

"OK, it was great, and I'm looking forward to seeing her tonight. It's just ..."

"What?"

"I'm kind of worried if I really do get to know her, I could really like this woman ..."

"Wasn't that the whole idea?"

"I guess," I said ... Not quite, I thought. "What if I find out I can't have her? Now that she's, well, a real person, it's occurred to me that with the ten-percent chance of anyone being queer, this could be a long shot. Factor that in with some of those people not willing to actually live it, and the odds get worse."

"Well, first off, I think it's already too late, since you're completely in love already, you idiot. And second, what makes you any different than the rest of us that you don't have to take a risk? If it doesn't work out, you lick your wounds for a while and then, when you're over it, we all goof on you. That's life. For Christ's sake, lesbians of all people shouldn't be afraid to lick wounds."

In spite of myself, I laughed at his joke. While he was wildly inaccurate about the head-over-heels assessment, I said, "You scare me most when you're the voice of reason, Vin."

"Me too. Let's eat before Aunt Aggie loses it. She practically kicked poor Uncle Freddie out of his chair when you finally got here."

Breakfast was very good, and in typical Italian tradition, we all ate more than we should have. The plan was to skip lunch so we could have dinner early. I was distracted, thinking about what dinner with Lorn would bring, when Dad tapped the side of his glass with his spoon to make an announcement.

"May I have everyone's attention, please? Other than the chance to spend time together as a family, it seems we're all here for another reason. Marie, we'd like to thank you for bringing us all here so we could share in the beginning of what could be a beautiful new relationship."

I spat out my drink back into my glass, and the gurgle-gag-spit sound made everyone turn to look at me.

"Sorry; swallowed wrong ..." I choked, glaring at Vince, convinced he had blabbed.

Vince was sporting his famous deer look again, and he indiscreetly shrugged his shoulders at me as our father continued.

"It has come to my attention that someone in our family has fallen in love and regardless of what happens, I think that fact alone is reason to celebrate!" He raised his glass as my mouth dropped open. "To the member of our family who has met the lady of their dreams ..."

Aunt Aggie thumped Uncle Freddie in the side and interrupted Dad, "Do you know anything about this Fred? You never tell me anything!"

My father looked at me and smirked as I braced myself, and readied to lay my face in my hands. Dad lifted his glass again. "To my brother ... who swears to me that one day soon he'll marry the lovely Katherine!"

Lisa and all the men at the table erupted in cheers, and Uncle Tony looked proud, as if he might make a speech, and I heard my mother say, "Who's Katherine?" and Aggie answered back, "I have no friggin' idea!" I breathed a heavy sigh of relief as Vince and Lisa started laughing hysterically at my panic.

Uncle Tony was convinced he would marry Lorn's mother? Christ ...

Lisa answered Mom and Aggie's questions with her favorite quote from *The Big Chill* movie, "If you're going to sleep late, be prepared to miss a few melodramas."

Uncle Tony said in a loud but tender voice, "My brother thinks I'm kidding, but I was serious when I said this to him after meeting Katherine yesterday." This silenced the table in an instant. "Not since my Celia left me have I ever felt such *contentezza*, such happiness. She was the light of my life, and I knew I would spend the rest of my life with her from the first day that we met in grade school here in America ... and when she died, I was certain the part of me that could love had died with her."

The other tables around us now grew quiet, and Dad, who had started this as a light-hearted joke, had gotten up from the table and was now standing behind his seated brother, with both hands placed in affectionate support on the older man's shoulders.

Like the rest of us, Uncle Tony's eyes had filled, but he continued cheerfully while raising his glass of orange juice into the air. "I knew it instantly when I met Celia, and I know it now after meeting Katherine too—I can feel love again. And even if Katherine doesn't choose me, I will always be grateful to her for making me feel alive again. To life and *amore*!" he said, raising his glass of orange juice.

"To life and to love!" Dad said, giving his brother a quick hug before grabbing his drink and raising it with ours across the table. I clicked glasses with Lisa and Vince with direct stares into their eyes, since long ago we started the tradition that if you clicked glasses without making eye contact, you'd run the risk of going seven years without sex. We gaped at each other with wide, watery eyes and smiles as our glasses clinked. The people around us gave Uncle Tony's sentiment scattered applause and some raised their drinks as well. I thought about how strangers don't act like strangers when they're on vacation; you had all the time in the world to connect with people. In their busy lives back home (for people unlike myself who held jobs) it would take weeks to carve out enough time to get to know someone ... an hour here or there, a ten-minute coffee break at work ... maybe this explained what was happening to me as well. Back home it might take years before you would feel you know someone well enough to take a walk alone to talk with them ... and to plan having dinner to boot. Here, things seemed to be happening in a heartbeat.

Our family had witnessed Uncle Tony's tremendous loss, so when we realized this was the real deal for him, there was not a dry eye left at our table. I thought, too, as I raised my drink, life is too short; love is too important ... It was up to me to find the courage to do something about my life too. I had an opportunity to get to know Lorn here on this trip, and maybe I should see where that might lead. She was the first person who had turned my head in years ... Oh, and of course, there was the screenplay. The screenplay I had been fixated on ... and strangely hadn't thought of all day.

Before lowering his glass, Uncle Tony hastened to add in a quieter voice, "Make sure you bunch of *minchiones* don't fuck it up for me!"

Minchiones is Italian for idiots. Ditto, I thought.

Chapter Eleven

From Coffee to Merlot

After Uncle Tony's speech, he inspired me to find the nerve to ensure I would sit next to Lorn this evening, even though Uncle Freddie had insisted we sit "boy, girl, boy, girl." Obviously with six women and four men, this was a rule we voted to abandon, even though Lisa had volunteered to be a boy, just for the sake of keeping order. Mom rolled her eyes at her but she could not completely stifle a smile.

Since Lorn and her mother hadn't yet arrived, I sat next to the two empty seats near Uncle Tony, who had the whole table working toward his love match. Mom and Aggie insisted we arrive forty minutes early, so we were all on our second glass of wine when Lorn and Katherine walked into the restaurant. They were a stunning pair of women, and more than our party noticed. I wondered if some people recognized her, or if they were just enjoying the sight of a beautiful mother and daughter walking elegantly together across a room ... I know I fucking was.

Lorn was wearing a black dress that perfectly showcased her full figure and brilliant auburn hair, which she wore loose in waves brushing against her exposed shoulders. Yikes, she looked good ... too good. Katherine was also radiant in a blue dress that showed off her lovely silver hair, which she elegantly wore up for the evening.

No one questioned who'd escort them either, because Uncle Tony's eyes hadn't left the door for a moment. When he saw them he bolted for the door and met them halfway across the restaurant to walk them to our table, where we all made our greetings. I found it difficult to look Lorn in the eyes as I said mine. As I had planned, Lorn sat next to me. Vince winked at me from across the table, and I glared at him with scolding eyes. A useful trick I learned from Mom.

"Thank you all for inviting us to join your family dinner," Katherine said. "Perhaps the right thing for us to do would've been to politely decline; but you're all so very gracious and have made us both feel so welcome."

"Nonsense, my dear." Uncle Tony amazed me again with his perfect hearing. He then spoke in his most pronounced Italian accent, "Tonight we are all *La Famiglia Santora!*" He was still standing and he raised his glass to Katherine, who reached for the glass of red wine he'd poured for her. My family simply never entertained white wine as a choice. In fact, my grandmother had referred to it as if it were a new-fangled type of wine they cared not to explore, referring to it as *"profumazione"*, the Italian word for perfume. Katherine and Uncle Tony clinked glasses while we all smiled at them.

I could see Mom and Aggie comparing notes as they smiled and assessed Lorn and Katherine. Lorn unexpectedly turned to me and said, "You have such a warm and charming family."

"Some of the time," I responded. "Hopefully, they'll all be on their best behavior."

"Well, I hope not on our account. This is Jamaica, and they should be having fun, not behaving for two strangers that have crashed their party."

I smiled at her, "Don't worry about that. Even if they intend to, the Santora family never deprives itself of fun for very long." This was a fairly complex sentence for me to get out, since I was drowning in the intoxicating smell of Lorn's *profumazione*. "Besides, you didn't crash; you're invited guests."

"Thank you again for that." She lowered her voice. "I hope this doesn't sound crass, but my mother just simply adores

Italian people. She wouldn't stop talking about what charming men your Uncle Tony and father are." Maybe it runs in the family, I hoped, but with the way my luck was running, it would probably be the men only. Still, there was something ... she was very attentive, although that was probably due to the location of my seat. If Vince or Lisa had sat by her side, they may have had her immediate attention instead. I was actually surprised Lisa hadn't arm-wrestled me for it.

"Well, Uncle Tony and Dad both love the ladies."

"And is your mother OK with two unattached women being invited to a family dinner?" The word "unattached" rang in my head like a school bell in early June. I pictured myself flying victoriously over one hurdle, on a long, outstretched track. I reminded myself that this was not the hurdle I had originally set a goal to leap over. As inspired as I was with Uncle Tony's speech, there was still the screenplay ...

I answered her, "My mother is so used to it by now, she barely blinks if Dad happens to stroll on by with a woman on his arm. She knows he's just a harmless flirt; it's the Italian male's birthright after all. It's written somewhere I think. Could be the Bible ... or maybe *The Godfather*."

I congratulated myself for making her chuckle.

"I heard that," Vince said.

"Are you a flirt with the ladies as well, Vince?" she asked him.

"Nothing compared to Lisa," he answered, as Lisa swatted him hard on the back of his head. All those at the end of our table, especially Lisa, burst out laughing. The feeling I had from sharing a laugh with Lorn and my brother and sister felt warm in my chest. I could tell Vince and Lisa both liked her, and I knew Lisa especially enjoyed how Lorn didn't shy away from their off-color jokes—a must for survival in our family. Our family ... I glanced around the table and wondered if some day what Uncle Tony said could possibly come true. Some day, could we be one family linked by their just-under-the-wire romance? Katherine seemed flattered by Uncle Tony's attention and was now speaking softly

113

to him, rather than to the rest of the table, and he was rapt with attention.

The wine flowed and despite my fears, the conversation was easy over the resort's diligent, though not entirely accurate, attempt at Italian food. The table had naturally divided between the young and the older, with Lorn sitting squarely between the two sides. I knew Dad wanted to be closer to our end of the table, since Uncle Tony was monopolizing all of Katherine's time, and Lorn was too far away for him to engage in conversation, although it didn't stop him from shouting several attempts.

At our end, Lorn asked questions mostly to Vince and Lisa since they were directly across from her. It was probably also because my siblings were more adept at small talk than I was. I found myself envious of how easily the two of them kept the conversation going. Meanwhile, while they chatted away, I was still dreadfully distracted by her perfume and sleeveless dress with her smooth, lightly freckled arms in such close proximity to mine. There seemed to be a vibration along the entire length of my left side, like an invisible, body-length antenna, constantly monitoring her presence. *This could be trouble*, I thought.

Lorn was a great listener, and in the Santora crowd this was yet another requirement for survival, since it was tough to get a word in unless you talked right over people (which was perfectly acceptable and necessary behavior). Lorn asked Lisa about her house in Maine, and shared that Ogunquit was one of her favorite places to visit in the summer. A pink triangle flag arose in my brain, and started waving wildly. A fair amount of gays lived and vacationed up there, with my sister being the troop leader ...

"I heard from a friend who visits there even more often than me that the best place to eat was, believe it or not, at the house of one of the locals. I have been told it is the best authentic Italian food you can get in Maine." Vince, Lisa and I all looked up at the same moment. Lorn continued, oblivious, "Apparently, this woman does all the cooking herself and the seven dollars she charges is cash only and on the honor system, so it's completely off the books. There are some real wacky characters up there, I guess." Vince started laughing so hard he had to choke back his food from behind a napkin. I just waited.

Lorn looked at Vince. "I don't get it ... did I say something funny?"

Lisa finally spoke, "I had to raise the price to eight bucks. The homemade wine was a friggin' bitch to keep up." Lorn thought she was kidding but cut off her short laugh when she saw Lisa staring at her deadpan, until Lisa she couldn't hold her laughter in another second.

Lorn was mortified. "Forgive me, Lisa, I hope I didn't sound ... I mean, I heard the food was excellent ... I said that, right?" With every word she uttered as an apology, we all laughed harder, until Lorn finally joined in. "I'm so sorry," she kept saying, "I really heard the food was superb," and we started laughing all over again.

"What am I missing down there?" Dad kept shouting across the table. And soon, due to the help of three bottles of dark red wine, everyone at that end of the table was laughing too, without even knowing what had happened.

"What a wonderful evening!" Uncle Tony declared as he stood up with his glass of wine, and, once again, a small group of people at a nearby table gave a cheer of approval to egg him on. What was it about a little old man that could charm people so? He certainly appeared to be charming Katherine, who beamed up at him as he turned his attention away from her for the first time that evening, to address the table that was encouraging him. "These people also know how to live ... they must be Italian, too!" he declared, and they cheered again, raising their glasses (although they looked like Irish Bostonians to me).

I looked at him, and then at Katherine, and realized he was holding her hand, discreetly and delicately by the tips of her fingers ... just as I had seen him do so many times with Auntie Celia. We saw him do this at her bedside, when she was so weak he was afraid to touch her, for fear of causing her more pain. He was holding Auntie Celia's hand in just that way as she lost her long fight, trying right until the end to stop herself from slipping away from the man she loved for so long. The doctors said she was on borrowed time for six months when, finally, early one morning, she could not hold on to her husband's hand any longer.

I wanted more than anything for Uncle Tony to have a love like that once again. Vince and Lisa were seeing it too. I felt my eyes sting and fill, and I tried to wipe a tear before it fell onto my cheek, but Lorn stunned me by intercepting my hand and giving it a soft and friendly squeeze. I turned to her to find her close, with her eyes fixed on mine. She asked softly, "Are you all right?" I nodded, but couldn't speak. How could I explain it to her, when I could only smile? And how could I stop myself from following in Uncle Tony's path, when this woman looked so damned beautiful?

Lorn turned to look at her mother and Uncle Tony and when she turned back to me, she hesitated, then softly said, "It's beautiful, isn't it? To witness what could be a brand new beginning for two people."

I hoped she was right.

"I fear my mother may ditch me for the rest of this trip," Lorn said when she saw me the next morning by the pool alone. We had miraculously been placed together once again; or rather, that's what she believed. It was only my third day in Jamaica and I had already slipped back into my old California-stalker ways, and had gotten up even earlier than the first morning to make sure I didn't miss her leaving for her morning walk. I had hoped the first walk was not just a fluke and sat near the pool closest to the stairwell leading to her room (I learned which staircase was hers—additional proof of my stalking prowess). I held a magazine so that I might appear like a person relaxing by the pool, in a really cute "beach walking" outfit ... or so I hoped. It worked, and I even let her spot me first, as I pretended to read *Yeah Mon*, which I guessed was the Jamaican equivalent of *Newsweek*, only with many more piña colada recipes and advertisements for Cuban cigars that could be discreetly shipped to the US in plain brown boxes. Thankfully, I realized I was holding the magazine upside down before she did.

Lorn asked if I'd join her, and we began our second walk. I liked learning small details about her, like which seashells caught her eye, and which ones she couldn't resist picking up. Also, that for some reason, she walked on my left side, always. I knew this, because I tested my theory, and within seconds after I switched lanes, she floated back to my left, just as she had been at dinner last night. Maybe this was her place by my side, I thought foolishly, and later, just to be sure, I had to test it again ... and she stopped for a pink-colored shell and took her place to my left again. I liked this ... I liked this a little too much ... and could not imagine it feeling more perfect if she had picked the other side.

She wanted to talk about my family, and even after spending the entire walk talking about dinner last night, she still wanted to know more about them all. When we reached the café she chose a small table and said, "Tell me more about your sister."

"How much time do you have?" I asked.

"About eight days," she said, smiling as my stomach did a triple gainer off the highest diving board. I started making lists inside my head. Maybe there was a way to get her to change her plans to stay longer ... eight days wasn't long enough. Enough for what, I wondered?

"My sister's an original," I said. "She's the strongest woman I know and I was fortunate to have her as my older sister, although I didn't always feel that way growing up. I think when you're a kid you see your older siblings as extensions of your parents; another person to tell you what you can and can't do. She was a bossy and very confident child and I tease her that she is frequently wrong, yet never in doubt—a brutal combination. But she's very protective of Vince and me, and although I tease her about it, I've learned a lot of important life lessons from her."

Lorn said gently, "Tell me more."

"When I was younger I didn't really understand that she was growing up and learning too, just doing it a little bit ahead of me. It took me years to figure that one out. I had always assumed she was born with all the answers."

"And I get the benefit of this wisdom all in the time it takes to finish a cup of coffee." Lorn lifted her cup and we clinked mugs. I was superstitious enough to take care to look her directly in the eyes. The thought flashed through my mind, *some day ... from coffee to Merlot ... every day.*

"Your entire family seems very comfortable with Lisa's sexuality; that's quite rare, even these days, don't you think?" I watched her intently, trying to read her for any signs ... but there were none I could see. I nodded and she kept her eyes directly on mine as she spoke, and, try as I might, I heard nothing more than a purely casual tone in her voice. "Vince is wonderful. I wish I had a brother like him."

"I'll be happy to share him with you," I said. "He can be a real handful."

She took a long pause before speaking again. "I wouldn't think you'd share him at all. I think you're very protective of him as Lisa is of you ... but perhaps one day you'll share him with me as a brother-in-law."

I sputtered my coffee, but somehow managed not to send it flying into her face. That would have been a smooth move. She asked if I was OK as I reached for a napkin. I had not managed to spill coffee onto the table. "Excuse me," I said, finally.

"If your Uncle Tony marries my mother, like he has told her he's going to, then Vince would sort of be my brother-in-law."

I thought: *I'm such an ass. It's not all about you, Marie ...*

"He actually told your mother that?" I asked.

"Yes he did, moments after they met, while they watched that first sunset together. And since my mother thinks he's the most charming man she's ever met, besides my father, of course, you just never know, do you?"

"I guess you don't," I said. "Since he announced his plans to marry your mother to our entire family last night, I'm relieved we don't have to keep his prediction a secret. Italian families are not the best at keeping secrets."

I tried to get her to talk about her work, but she wouldn't budge. "It is just a job, and unfortunately one whose success hinges mostly on the superficial. Tell me about your uncle Tony next," she coaxed, leaning closer. "I assure you, I'm not spying on my mother. She's her own woman. I just sense such sweetness from him ... and such a deep appreciation for life, too."

"Born from losing the love of his life, I'm afraid." I shared with Lorn the history of Auntie Celia, and the special life they had shared. "They were made for each other ... they spent every minute together, and not just after Auntie Celia got sick. They worked together at a textile mill, shared one car, did the grocery shopping together, everything. I never saw one without the other until after the day she died, and it was devastating to see him without her. It looked ... unnatural, since it had been that way for as long as I can remember. He was at her beck and call, long before she ever needed him to be."

"Have you ever experienced that kind of love?" Lorn asked, surprising me, but she looked away from me toward the ocean while she waited for my answer.

Suddenly shy? I wondered.

"I once thought I did. But I guess we all think we do in the beginning, don't we?"

"Not necessarily even then," she said, and I heard a trace of desolation in her voice that sounded familiar. I realized it was much like my own voice when I spoke of relationships. It was the first clue I had picked up on since the mention of Ogunquit that she may share some common ground with me, but I could not bring myself to ask her.

The annoying thing about being gay is that if you come out to someone right away, you run the risk of looking like that's all you believe your life is about, especially if the other person is straight. On the other hand, if you don't come out right away, you run the greater risk of looking like you're ashamed of your life, especially if the other person is gay. It's a dilemma that straight people enjoy the luxury of never having to consider. They walk around in this world with the confidence (of ... well, Lisa, but that just confuses the point) that of course they like the opposite sex, and why yes, I assume you do as well; and well, doesn't everyone?... And goodness what a surprise to find out that you don't, and why didn't you tell me sooner, even though it was my wrong assumption that led you to be silent in the first place. I felt I had hit that wall with Lorn after only two walks on the beach, one Italian dinner, and a light breakfast by a pool. I sighed quietly to myself.

Then I realized I usually hit that wall much sooner. She had not only avoided talking about her own personal life, but had avoided asking me personal questions, too. Maybe this indicated hurdle number two. Plus, Lorn had not (yet) assumed I was straight, since she hadn't asked the traditional "Do you have a boyfriend" question. It wasn't much, but this I would happily claim as hurdle number three.

Chapter Twelve

Dinner for Two(s)

"You whore."

"Shut up Lisa." I snapped, but it was hard to hold back the smile. "I told you, *she* asked me."

"So, she is ditching her poor old mother for dinner with a dyke. Now what does that say about this woman you have chased across our entire country and now to the Caribbean?"

"Hey, I didn't chase her ... here. And you're wrong again; her mother ditched *her* ... for a private dinner with Uncle Tony."

Lisa softened instantly. "Really? I really admire how forward that little old guy is being ... let's face it, at his age, you need to strike while the iron is hot."

"And still stiff." Vince had snuck up behind us on the beach. "We must be dishing about Uncle Tony. Man, what a player, huh?"

"You could learn a few things from him," I said.

"Or he could learn from you ..." Lisa said back at me.

Vince said, "How to tail a subject without getting made; no thanks ... I don't have the patience."

"Somebody else has herself a dinner date," Lisa said grinning.

Vince looked confused for a moment. Then shot me a look. "You *WHORE!*" he yelled over the surf.

"Shhh, for Christ sakes Vince! I'd better have dinner with her somewhere off this damned island before you both make a fool out of me. Can we just go snorkeling, please?"

"OK, but you'll have to agree to stop looking for her once we're underwater ..." he said. He'd noticed I'd been scanning the beach like a starved gull on French fry patrol to possibly catch a glimpse of her.

"You do realize it's Mom's sixtieth birthday dinner tonight?" Lisa said.

"Oh shit!"

"Guess she didn't realize," Vince said to Lisa, shaking his head like there was no hope for me.

"I suppose you're going to leave Vince and me alone with Mom and Dad to go on your hot date?" Like most siblings, we'd always tried to face our parents together whenever possible, to lessen the focus on any one of us in particular. It was an unspoken pact, and one that I couldn't honor tonight.

"I'll have to bail on Mom ... you think she'll be pissed?" I asked, already knowing that of the two of them, Dad would be the pissed one, as Mom preferred to forget the fact she was getting older.

"Do what you gotta do, Mare, she'll get over it. You took her to Jamaica for Christ's sake," Vince said. "But Dad is liable to make a fuss ... you'd better think of a good excuse. Shall I pelt your foot with another steaming ball of meat?"

I ignored the comment since I was busy trying to think of a good excuse. Ironically, I had already considered the meatball concept but decided it was too derivative. I would just have to think of something as I passed the time today. It had only been two hours since I sat with Lorn together over coffee, but the slow pace of the Caribbean made it seem like an entire day should already have passed.

Lorn's dinner invitation (which I counted as hurdle number four) had been offered as she, once again, avoided looking me directly in the eyes. She had asked very casually if I was having dinner with my family tonight. I decided to gamble and say no, that I needed a night off from the group, just to see where her question was going. But before I could answer, a man standing nearby snapped a photo. I said, "I think that man took a picture of me. Why on earth ...?"

"It happens sometimes," Lorn said. I realized he'd taken a picture of her, not of me, and I felt rather dumb.

"They don't understand it's rude to do that when people are on vacation and it's their own personal time."

The man drifted away, looking back several times as he walked; clearly regretting he'd not gotten closer. I regretted not kicking him in the balls, since Lorn seemed troubled by him. She changed the subject quickly. "My mother has a dinner date this evening and your uncle was too much of a gentleman to exclude me, so I lied and said I already made plans ... with you. You would be doing me a favor, just so I don't look like a liar. I also really wanted to give them some time alone." I wondered if she fussed a little too long with the explanation, as well as the re-positioning her chair, all so she wouldn't have to look up at me.

"I would love a night off from the Santora clan," I said.

"I don't want to take you away from anything special," she politely offered, "you probably have plans."

"No, no. Nothing special."

Just my mother's sixtieth birthday dinner, but I hadn't remembered that at the time. This was not going to go over well at all, but I would deal with that later. Besides, wasn't I the rich bitch with all the money? If money cannot buy you out of an obligation or two, what the hell good is it?

"OK, it's a date," she said a bit too easily, when I had hoped for signs of more shyness. *Straight girls can use the word date and it means nothing*, I thought, imagining me tumbling into hurdle number five, landing right on my ass.

We were interrupted by a woman who approached our table with a piece of paper and a pen outstretched. "Are you Lorn Elaine?" she asked meekly. When Lorn said yes, she politely asked for Lorn's autograph and Lorn smiled and obliged. As I watched the woman stare at her in awe, I hoped I had not been looking at her in that same pitiful way.

123

When the woman finally left our table, we settled on dinner at 7:30 at the Italian place again, since I was betting my Dad would win out by insisting on trying a different restaurant, regardless of Aunt Aggie and Uncle Freddie's likely protesting. I confessed to Lorn that I was dodging them, but left the sixtieth birthday information out for fear she might insist that I go, since, of course, I knew I should.

Once, when Lisa, Vince and I were kids, Mom gave us a ride to our Little League game, along with a friend she had begrudgingly agreed to pick up. The friend was a little girl named Nicky and she was close to our age, but about half our size. Looking back, she may have grown up (so to speak) to be a dwarf, but alas, we lost touch around age eleven and I would never know. Nicky was very little, and shutting the big rusting door of an old wood-sided station wagon probably required a bit more strength than she had to give. Hindsight told us this, but at the time, it was Nicky's rolling out of the moving car's door that gave us our first clue that it had been too heavy for her to close. Meanwhile, Lisa and I were fighting over who got to use the "good" baseball glove this game, so we never actually saw her roll out. It was the door slamming closed as Mom completed the turn at end of our street that finally got our attention. I looked over and, rather curious, asked, "Hey, where's Nicky?"

"Good God!" Mom yelled angrily into the rearview mirror. "She fell out of the damned car!" I remember wondering if Mom was angry at Nicky, or at Lisa and me, or simply at the fact that she had to backtrack, which she hated to do whenever we forgot something at the house. She screeched the car to a halt, and, since it was not in vogue to bother with seatbelts back then, my face hit the back of Mom's car seat. "Stop clowning around," she yelled at me over her shoulder. She backed the car up to where Nicky sat in the middle of the street, a little dazed. To Nicky's credit, she wasn't crying. (Thankfully, since Mom hated crying even more than backtracking.)

I'm sure Mom didn't mean it exactly like it sounded when she muttered, "Of the three of you, why did it have to be someone else's kid that fell out of the damned car?"

We understood she didn't actually wish it were Lisa or me, but that she was simply worried about being sued. This was a worry we heard often expressed when kids played football in our front yard, fell from a skateboard, or bloodied a nose from a stray baseball. Mom had made a second career of worrying about things that would never actually happen in our lifetime. While it may be true that community is an important part of life—you know, the whole "it takes a village" thing—my mother, nonetheless, had always been the "it takes a fence" type.

She was not, thankfully, the type to worry too much about how her birthday would be celebrated, so I tried to keep my guilt in check. Had it been Dad's birthday and I had tried to weasel out, my actions would have been met with much disapproval, since Dad was always of the opinion that the date of his birth was reason for the world to celebrate.

It would be many hours before I'd meet with Lorn, so it had been me that rallied Lisa and Vince for the snorkeling outing. It was a perfect day for hitting the beach, and the sky was a vast and unmarked blue, which improved the visibility below the water's surface. After we had swam out a good distance, it was Vince who was the first to spot a school of fish and signaled Lisa and me to join him further away from the reef. I worked hard to ignore the *Jaws* theme pounding loudly in my ears, and thought for the millionth time: If I could take back seeing one movie as a kid ...

The surface of the water rippled around Vince as the school of fish zigzagged past him. Eventually the spectacular view below provided the distraction I sorely needed, both from Bruce the Awaiting Shark, and from Lorn, the Awaiting Date. The colors of the fish were intense, and even the ones that were shimmering white seemed to have a neon thread of light glowing inside them against the backdrop of the clear water.

For some reason this outing reminded me of when Vince and I

125

were kids, and we'd go snake hunting in the woods near our house. I hated snakes, but it was a secret I kept hidden fairly well from Vince; or, more accurately, he let me believe I had kept it hidden. He respected my no-snake-touching rule because I was the only girl in the neighborhood that would help him lift the rusted metal piano top in the woods, where there was almost always a snake coiled beneath. It was our secret spot. Lisa hated snakes worse than me, and so I relished the fact that in this one thing I was braver than her, since she seemed utterly fearless in every other aspect of life.

I'd make a big production out of going out on a hunt, as if our family's very survival hinged on us coming back with the bounty, instead of it being simply for neighborhood bragging rights. The end result was keeping the snake in a pail to show everyone in the neighborhood our hunting skill until I grew afraid the snake was starving to death. Next, I'd spend the better part of the day convincing Vince to let it go back near the piano top, in case the snake had a family to get back to. We may have caught that same snake dozens of times, but each time we would both say, "This one is huge!"

Now, hunting for sights under the Caribbean sea, I couldn't help but hope we would see something spectacular, just hopefully not of the shark variety. Lisa was the first to call it quits from snorkeling, not coincidentally right after I pointed out a hairy-looking eel. I knew it was a mistake as soon as I did it, but it was too late. She'd laid eyes on it and immediately indicated that she was heading in to shore. Anything snake-like (and that, of course, included a certain portion of the male anatomy) could send Lisa quickly heading for the hills. Vince and I stayed out for another hour, floating, pointing and grunting under water until we had nearly constructed another sibling sign language. Over the years, we developed a sign language for loud bars and silently mouthed or cleverly disguised code words for coordinating the exiting from family events. We also developed a rating system for sharing the fuck-ability factor of Vince's dates as soon as their backs would be turned. (Lisa invented the victory sign with her tongue laid in between the finger-shaped "V" to demonstrate her approval.) And now, in just a few hours, we had developed underwater grunts which had clear definitions for, "Big, huh?" and "Wow, look!" and "No, this one ..." and even "Yucky" and "Eeew" (we eventually had to drop "Eeew" since it kept getting misconstrued as "eel"). When we spotted a toothy barracuda with huge, flat, saucer-like eyes circling nearby, I called the exploration to a halt, since I was wearing a silver bracelet despite the warnings that wearing jewelry could entice a fish like a barracuda to attack.

After snorkeling, Vince and I grabbed frozen cocktails and sat in the sun to dry off as we rehashed everything we'd seen. In our enthusiasm, we agreed to snorkel every day and always in the morning when visibility was best. There was a long pause and then we both turned to each other and spoke in perfect unison: "Gym Promise."

A "Gym Promise" was one made under the adrenaline rush of an activity, usually involving some sort of exercise, which included a vow to repeat the activity on some regular schedule. It didn't stand a chance of being honored, once sanity and aching muscles kicked in. Vince informed me it was exactly the same phenomenon that happens after a man has casual sex and promises the woman a future date when he has no intention of following through.

Vince was jealous after he tasted my drink. I had smartly ordered a frozen margarita without salt, since there was already plenty of salt on my lips. We named the drink "The Jamaican Deep Sea Salt Margarita" and made a pact to have one every day. This was probably not a Gym Promise.

"What do you mean, you're not going?" Dad asked me.

"She doesn't have to go if she doesn't want to, Sal," Mom said. "We're going to be together for two weeks."

"I said I wasn't feeling well, not that I didn't want to go." Not much had changed since the last time I had done it; it was still difficult to defend yourself when you were lying to your parents.

"So what the heck is wrong with you?" Dad demanded with his usual tact.

"Not sure ... I just think if I don't make it an early night, I'm going to come down with something. Or, it could just be nothing. I just really don't want to get sick here."

"It's fine, Sal," Mom said, surprisingly lacking in sarcasm. "Let her rest if she doesn't feel well enough to go. Tony has already made plans, so let's just you and I have dinner tonight."

"That sounds very nice!" I sounded a bit too enthusiastic, so I took it down a notch. "This could be a very romantic place—don't you think it would be nice to spend your birthday alone with each other?"

"I suppose so," Dad answered. The problem was, Dad loved an audience and his personality thrived in groups. He loved nothing better than to be in the middle of a crowd, entertaining and being entertained by them. Still, he was not about to tell his wife he preferred to spend her birthday dinner with a gang of people.

"Yeah, screw you kids," he said, "I am taking my best girl out for an All-Inclusive dinner ... and I'll spare no expense!" Dad wouldn't be tiring of the 'all-inclusive'-themed humor anytime soon. Vince and I had already discussed bribing him with cash to get him to stop saying, "The drinks are on me!"

He curled his arm around Mom as if posing for a photograph and she looked equally amused and embarrassed. It occurred to me that I could not remember the last time I had seen them demonstrate physical affection towards each other, even in a light-hearted way like this. He squeezed her again, and said, "What do you say? We'll ditch Aggie and Freddie too."

Mom liked that idea.

"Don't you look nice," I said, as I met Lorn at the restaurant door. I was lying. She looked exceptional. I had planned to dress more casually, anticipating that she probably would as well, since last night she had dined with my whole family and tonight it was just the two of us. Thankfully, I had changed at the last minute into a summer skirt and one of my favorite blouses to hopefully show some tan. I felt sadly underdressed. Lorn was in a beautiful white suit with semi-transparent lace trim, which was gorgeous against the contrast of her hair. The skirt on the suit was just above her knees and made her look like a much younger woman.

"You look nice too," she said. I noticed that she appeared a little tense. *Hurdle number six?* I wondered.

"Is everything all right?" I asked her when I saw her glance around the lobby for the second time.

"I thought I saw that same man with the camera this morning," she said. "Never mind, I don't see him now. The paranoia of an actress is not a pretty thing."

"Sure it is," I said before I could censor myself.

"Sweet of you to say," she said, the flirtatiousness of my comment seemed to go flying undetected over her head.

"Nothing sweet about it," I said, only half under my breath. I could be brave if she was that clueless.

To my disappointment, she just gave my arm a quick pat, just as you would a thoughtful child, neither threatened nor enlightened in the faintest way by what I had said. This was going to be very difficult. Hinting wasn't going to work with this woman, as I was clearly flying under the radar ... if she even had a radar. I was battling with my impatience, and, as usual, my impatience was winning. By the end of this evening, for better or for worse, I promised myself she would see me differently.

An elegantly dressed Jamaican man opened the door for us. "Table for two?" he asked.

If I hadn't been so mesmerized by Lorn, I might have noticed Aunt Aggie and Uncle Freddie as I passed right by their table. "Well, don't you two girls look ravishing tonight?" my uncle said, startling both of us.

I froze as if I'd been caught stealing cookies from a jar ... For someone vacationing in the warm Caribbean, I sure had been doing a lot of freezing lately. Aggie said, "Your mother said you were sick." She scanned me up and down with a look that clearly said, "You look just fine to me."

"Nice to see you both again," Lorn said, rescuing me from my stupefied silence. "I'm afraid it's my fault. My mother had a date tonight and I begged Marie to come eat with me even though she wasn't feeling well ... just so I wouldn't have to eat alone."

I could love this woman. Gorgeous, and could think fast on her feet as well. A damn fine catch if you ask me ...

Screenplay ... Screenplay ... Screenplay ...

"A woman so pretty should never have to eat alone," a voice said behind us. It was Uncle Tony, escorting Katherine in on his arm.

"I guess we all liked this restaurant," Aggie said, inspecting Katherine. "Don't you two look lovely this evening as well? Fred, I told you we weren't dressed fancy enough," she said, swatting him. He put his hands up in his familiar pose of surrender and just laughed.

Katherine said to Aggie, "That blouse is perfectly lovely on you, Mrs. Bellatoro. The coral color is so flattering with your flawless skin. Later, you must share with me the name of the skin cream you use." Aggie beamed and dropped all her defenses so abruptly I swore I heard a thud.

She said warmly, "Please call me Aggie, dear. We just finished dinner, but we've decided to stay for dessert. Would you all please join us?"

"We have?" Uncle Freddie rubbed his round belly in a gesture of being over-stuffed.

"Yes, we have, dear," she said.

"Sometimes I forget what we decide. Old age I guess," he said, winking at me.

Katherine looked to Uncle Tony to answer, and he took the cue. "*Grazie, grazie*, but I called for a special table reserved by the window. If you don't mind excusing us?" he said as they gracefully made their exit.

Aggie said, "Well, clearly they wanted to be alone."

"I don't blame him," Uncle Freddie said. "That mother of yours is a beautiful lady." Aggie swatted him playfully again and this time he feigned being wounded.

Aggie ignored his theatrics and asked, "So will you two join us, then? I would love to ask Lorn all about Hollywood. We've never been to California, but we may have watched your program. Only once though. Why is it always on so damned late?"

In the same way that Katherine had looked to Uncle Tony, I noticed Lorn was looking for me to answer. "I think since you've almost finished, we'll probably just take our table." I confessed, "I had also called to see if we could get a table with an ocean view, so I feel it would be rude not to take it." I felt Lorn's eyes turn towards me, but I didn't look back.

"Let the kids go eat, Aggie," Uncle Freddie said, "I couldn't eat another bite anyway."

"Well, it seems like everyone just wants to be alone tonight," she said, finally giving up. "I guess us old folks should call it a night."

We wished them a good evening, and as we walked to our table, I quietly thanked Lorn for her help. From a sideways glance I could see she was grinning. I think she had enjoyed the challenge, or maybe just watching me squirm.

"Well, look who else is here!" we heard as we entered the ocean-view side of the restaurant. It was Lisa, with Vince sitting next her, and she looked quite proud of herself as she tried unsuccessfully to hide a smirk. Vince, at least, knew enough to keep quiet under my glare.

"Oh, hello, nice night, huh?" I said, but I didn't stop at their table as we passed, and Lorn looked puzzled for a moment before moving on since I was not stopping. I dipped down low to whisper in Lisa's ear, "I'm going to strangle you." I had made the mistake of telling Lisa which restaurant we were going to and she was the one who suggested I reserve a seat by the window.

"With any luck, you'll be sitting right near Mom and Dad," she said back with a smile as we went on to our table.

I looked across the room. There was an empty table right next to Uncle Tony and Katherine, and on the other side were my father and my mother, both forcing smiles as we approached. Lorn whispered in amusement, "Doesn't your family eat anything besides Italian food?"

"It appears not," I whispered back. "I'm so screwed ... confession time ... I faked sick to play hooky from my mother's birthday dinner!" I saw the back of Lorn's shoulders stiffen to suppress a laugh as I walked behind her. This was not turning out to be the evening I had imagined.

Thankfully, Lorn took charge this time. "Mr. and Mrs. Santora, it's so good to see you again."

"Please call me Sal," my Dad offered. He positively glowed around beautiful women. I thought I saw him shoot a raised eyebrow towards me.

"Happy birthday, Mrs. Santora," Lorn said to my mother, as I hid behind her.

"Thank you Lorn, please call me Helena," Mom said.

"Well Helena, when your daughter said she was starting to feel better after having to cancel on your dinner celebration, I convinced her to come to dinner with me, since I was left all alone this evening."

My dad instantly warmed to her. "Well, of course, but Lorn, you could have joined us as well," he said gallantly, and then added with just a little too much effect, "Marie, I'm so glad to hear you're feeling better."

I peeked around Lorn, whose perfume was making my head fuzzy, and it didn't help me think any more quickly. "I was a bit light-headed earlier, but it passed," I said, "then I got hungry, I guess." It wasn't the worst lie I had ever told.

"She's just being polite. I simply had to beg her to come out with me tonight," Lorn said, placing her arm just for a moment around my shoulder before quickly dropping it away. (A little nervous to touch me, perhaps?)

"We'll not interrupt your nice dinner for another moment,"

Lorn said. "Would you prefer we find another table to give you some privacy?"

"Oh no, don't be silly," Mom said as she still studied me for signs of illness. It was the same look she used when we tried to get out of going to school. I glanced over and saw Lisa joyously whispering to Vince. Why was it still so much fun to enjoy your siblings getting caught by Mom or Dad?

We acknowledged Katherine and Uncle Tony again with a small wave and took our table at last. Thankfully, there was enough breathing room between tables that our conversations would remain private. I glared at Lisa once more before sitting, but they were at least pretending to ignore us now, and that was good enough for me. I decided to do the same, and after just a few minutes, I forgot that Lorn and I were not alone in the world.

As we talked, the wall of people surrounding us fell away, despite the fact that I was related to most of them. Each time the waiter came to the table to interrupt, I had to remind myself he wasn't being rude, but actually doing his job. I finally got Lorn to talk a little bit about herself, and drank in every word. I enjoyed being able to relax and watch her as she spoke. She talked about her mother and her work, and how she loved living in the city so close to the studio. Good, I thought. I didn't invest in property anywhere she was looking to move from. She also spoke at length about how lucky she was to have her career actually peeking at an age when actresses typically found it challenging to find good roles.

"Contrary to the belief of what all the tabloids say, not every actress chooses plastic surgery to try to lop off a few years."

"Of course not. You don't need it," I said, and meant it. The few laugh lines she had gave her the look of a confident woman who didn't want to hide that which she had earned through years of kind expressions.

"I never said I wasn't pressured to do it, though."

"Oh, well, if you did, you look great either way, and ... I'm sure you didn't need it if you did have it ..."

"And I'm sure I'm teasing you," she said, giggling to herself.

Lisa and Vince were the first to interrupt to say goodbye, and after they did, I boldly confessed to Lorn I'd forgotten they were there. Lorn said, "What a relief. I was afraid I was boring you with all this Hollywood talk." I assured her she hadn't. Soon after, Mom and Dad stopped at our table on their way out. "How was your dinner?" Dad inquired, wanting the lowdown on what we had ordered.

"Perfect," Lorn and I both said in unison.

Dad looked back and forth at both of us, but when we offered no more, he said, "Well, you two kids have fun. It is nice to see you finally met each other, and are becoming friends." I gulped a sip of water, and didn't look up until after they left. Since it was just the two of us at the table, I had to look up eventually. When I did, her gaze was quizzical. Lorn had not missed the panic in my eyes.

Chapter Thirteen

Fig Newton's Law

"Your Dad is happy we finally met?" she asked.

I took a large gulp of wine and decided to come clean about some of what I'd done, or risk looking like the liar I was. "I have a confession. I would've told you before now, but I feel pretty stupid about it. I'm actually a fan of your work, and my family knows that. I'm embarrassed to say I may have expressed wanting to meet you ... a few times."

Lorn raised her eyebrows at me but she didn't look too concerned. Instead, she listened with interest. Had I imagined a little sparkle in her eye? Or maybe meeting freaks amused her.

"OK, so maybe I mentioned it more than a few times. I hope that doesn't sound strange to you ... now that we've met, I feel a little silly about the whole thing. And, like everything else I tell my family, I *really* wish I'd shut my mouth about it." I sipped my drink again, waiting for her to say something. My heart pounded so heavily I was concerned the wine I was holding might show the tremors. I quickly added, "Don't be too flattered, though ... I'm not that hard to impress."

Her eyebrows lifted again.

"No, really," I said, as I looked around for something trivial in the room to be impressed about and spotted a half-full piña colada at the next table. "You'd probably never guess I'm the type to actually tear up over that piña colada song ... you know, that dramatic third verse, when the wife answers the husband's personal ad to meet in a bar called O'Malley's, 'to plan their escape' ... When she says: 'Oh, it's you,' I get the damned chills every time. Really."

She laughed, and my relief and the sound of her coupled to soothe me. I swore a few cherubs and unicorns must have fluttered through the sky to celebrate me getting off the hook ... or maybe, they fluttered by just to get closer to the sound of her laughter. Christ ... when had I gotten it so bad for this woman? Had one of those cherubs dropped something in my drink? While I was taking my victory lap with the chubby-winged baby and a horse outfitted with a horn shaped like a long Italian pastry shell on his head, she stopped me dead in my tracks by saying, "As long as you're not a stalker."

Although my stalking days seemed far behind me, the vivid memories of staking out her studio with binoculars, notebooks, and Fig Newtons flooded my brain. The thought occurred to me that the Fig Newtons were aptly named after the guy who dictated the laws of motion (example: when one car hits another car). My face was suddenly on fire at the memory of my car tapping into the back of her Lexus, and the insurance company's subsequent reporting of it to the police. It seemed a lifetime ago ... and, if I didn't blow this, I'd eventually have to come clean on that one. But not tonight. I put the wine down and hid my hands under the table, since they were shaking a little.

"I'm not a stalker."

Lorn studied my face for a moment ... than she smiled sweetly, as if she had been kidding all along, which she probably was since now she was chuckling at me. A rainbow appeared to form a backdrop for the cherubs and unicorns. Whew.

"I'm just a reluctant inheritor with too much money and time on my hands, I guess. I do enjoy your work," I said, and that part wasn't a lie. We didn't have to go into the weekend-long video marathons, now did we?

Lorn said, "Just assure me there isn't a cabin in the woods somewhere with photos all over the walls ..."

I laughed, as I thought, no, just a living room floor carpeted in clippings ... I never would have glued the photos to the walls like some insane person.

"No way ... if you use good glue, it's impossible to get off the walls."

"And you're not a member of the fan club, right?"

"Hey, don't knock the fan club. It's the only accurate source to find out when the cast of *Razor Falls* would be appearing on *Oprah*! But I swear, I never bought the sticker album, or the lunch box, although both seemed a mighty great value."

I made her laugh again, and I felt I could rule the universe with my powers. Perhaps I would command the cherubs to ride the unicorns and vault over the rainbow like a hurdle ... Not wanting to press my luck, I changed the subject by blithering on about the inheritance and about the free time it bought me, and how it had altered my family's petty annoyances into million-dollar dramas overnight. I shared with her the fact that I hoped this trip would help mend some of those issues. As she kept me talking about my family, it occurred to me she might be using the time to size me up as I spoke ... after all, it's what I had been doing when I kept her talking.

I never once thought she wasn't listening, but her gaze had grown increasingly fearless and now lingered about my face and shoulders, and I even caught her stealing quick glances towards my breasts as I spoke, but reminded myself it likely meant the exact opposite of what I hoped. While she was taking notice of me, she had no conscious worry of being attracted, or she'd attempt to mask it. (I didn't dare hope she was actually a bold-and-dirty-girl Hollywood actress in desperate need of a good spanking to teach her it was rude to stare, though it was a brief and joyous thought.)

Changing the subject to money issues with my family seemed to be a good decision, and she asked, "Wait a second, you aren't complaining about being rich, are you?" All traces of stalker skepticism seemed washed from her thoughts.

"Why, no, that would make me a spoiled brat," I said.

"Freedom is worth a lot, and dealing with a few family issues seems a fairly small price to pay."

"Agreed. I'll shut up now."

"Marie," she started, as I reveled in her saying my name as if we were old friends, "I'm going to pry a little. Tell me, have you thought about what you're going to do with your life now that you don't have to earn a living? I can't even imagine what that would be like."

"I don't know yet. It depends on a lot of things," I lied again, because right now, it only depended on one thing, and she was sitting across from me. I could feel the wine making me both warm and a bit stupid; a dangerous combination, and I felt a strong urge to confess everything to her. Although I was not quite that drunk, I thought I would test the waters.

"I actually love to write," I confessed.

"Really? What type of writing?"

I balked ... the stalker question was too fresh in my mind, and I retreated. "I can't believe I just told you that, since I haven't told anyone ... not even Vince or Lisa. You know, the typical plans to write the great all-American novel ..."

"Good for you. Now that you have the time, you can pursue it. I'm flattered that you shared something with me you haven't confessed even to your brother and sister," she said, and then she smiled at me in a way that made my stomach feel as if it had flipped out the window and over the restaurant balcony, hurtling towards the ocean ... yet in a good way.

"As a matter of fact," I decided to push my luck. "I ... a friend of mine is a screenplay writer," I said. "She's completed a great idea for a movie ... Have you ever considered trying to make the move to the big screen?"

Well, I had said it ... well, sort of said it.

This made me remember the time I got a tremendous sun blister across my entire bottom lip after my first Caribbean trip. I was too embarrassed to leave the house, but was eventually forced to go to the pharmacy when the throbbing pain of my lip felt like a balloon filled with poison. As I approached the counter, I saw the look of horror on the young pharmacist's face as THE LIP drew nearer ... I was mortified, but attempted to speak with my rapidly pulsating lip, which was now projecting at an unusual slant, distorting my speech and making me appear like a stroke victim with herpes and a sunburn. I was forced to slur my speech even more to protect THE LIP from cracking open again. Although I had to avoid all hard Hs and Ts, I attempted to be funny as I struggled to speak clearly: *"Do you ave any—ing for sun blis—ers? ..."* Then, impulsively I added: *"Iss not for me, iss for a friend."* The pharmacist didn't get the joke, and instead, ducked behind the counter to get me some ointment, while averting his eyes from the beast.

Just like then, I had now pinned the screenplay on a mythical friend and I instantly regretted it, since I was dooming myself to eventually having to confess to being a liar, on yet another point. But it was done now ...

Lorn said, "I suppose every television actor considers doing a theater release movie, but for me it has to be the right project and of course, you have to be real lucky just to be considered for a movie. Even with a good agent, it's not an easy jump to make, especially at my age. It's no secret that forty is considered old in Hollywood. Made-for-TV movies are teeming with actresses over forty ... the big screen, not so much."

I was about to protest her last statement as an opportunity to change the subject, when she asked, "So what is your friend's screenplay about?"

I had no choice but to dive in. I took a deep breath and quickly rattled off the well-rehearsed pitch, although it was the first time I had actually said it out loud.

"It's a ... gay theme, actually, although mostly due to circum-stance, since it takes place in a women's prison ... you know, like *Kiss of the Spiderwoman* was not *really* gay ... A female prison guard falls for an inmate. It's called *Unguarded Love* ... Kind of a

Brokeback Mountain thing only with girls in a prison setting, without the western theme, and no horses, of course."

I don't know if it was the wine, or just saying the premise out loud. But I had the complete and horrible realization that it was the worst idea for a story I had ever heard (that was not in a porno movie). I burst out laughing uncontrollably. Lorn joined me, relieved that it was okay to goof on my "friend's" idea for a script. Our peels of laughter continued until Lorn wiped tears from her eyes and choked out, "Unlike you, your friend had better keep her day job!"

We laughed even harder at this, but now I was recalling some of the dialog I had written, and laughed harder with the sudden clarity that it was my worst ever brain-fart gone awry. I even quoted some of the worst lines for her as I thought, *Thank God I had not claimed it was mine!* The one line that really got to her was, "Let's pretend we are in a playground together and not in a prison ... these are just monkey bars between us ..."

I planned to have another trash-barrel campfire with that script the moment I got home, before it fell into the wrong hands ... like my siblings' ... or Lorn's. It would ruin any chance I had with her. It had become painfully obvious that I wasn't going to be famous for *Unguarded Love* ... no matter how much I wanted see this woman who was sitting across from me kiss another female. And with that, my quest officially changed. Right there, over dinner, I let myself acknowledge that I wanted her ... and that the woman I wanted her to kiss was me.

As our laughter finally slowed to a halt, and we returned to our meals, the mood of the evening shifted into a quieter one. Lorn asked me a bold question, which contrasted with her shy delivery. "So tell me about the time you thought you experienced the love of your life."

"The short version is, I was wrong," I said, even though I hadn't intended to sound so bitter.

"You just haven't met the right person," she said, but she

sounded like I was a teenager and she was my counselor ... a counselor who was getting very tipsy on Jamaican Merlot. I decided this meant I could play a little, since she was in a slightly weakened state, and she seemed to be avoiding certain key pronouns.

"I may have," I said, watching her eyes still roaming all over me. She wasn't even attempting to hide it now, so why should I? But I was only teasing myself with my answer, because she remained totally oblivious.

"You have? So, what happened?" Lorn asked as she leaned closer to me and took another swallow from her glass. She was becoming more sensual as she relaxed, even though I cautiously watched the maroon liquid whirlpool unsteadily against the walls of her glass. There was relaxed, and there was drunk ... and there was a big difference. I poured more wine into her glass.

"I'll let you know," I said, as she watched me in silence. I bravely stared back. The wine was making me feel bold again. She looked blank at first, but then quickly averted her eyes to her drink.

"I won't ask any more questions," she said. "I think I'm getting too personal ..." She let out a small laugh that sounded unlike her ... more like a schoolgirl. I concluded beyond a reasonable doubt that she wasn't accustomed to sharing a whole bottle of wine over dinner. "I wouldn't want to make you uncomfortable," she said.

"You're not making me feel uncomfortable," I said, and I could read her clearly right then. She was considering that maybe I had been referring to her; but just as quickly, I saw her dismiss the idea, barely smiling to herself for thinking it.

I had a crazy vision of myself leaning over the table to kiss her softly on her wine-reddened lips. I further imagined taking her hands and placing them on all the parts on my body at which she had been staring. But really, how could I turn that into a smooth move, when I had no frigging idea what her deal was? I imagined myself saying, "Here Lorn, this is how a sight-impaired person

141

would look at me the way you've been all night ..." but I opted to wait it out for a better plan. Besides, she was staring again, and I was just drunk enough to resist the impulse to look away. Her slight smile faded, and she suddenly looked nervous; but she didn't look away either. Slow seconds passed between us as she gave an uncomfortable smile. I took another sip of wine, but did not take my eyes from hers.

"You're staring," she finally said, softly, and I wondered why the room was slowly spinning around us. It was downright distracting, but still, I kept looking at her.

"So are you. And at least I have an excuse," I said.

"What's that?" she asked quietly.

"I'm having dinner with my favorite actress."

She let out a full laugh, but it didn't change that something had passed between us ... and I didn't want to let the moment go, to only have to wait for another. So I asked, "I guess the question is, why were you staring back?"

She paused, and then said, "I was just thinking about how fortunate Italian people are."

"What do you mean? Because our families are so vast and imposing that you can't fling a dead cat without hitting a Santora in a restaurant?"

"I was thinking Italians are very attractive people ... I mean, your brother, your mom, your dad ... are all so ..."

I looked around the almost-empty restaurant. Only Katherine and Uncle Tony remained across the room at their table. "None of them were anywhere near where you've been staring," I said.

She looked embarrassed, and turned her attention back to her wine.

"No, I guess they weren't," she said softly, mostly into the glass, "I can notice an attractive woman, can't I?"

"I have no problem with that whatsoever. No laws against it—well, maybe in Jamaica."

Even from across the table, I could see that her breathing had quickened. Was this shaping up to be a *Brokeback Mountain*

142

thing, only with two women in Jamaica, and no western theme or horses?

"May I get you anything else?" our waiter interrupted. I imagined grabbing him by the neck and flinging him out the ocean-view window to search for my fluttering stomach.

"I think we're all set," I answered after Lorn nodded, and the waiter finally left us. Lorn turned to look at her mother and Uncle Tony, but they were oblivious to us, and were discreetly holding hands across the table, wordlessly speaking volumes. Their intimate moment mirrored our last except for the hand-holding, and when I looked back to Lorn, she was looking at me, and I was convinced she had thought the same. I wanted to hold her hand across a table. I might want to hold her hand across our entire lives, now that I actually thought about it. Things were happening fast on my side of the table ... I just needed to get the ten-thousand-dollar "are you a dyke" question answered before I made a fool of myself. But before I could ask, she spoke.

"I live in L.A., Marie, so it's not like I haven't been around enough gay people, but ..." she paused, and dropped her voice, which was odd in a restaurant that was almost empty, "... can two women actually expect to live happily ever after, like my mother and Tony probably will?"

Her question, and indirect confession, had taken me off guard, as had her wistful tone of voice. She wanted it to be possible. Was she asking me to assure her that it could be true? Was it possible for two women to spend their lives together? I paused for a moment, thinking the delay might lend weight to whatever my answer was so she would know I had thoroughly considered the question.

Jess and the others before her had not worked out for me. Lisa was still in her conquistador phase when it came to women, dividing and conquering her way through the Maine locals and tourists alike. She used her Italian sausage and meatballs as bait, and the ladies came running for it. She always seemed to get the extremely feminine women too, the "lipsticks" that were

143

attracted to the contrasting more masculine look, the ones that were a bit too straight to be with too feminine a woman. Maybe her football jerseys and big bone structure bridged the gap in a familiar, masculine way ... a female starter kit, if you will. But, as with easy bake ovens, and most other starter kits, the dabblers moved on, seeking a connection that is less easy bake, and more like real cooking. They typically ended up back with men, armed with a darned good story to make them feel liberal, and vivid confessions their husbands could jerk off to for the next decade or so.

But then I thought of two friends (really just acquaintances, but why quibble when making a point?), Rebecca and Jackie, who had been together for almost twenty years. Jackie was alone now, but only because Rebecca lost her battle with cancer, which had plagued her with a cruel game of hide and seek for over eight years. I felt downright self-righteous in answering Lorn's question after thinking of Rebecca.

"Women do it all the time," I said, "I just haven't been fortunate enough to be one of them."

She looked at me for a long time, not speaking. She looked for a moment as if she may want to argue the point, but then she connected with me again, and the staring got intensely heated.

Whether she intended for me to know or not, I now knew the deal.

I finally spoke, "My brother would say, leave it to a couple of lesbians to talk about the happily ever after even before the first kiss."

The expression on her face warned me that my smart-ass remark was about to backfire.

"I never said I was a lesbian," she answered, straightening her back to her chair. I wanted to tell her it was too late to try to appear looking straighter, but she was not going to do well with a comment like that. The last time I saw someone looking that uncomfortable, seconds later they had vomited their lunch across an airplane seat into another passenger's hair. I pictured my unicorn crashing head first into that fucking rainbow, while the naked fat cherub laughed so hard he shit out candy conversation hearts and they all read NO WAY.

"You never said you weren't either," I said.

"Why would I have to say anything? I think we should go." Lorn said, standing up rather unsteadily.

We walked together from the restaurant into the darkness to find the resort was deserted as well. It would have made the perfect romantic postcard if it weren't so dark, and if I wasn't with a woman who wanted to sprint across the resort to get away from the well-disguised dyke who had accused her of being the same. The cool breeze helped me to gather my thoughts, but the fact was we both had had a little too much to drink, and I feared saying the wrong thing again. I wanted to reach for her hand, as it was so close to mine, but I appeared to be just one drink short of finding the courage to play out that last card.

I had said the L word. Too damned fucking presumptuous of me, I guessed. But what was all that staring ... and the happily-ever-after question?

It was unfair that, unlike Katherine and Uncle Tony, this whole gay thing was so much more fucking complex. Did I misread her signals, either due to the Merlot or to my own abrupt and intense desire for her? Maybe she had been conducting a survey about gay people, and hadn't meant to include herself at all. You know, just taking a poll to see how the other half lived ... and I had let my clit do the talking.

We walked along the dark beach in silence but, unlike our peaceful morning walks, the silence was now painfully awkward. *Something* intimate had passed between us; after all, it was Lorn who had asked about the gay thing. Had I just talked myself into believing she was interested?

She stopped and turned to me. "I'm sorry," was all she said.

I stopped walking as well, and it seemed the breeze and ocean grew still with her, in anticipation of what she would say next, but she remained silent and stared at me in that same way she had at the restaurant.

I said, "I'm not sure what you want, or what you expect me to do."

She whispered, "I was having the exact same thought."

There was an arm's length between us, but the wine-induced courage finally kicked in and I reached out to barely trace the side of her face with my fingertips, and she let me ... it was hard not to notice she was the softest thing on planet earth. She shuddered even though the air had warmed near the sand, which stored some heat of the day under the thinnest layer of cool beach sand. Lorn looked petrified, but I noticed her breathing quicken again. Petrified was not exactly the look I had hoped for ... petrified is usually bad. I wanted to kiss her, but remained caressing the side of her face with my hand, waiting. Petrified looked very sexy.

Gay people are forever waiting for signs. It comes from spending your life watching for signs that the person of the same sex you've fallen head over heals with might feel the same, but never having the luxury of being able to assume, or even simply ask, in case they don't ... which could send them running and screaming from the playground, slumber party, college dorm ... or Caribbean beach.

Lorn closed her eyes and barely leaned her face further into my hand ... her warm skin against the palm of my hand made the breeze around us feel cool again by comparison. Was I imagining this too? Or, maybe she was she about to pass out from the Jamaican-Italian–blended food or the Merlot with the heavy cherry and chocolate notes? Now I was the one that was frightened. One false move and it could all end here, before it even had a chance to begin.

Damn this fucking lifestyle. As I waited for a billboard sign to assure me that my next move wouldn't earn me a slap to the face or an outraged cry, Lorn slowly turned her face and opened her mouth to gently kiss inside the palm of my hand. Perhaps this was the billboard I was waiting for?

I melted from the heat of her mouth and it sent a chill up my arm and across both my breasts, the shiver ending simultaneously like a pair of lemmings perched at the tips of my nipples; only they did not jump off. Instead, they danced like they had a new lease on life, their furry toes prickling me into delirium.

And yet, I still debated if it was OK to kiss her.

I was really good at this. Even when the all the planets had finally aligned, and there were no more signs left to signal me to go for it, I could somehow invent doubts to freeze me into inaction. What I wouldn't give for a neon applause sign that read, "KISS HER YOU DUMB FUCKING ITALIAN DYKE."

Lorn interrupted my thoughts by opening her mouth further against my hand, her warm tongue now burning my palm. She breathed hot against the inside of my hand, and I thought I heard her say, "I want this."

Then, while as I was wrapping up the debate, she lunged towards me, her first kiss half missing the target and hitting my cheek, but our lips crawled towards each other until I found her mouth, at first timid, yet blistering hot against my lips. Her trembling hands were now on my shoulders, pulling me closer, or possibly holding herself up. I gave security clearance to myself to kiss her harder and finally she whispered, "Yes ..."

I wondered if she wanted to say, "Yes, you dummy, you call yourself a dyke? Took you long enough ..." I embraced her and felt the length of her body against me, her breasts full and soft on mine. Her mouth was perfect, and her kiss didn't stay fearful, but launched instead into the starved kiss of a woman claiming something she had wanted long before we had met. Maybe something that had little to do with me ...

She stopped to catch her breath and whispered against the side of my face, "Is this what it's supposed to be like? Kissing someone? I can't believe how much I want this ... with you." She stopped there for a moment and then said, "Would you think less of me if I asked you to come to my room?"

"No, but I might think less-bian of you." She stared at me, as that petrified look came roaring back.

Why do I have to be such an ass?

"Sorry," I said, reaching for her hand. "You surprised me, that's all. I thought I had misread some signals ... I couldn't tell if you wanted anything to happen. By the look on your face I still can't tell," I said.

Her look finally softened. "Actress," she answered.

"Ahh," I said.

"I can't promise I know what this all means right now ... I only know I need to find out," she said.

I chose to ignore the warning of her latest comment.

We broke apart from each other to walk back to her room, and I noticed she kept her hand a safe distance from mine. Had she sensed I wanted to hold it? I probably wouldn't have had the courage to reach for it, since, left to my own devices, I would still be standing on the beach waiting for the billboard and wondering if a how-dare-you slap would come my way if I dared to kiss this woman.

"How do I know you aren't just star-struck," she said in a teasing tone, but there was something in her voice that made me want to reassure her.

"I'm not," I said firmly. Maybe it was a bit too firmly, because she stopped walking then.

"You're sure ... right?" she asked softly, the petrified look returning a third time.

"Lorn, no. I'm not a star chaser," ... *Anymore*, I thought. And that was the truth. I knew myself well enough to know I would never need to chase another thing if I could just have this woman.

"Several years ago ... there was a person I cared about, a woman ... but I didn't let myself trust her. She was too enamored with Hollywood that I convinced myself it would be a mistake; I wondered if she wanted to get close to me for the wrong reasons. I guess I'll never know." Her voice had trailed off as if the memory were replaying in her mind, interrupting her thoughts. I stopped walking and held her face with both hands this time.

"Your celebrity has nothing to do with why I want to be with you ..."

Lorn became aware that we had strayed into the lighted area at poolside, and pulled back to let my hands drop from her face. "Please, let's go inside."

There was nothing I wanted to do more. I wanted very, very badly to go inside.

When we reached her room, she unlocked the door and reached for my hand, just as a flash went off from behind us. For a moment, I assumed it was lightning until it happened twice more in rapid succession, and I registered the machine-like sound of what I heard. When my eyes adjusted, a saw a man scurry away down the stairs holding an absurdly long camera.

"Oh my God ..." Lorn said in a panic, "I'm sorry, Marie."

"Don't apologize to me," I said. "I don't care what he does with that picture." But then I realized she cared very much, and was backing into her room as if she were backing away from a cliff. It was as if she was the reluctant lemming now, but this one had no intention of jumping into what trouble I might bring her.

"No ..." she said, "I'm so sorry ... but I can't do this. Please forgive me, because I can't. I knew I shouldn't have let things go this far, but ... I couldn't help myself. I'm so very sorry." She backed away more swiftly now, and before I had fully registered all that had happened, the door was closed softly between us. I heard the muffled words behind the door before I could even ask her to open it, "I'm sorry, Marie ... I just can't ..."

Chapter Fourteen

Running Out of Fingers

In my eleven-year-old mind, Juliet was the first time love had gotten away from me. Now, at thirty-two, I realized it was only the first of many times that I vowed it would be the last. There had even been a couple of boys after Juliet, since I couldn't put a name to how my intentions were leaning at the time. I only knew they had not been right for me ... and I never counted any of them among the loves that got away. When I was late into my fifteenth year I met Anne, and all my questions, if not my passions, became answered.

Anne was seventeen, and by some miracle (because that is what it took for a seventeen-year-old girl to become friends with a fifteen-year-old girl) for exactly eight months Anne and I were best friends. We had crossed paths when I joined a community theater group after suffering a rejection from my high school play selection committee. I wasn't pretty enough to get the votes I needed to outweigh the friends I didn't have at my school, but in community theater, it was not a popularity contest, but instead, I was chosen because I was the girl who could shed real tears on cue, and was the only one who had tried out who looked young enough to play the daughter of the lead character in the play, Sir Thomas More. In this makeshift troop of school secretaries, dental hygienists, and restaurant workers who had been bypassed by management training programs, I felt blessed to be the only person close to Anne's age. It was a friendship that wouldn't have worked if Anne had attended my high school. We both knew the hard and fast rule on this one: While you aspired to hang out with those that were older, you never would risk hanging around with someone two entire grades younger than you. However, in this non-school environment of community misfits, we became fast friends who bonded over the same music, food and most importantly, likes and dislikes of our fellow actors. We agreed that we loved the gay guys, hated the secretaries, and felt leagues cooler than the restaurant people, except for the one cool gay guy who worked at Wendy's and had a pierced eyebrow.

I fell desperately in love. Anne looked nothing like anyone I knew and if you were to design the polar opposite of my dark Italian features, you would be left with a portrait of Anne, with her light eyes and gold hair, so smooth and straight that it shimmered and moved like a waterfall all the way down to the middle of her back.

For years, when I looked back on how intensely our friendship developed, I convinced myself she had fallen hard for me as well. What else could explain the small gifts she'd buy me (she was old enough to have an after-school job) and our desire to sleep over at each other's houses as often as our mothers would allow? When we were denied the right to sleep over, we had insanely long phone conversations that soon had to be kept secret from my mother, who had started to ask questions. Anne had her own phone number and her own bedroom, but I would have to sneak the telephone under the covers of my bed to talk into the night with her. Since we often talked graphically about sex (although it was always about boys), after our phone calls ended, I would often have to touch myself, imagining it was her as I tried to remember each detail of how pretty she looked the last time I saw her.

I couldn't stop thinking about her. I wanted Anne in ways I'd never desired with a boy. With boys my desire had been an odd curiosity, mainly about body parts I did not own and have access

151

to, and for recreating kissing scenes from the movies I'd seen. My crush on one boy could be easily traded in for the next. With Anne it was different. What I felt for her was a desperation that would leave me inexplicably in tears if I missed her faithful midday call between school and her job as an office assistant. During the one summer of our friendship, every Friday she would take an extra fifteen minutes for lunch so she could drive to my house where I had her favorite macaroni and cheese waiting for her at a table that was all set with napkins, potato chips and Coke, which I would ice at exactly 12:13 so her drink wouldn't get watery. My mother observed me with first a puzzled, then an increasingly worried look after the first lunch I prepared. In the beginning, Mom had enjoyed seeing me set the table, commenting, "I never thought I would live to see the day that a table would get set without me having to ask." But soon she started firing questions at me like: "Why all the fuss?" and "Are you going to do this every week for this girl?"

When I asked her why she cared, she made an excuse about feeding an extra mouth, so from that point on, I spent all my allowance money on the boxes of macaroni and cheese and other lunch treats I knew Anne liked. When I had taken Mom's excuse away, she started asking why I gave up beach invitations from my friends and cousins, to stay inside a hot house to spend an hour preparing a rushed twenty-minute lunch for "some girl." This caused me to wonder as well. *Why was it so important to me?* Why, when I'd see the rusted blue Honda CRX pull up my driveway, would my heart pound so deliciously in my chest as I waited by the window to see Anne emerge from the car, her hair gleaming in the noonday sun? Why would the sight of her dressed up in a professional skirt, crisp blouse and heels walking carefully up my front steps send my head into a dizzying spin? I slowly, but very surely, realized that I'd fallen in love with her. And what that meant I'd become didn't concern me nearly as much as planning my next stolen moment with her.

I began to obsess over her. The number of minutes of our

morning phone call had the power to set the tone for my entire day, until I could see her on the weekend or at our Friday lunches. The lunch ritual had me laying out the vinegar potato chips as if they were the Eucharist host, onto oversized downy dinner napkins which I had paid extra for, and kept hidden on the floor in my bedroom closet. I had bought the expensive Vanity Fair ones by accident and Anne commented on how fancy they were, so I bought them ever since. Sleeping over became an agonizing and glorious torture that kept me up all night long, awake in the dark and staring at her, sometimes with only one eye open, in case she woke up. My logic was that one eye would be quicker to shut than two.

One morning I did get caught staring at her, mesmerized by the sight of her hair spread out on the pillow like an Asian fan spun of golden silk, so close to my face, the strands like fairytale threads of gold and smelling like summer peach, which was the scent of her shampoo. She laughed a huge belly laugh when she saw me, since I must have looked pretty dumb staring intently at her hair with only one eye open. She hit me over the head with her pillow. I joined in with her laughing and we continued until we were crying stupidly into our pillows, and I had to fight the urge not to kiss her, even with the post-braces night retainer she wore to keep her teeth straight. I realized it would take something much more powerful to keep me straight.

It was shortly after that I realized I should avoid the sleep-overs, and that her sleep-induced tossing of an arm against mine did not mean to her what it did to me. And yet, there were times when I could easily convince myself she felt the same way. She had, after all, endured the taunts of her bratty younger sister (who, I tried to forget, was closer in age to me than Anne actually was) about how she was babysitting me. Anne also defended our constant companionship to her own mother, whose face had assumed the same worried look as my mother's when we would spend entire weekends at each other's houses.

It was my impatience that finally scared Anne away from

me, although there may never have been a real chance. It was late at night and we were talking in low voices on the phone, bemoaning that our mothers seemed to be conspiring to keep us from sleeping over so we couldn't play a proper round of Ouija board, which required both sets of our hands on the Ouija. While we talked, I was spelling the invisible words "I LOVE ANNE" in all capitals with the tip of my finger on my bed sheet. I wrote in a more formal typestyle, "I love Anne Mulligan" just as she whispered the something to me that stopped my heart.

"Why can't I find what I have with you, only with a guy?" My invisible pen sputtered and disappeared back into a finger. My silence must have made her feel she should explain further. Her voice grew softer as she said, "Don't take this the wrong way, but sometimes I wish you were a boy."

I swallowed away a lump that felt like a giant fist in my throat. What was "taking it the wrong way," I wondered? A list of possibilities formed in my head:

1. Did she love me like she should a boy?
2. Was she worried I would think her a lesbian because she wished I were a boy?
3. Or was I too much like a boy and maybe it was my fault that she liked me like a boy?

My eyes stung with tears, but they were teetering between elation and devastation ... should I have been happy that she felt so much for me, or wounded that she couldn't feel more because I was a girl? Before I had decided, I spoke the words that had been blaring in my heart.

"I wouldn't want you to be a boy, Anne. I wouldn't like you as much."

She was silent for a long moment, before launching into another explanation that was identical to her first, except now she was adding things about how she didn't want me to think she was a sicko, or worse, a *queer*. She confessed that her sister had been calling her that for weeks now. It made her so angry because (despite what she had just said, and the fact that she loved the gay guys in the theater troop) she "could never, EVER, be one of *those lesbians.*"

Although my hearing was just fine, and what she was said was crystal clear, I convinced myself that she was simply afraid, and that she just needed me to be the one to say it first. Just two days ago I had sat alone for hours, pouting and bored, taking an extra long bath because Anne had to go to dinner with her family instead of coming over as we had planned. This was the day that I ran out of fingers, and concluded that I was gay. It's not as bad as it sounds, the fingers part (and the gay part, as it turned out much later). I had counted on one hand the boys I really liked from grade school through high school. When I could only count three, I decided to include Robert Redford and Andy Gibb. Then I counted the girls. Anne, Juliet, Kendra (but only for two weeks of a three-week camp), Linda (the Australian girl who went to our school for a year and drew a purple heart on my sneaker that I now realize had nothing to do with the military), three grade school teachers, two high school teachers, plus Sally Field, Jane Fonda, Mary Tyler Moore, Madeline Kahn, Dolly Parton, the nun on the soap *Another World*, K. T. Oslin ... and then, I had run out of fingers.

Face it—you're *queer,* I thought. Or g*ay,* I tried, which sounded a little better, but not much. But if it meant I could love Anne instead of a boy, then I very badly wanted to be a queer.

Should I tell someone, I wondered? The problem was, Vince was too young to talk to about these things, and if I told Lisa she would hit me real hard on the shoulder and scream, "I KNEW IT!" as if she herself had created my gayness. She would have said, "I told you! I knew you liked Anne!" and she would have been right. That coming from my older sister, who'd come out before even getting her first period, would feel as if I were trying to copy her, as I had with so many other things ... except this felt very much like my own thing. This was deep inside me, and had nothing to do with anyone except maybe Anne, and now, in the only way that I could, I was telling her.

Carefully, I said, "Anne ... I understand what you mean, but if you were a boy, I wouldn't like you like this." *Like this*, I had said. There it was, as "out" a statement as I could imagine saying at the age of fifteen and three quarters.

"It's late, and I should get off the phone," Anne answered after a long silence.

"Why?" I asked, but I knew. "We haven't even passed yawns back and forth."

"Because it's late, and if my sister heard me having this conversation with you, she'd call us Lezzies for sure."

"I don't care," I said.

"I do," she said.

Anne drifted from me quickly after that night. Two months later, I visited her at Christmas to give her the perfect present I'd bought several months in advance. I'd tucked it away and had fought the urge to give it to her every time we'd been together since I had bought it. But by the time Christmas came around, I hadn't seen her for weeks. I went to see her in the hope that things might change. After all, I had this perfect present I'd spent four allowance weeks on, and maybe, if I gave it to her, she'd see how much I loved her and things could be the way they were before. When she agreed to let me come over, it was not the awkward silence that made me realize any friendship we had was over. It was when she gave me my present. It was a generic gift and she had forgotten I had been with her when she bought it.

It was one of several necklaces she'd bought for a dollar, made from bits of white plastic that were supposed to be shells, on a thin elastic strand that we agreed would probably break the first time you wore it. I had laughed at her, "If you don't like them, why on earth are you getting three of them?" She had answered, "I always pick up a few cheap gifts for people I forgot about at

156

Christmas who give me a present." I'd thought this was clever at the time, and even a little thoughtful to spare some poor sap's feelings. Who hasn't been surprised when the random girl at school you were nice to once embarrasses you with a Christmas gift? I wondered for years who the other crushed souls were who got the other two necklaces. I got her throw-away gift in generic Christmas wrapping that was carefully chosen to be not too cute, in case it had to go to a teacher, and not too adult, in case it went to the papergirl or a classmate; with absolutely no name tag at all.

Chapter Fifteen

For A Good Time: Dial 1-900-Closet Case

I stayed awake consciously replaying the entire evening with Lorn, until it looped automatically in my mind. The truth was I really didn't know her at all. Her reaction to the man with the camera was so severe I feared she might not simply be a closet case (as I had assumed her career might require)—she may also be ashamed and in deep denial as well. A closet case is better than a head case. I could take a lot of things, but even as I lay there awake, aching for her in only the way you can ache after having a taste of something you want so desperately, I knew that I could never be with someone like that. Not even Lorn Elaine ... not that she was mine to reject, I reminded myself. She had closed the door between us, quite literally. However, the sad truth was if she came knocking at my door, I wouldn't hesitate to yank her across the threshold to have whatever I could with her.

What had I expected? That eventually, I would confess everything and she would just accept that while I'd initially stalked her for career reasons, I'd since decided to make her my project instead of the screenplay? Now, alone in my room, the idea that it could have worked seemed absolutely absurd. I wondered, as I stared up to the ceiling, how could I make sense of any of this, when there was a painting of three parrots dressed in pirate hats looming over my headboard?

I don't remember falling asleep, but I do remember that at some point I noticed my pillow had been cried on. I wondered in my state of half-drunk sleep, now who would have gone and cried on my pillow?

My phone was ringing ... it was 2:33 a.m. and my money was on Jess.

"Hello?" I said.

I would have lost my money.

"Marie ..." It was Lorn. I sat up in bed but could not find the light.

"Are you all right?"

"Yes ... no ... I'm so sorry," Lorn whispered.

"So you said," I answered. What else could I say since we had clearly covered that subject?

"I had a lot to drink tonight ..." she said.

"It's OK, it was paid for. Plus, you don't need to make excuses on my account." Is this why she called? "If it will make you feel better, we can pretend it didn't happen ... since actually, it didn't happen."

Long silence.

"But I wanted it too ... very much," she said softly.

This got my attention. I sank back down into my pillow and closed my eyes and waited, but she said nothing more. I could hear her breathing, and the intimate sound sent a shiver down my back. My horny Spidey senses were tingling ... what was she up to?

"Are you in bed?" she finally whispered.

Horny Spidey was never wrong ...

"Of course ... it's 2:30 in the morning," I whispered back.

"I'm in bed too," she said, and then I heard her exhale, very slowly.

Oh, I could see where this was going ... and I couldn't stop it for the life of me. "I can be at your door in five minutes," I said, but I didn't move, since Spidey sensed a different web.

"I'm sorry, Marie, I can't," she whispered.

Did she have to sound so friggin' sexy right when she was reminding me how very sorry she was I couldn't have her?

She continued, "But … if I *could* have you here … right now …"

Danger Will Robinson, Danger, Danger! … But I couldn't help myself from diving in further.

"Tell me …" I said, squeezing my eyes closed, although it was plenty dark in the room. I was melting into the sheets, and asking … no, begging, for big trouble.

"I would kiss you again," she said. Her voice sounded raw and sexual … she was in a very, very, weakened state … and everyone knows what spiders do when that happens …

"Is that all?" I asked, softly baiting her.

"No … God no …" she said.

"I wish I could see you …"

"I'm not wearing anything," she said.

"Christ, Lorn …" I said.

I could hear her breathing quicken, and suddenly, Spidey figured it all out. She was being a very, very bad girl …

"Lorn … I think you need me to come to your room so I can touch you," I said.

"It feels like you already are …"

I sank further in my bed as if my bones had taken hasty leave of my body … I was now the one caught in the web as I waited to hear her. "I know what you're doing," I said, as I joined her, because I was often a very, very bad girl myself. I could tell from her breathing that it excited her I knew exactly what she was doing.

"I want you … so much," she said, and I could tell she was so close to the edge.

I would have thought hearing someone deeply panting on the other end of a phone line would be somewhat comical, or even creepy, but this was not at all the effect it had on me. I knew she would take me down with her, over the echoing static of a Jamaican telephone line. I did a fair amount of panting myself.

"Are you …?" she asked in a ragged breath, and I knew what she wanted to know.

"Yes … I'm coming with you."

Now that was some safe sex. What a challenging way to begin a relationship ... she must have thought so as well, since what I now heard was deep breathing morphing into tears.

"I'm so sorry, Marie," she said softly, before she quietly hung up the phone.

I'd never been dumped so quickly after sex, and I consoled myself at least it couldn't be because I wasn't any good. Now that was some bad reception ...

When I awoke, I felt hung over from lack of sleep, more than the wine. I found Lisa by the pool and convinced her to leave the bar to have coffee with me, even though it was almost noon and she had already started on her first frozen drink. I must have looked pretty pathetic, because I've never persuaded Lisa to abandon anything, unless I first took the time to convince her it was her idea. She managed to get most of the drink down before we had reached the café. Since my sister knew I first required caffeine to speak, she let me walk in silence until we reached the coffee bar. The sun glared across the light blue and gray stone patio, burning my eyes. Sunglasses typically rendered my dark eyes blind, so I only used them as a stalking disguise.

"You look like death," Lisa finally said.

"Thanks. I wish I was at the moment."

"It didn't go well, I'm guessing," she said.

"You think?" I hadn't meant to snap at her, but she seemed not to mind.

"Bet she's the flirty, straight variety, eh? Unfortunately not the rarest of breeds. They feed off the sexual tension of being around a chick who has the hots for them, but when push comes to pussy, they can't do the deed. Paranoia ... it's a fucking shame, really."

"That's quite a friggin' leap," I said, amazed that her leap landed so close to reality. I grasped my coffee mug and sipped, grateful that Lisa didn't know the details.

"She knew you had a thing for her," Lisa said.

161

It was so easy to let her continue to think this was the case, since now it was the case, and I certainly did have a thing for her. It was especially easy after recalling the laugh fest I had shared with Lorn over that horrid screenplay. Better to look like a lovelorn fool than a no-talent writer with a childish dream ... that is, if a child dreamed to someday write a screenplay about women prisoners.

"She may have guessed, since I acted like a complete idiot the first time I saw her, what with the wayward meatball and all."

"That, and Dad told her."

"What?"

Lisa shifted a little in her seat. Lisa is not a shifter. She was more the type to squirm with delight over the unraveling of an interesting story. There is a vast difference between shifting and squirming with delight. If Lisa was shifting, this was going to be very, very bad. With a forced calm, I placed my cup down, and rested my aching face into my hands. The calm came easier than expected, since I couldn't imagine anything going more wrong than it already had. There really was nothing left to ruin.

"Dad assumed, like Vince did at first, that you'd either invited or maybe followed her here ... and he tried to have a laugh about it with Lorn ... but it wasn't really his fault," she said, "we all thought this was what happened. Vince kind of blew it on the first day, despite his trying to cover it up afterwards with the college teacher story, which Dad was clueless about."

"Oh, God ..." I said.

"Mare, don't worry about it ... we just told her you were a big fan of her work and I think Lorn took it really well. We all thought you'd be ridiculously self-conscious if you knew, so we all decided to—"

"WE ALL?" I demanded. "So instead, you all decide to leave me clueless that she thought I might have followed her here? *This* was the better option?" Lisa shifted again as I felt my calm evaporating with the sweat on my forehead, dissolving into steam in the noonday sun.

"Well, Dad loves a good story. Especially one that makes him seem like a liberal-thinking man of a younger generation. You know, someone who accepts people of 'our kind' ... so he told a few people. I think he thought it was cute you had a crush on your favorite actress ..." Lisa then went on to indicate it was safe to assume everyone knew, with the possible exception of one part-time resort bartender.

"Jesus! But it's not even true! I didn't follow her here!"

"Well, you have to admit, it was a *huge* coincidence," she said.

I had to admit, it was huge.

When I snapped and told Lisa I needed to talk to Vince, she took this as an opportunity to escape from the table, scrambling away like a stray mutt squeezing out a gap in the back of the dog-catcher's truck. I sat staring into space, and forced myself to sip the hot coffee as I ignored my churning stomach.

Vince showed up within twenty minutes, in swim trunks and T-shirt dripping with seawater. He had his snorkel gear in his hands. "Are you OK?" he asked me. "Lisa said for me to come. I was snorkeling and she threw shells at me in the friggin' lagoon; I thought I was being attacked by heard of conches. What's the matter?"

I glared up at him. "Did you get Lorn here somehow? Send her a hotel voucher or something? How did you do it, Vince?"

"What? What the hell are you talking about?"

"Lorn! Did you get her to come to Jamaica somehow? You're the only one who knew the plans in advance. Did you?"

"Mare—no ... Of course I didn't! What on earth has you so crazed? You aren't even making sense. I was the one who thought *you* had invited her!"

I took a deep breath. Of course he didn't, I thought, now feeling guilty as well as foolish. "I'm sorry. Very rough night. I just need somebody to blame." He stared down at me like he had no idea who the fuck I was. I had no idea either.

"Can't I just blame you?" I asked weakly.

He sat down, dripping salt water on the table, and signaled

163

the waiter for two Red Stripes and two Red Bulls. "Blame away. I can take it." He paused, before explaining, "I should have told you. Dad had already opened his big mouth and told her you were a big fan of hers, so I lied to you when I told you I'd fix everything with the story about her looking just like your college teacher. I told Lorn you'd kill me for not fixing things, and, well, she took pity on me ... plus, we all thought you would freak out ..."

"You're right about that!" I wanted to walk into the ocean in Italian-style cement shoes and not look back. What a mess ... no wonder she was so damned paranoid last night ... she probably thought I brought the fucking photographer as well!

Vince continued, "I'm sorry Mare, but I asked her not to say anything to you ... I said you would be mortified if she knew you were a fan and you wouldn't be able to face her again ... I guess she must have wanted to see you again ... That's good, right?" he asked hopefully.

"No ... not speaking to her would have been better," I said, thinking about how deeply this woman already had a hold on me.

I didn't see Lorn at all that day, and it was actually an enormous relief until that evening, when I met some of my family for dinner. It was then I realized, despite the hopelessness of the situation, that I was continually scanning the restaurant for her, desperately hoping to see her. We had talked Aunt Aggie and Uncle Freddie into trying the Caribbean-style restaurant, and it had a clear view of the Italian place across the lobby, so I was able to keep vigil for any sign of her. When she was nowhere to be seen, a pit settled in my stomach that made eating seem impossible, despite the fact that I'd avoided food all day. Not seeing her was worse than being embarrassed to see her. The memory of her voice last night on the phone replayed again and again in my head all day. The wine had made the details blurry ... but there was no mistaking the ending to that call. She would not let herself go where she wanted to go.

Around 8:00, I saw Katherine and Uncle Tony at the entrance to the Banana Hammock and my heart pounded until I confirmed they were dining without Lorn again. She was alone somewhere. I reminded myself that she was the one who had closed the door, and that I had no business thinking I should go find her ... but the nagging thought remained; she didn't know the real reason why I had been following her career ... if my whole family wasn't convinced I hadn't followed her here, why would she think anything else as well? And if she did think I followed her here, could I really blame the woman for being paranoid?

I tried to focus on dinner with my family, since, unlike any other time in the Santora family history, everyone was getting along perfectly, but I could not. Even Aunt Aggie was on her best behavior, and asked me with genuine concern if I was feeling better. I said I was, but only Vince and Lisa knew I was actually feeling worse with each passing hour.

I decided to skip the after-dinner drinks, and walked back toward my room with Aunt Aggie and Uncle Freddie, who were calling it a night as well. After saying goodnight to them, I found it impossible to go back to my room and instead doubled back to the beach to take the long walk along the shore in the darkness. I was still looking for her, and the question occurred to me: would I forever be looking for this woman? The replay of our first kiss came back again and again, ignited by being on the same darkened beach, with the same sounds and smell of the surf. Finally, the memories drove me away from the shore. While I hadn't made a conscious decision to go to her room, I arrived at her door anyway. I knocked quickly before I lost my nerve.

Lorn answered the door dressed in her nightgown, with her hair pulled back in a thick ponytail. She wore reading glasses and not a stitch of make-up; and I thought she was the most hand-some sight I had ever laid my eyes on. Such an intimate view of her ...

"Oh ... I assumed you were my mother, coming to tell me how her dinner was," she said.

"Or you wouldn't have opened the door?"

"No, of course not. Please come in, Marie."

Before someone gets a snapshot, I wondered, surprised at my own irritation.

I walked by her, trying to ignore her semi-sheer nightgown. I focused on keeping my eyes fixed on hers. This wasn't much better, since the green color bored into me, weakening me further. I realized she looked much like Anne might have, twenty years after she gave me the cheap necklace. I'm in trouble, I thought. Why had I come? What was there to say?

She spoke first. "I'm sorry," she said.

"I didn't come here for more of that."

"For what then?" she asked, with just a trace of defiance as she put her book on her bed and placed her glasses on top of it. The nightstand light shone from behind her gown and I saw the silhouette of her body in cruel and beautiful detail. My irritation abandoned me.

"Can I sit for a moment?" I asked.

"Of course, excuse me for being rude. Please." She signaled me to sit on one bed while she sat on the other. A chair would be so much better, I thought, but I sat down, gratefully. Why did she have to look so damned good? She was avoiding my eyes; avoiding all of me, actually.

"I'm so embarrassed," she began, "for last night ... for now," she said, self-consciously smoothing her nightgown. "And now you've ruined my plan to hide here in my room for the rest of the week, so I wouldn't have to face you ever again."

"That was my plan after the meatball. It didn't work. Lorn, what happened last night? I mean, before the sexy 1-900 phone call ..." I tried to give her a little smile to assure her I was not being mean; but that only works if someone is looking at you. She kept her eyes on her nightgown, so I did too. "When that man took your photo, I know he invaded your privacy, but why would you—"

"Panic? Lots of reasons. My career is everything to me and I can't risk losing it. It's why ... I've been alone for many years. It's a hell of a price to pay, but it's the decision I've made."

"Has it ever occurred to you that your career means everything to you because you haven't pursued a relationship? Can you even admit out loud who you are, Lorn?"

"I thought I just did."

"No, if we roll back the tape, you really didn't."

"Maybe I didn't know exactly who I was, until we met," she said, appearing shaken at the confession. "I only considered being with a woman just one other time, and that was a disaster. She had an agenda I wasn't aware of, but I got out before it was too late. Before her, honestly, I was still attempting to find the right guy. I was trying to find one that could make me feel ... something ... anything. Now I've realized that it wasn't a problem with the men I'd dated; but that it's me ... but I've never ..." She trailed off and looked at me at last. Lorn looked scared to death again.

"You've waited a long time," I said. "Is any career worth not experiencing such an important part of your life?"

"This one is. I've supported myself as an actress since I was seventeen. I don't know if you appreciate how difficult that is when you're not married and on your own; especially living in Hollywood. Other women who are part of a two-income family can afford the time off in between acting roles; I've never had that luxury. I always had to worry about supporting myself."

"But you have done that, fabulously in fact."

"Because I've been careful not to let it get taken away. This business is very fickle." When she said the word "fickle," I couldn't help but raise an eyebrow at her. She caught this and attempted to defend herself. "I know what you are thinking, Marie, but I'm not a fickle person ..."

"You just play one on TV?"

She briefly forfeited a smile. "Can I at least get credit for admitting the whole gay thing?"

"We only give partial credit for that, because you're still avoiding the L word."

"'WE' as in the other club members?" she asked.

"'WE' as in me and my breasts. I speak for all three of us, except on weekends. Then, they speak for themselves."

Lorn shook her head to barely avoid laughing at me.

"It's not that I don't know what I want ... finally," she said, and immediately, the sexual tension grew between us. She turned away and said, "I don't want to lose what I already have. I hope you understand. And I can say the L word ... I do *like* you ... very, very much," she teased. Then she added sadly, "I wish things could be different."

"Things could be different," I said.

"No, they can't."

Well, there it was. She had chosen to let the world dictate what type of life she'd lead; that was her choice. I felt my heart splitting in two pieces as the thought overtook me: if she wanted me as much as I did her, she wouldn't have any other option than to reach out to me. I felt the sting of tears burning at the corner of my eyes, so I got up quickly. I reminded myself, she has made her choice; now get out before you make a bigger fool of yourself. Lorn stood up with me.

"I understand," I forced myself to say as I headed for the door.

"Wait, please Marie, don't leave, I really don't want to leave it like this ..."

But I was determined not to let her see me break down, and the breakdown was approaching fast. When I got to the door I didn't look back when I said softly, "I want you to know that I loved meeting you, Lorn. I don't regret that part at all." I closed the door behind me just as the tears started flowing. I walked quickly down the hallway and took the stairwell that led to the darkness of the beach.

Once there, I let the real sobs begin. The sounds were barely audible so near the surf, even to myself. The wind whipped the tears away as quickly as they flowed, and I imagined how I must

168

look. A thirty-two-year-old woman, walking on a dark beach, tears flying off her face in every direction ... like a crying dyke cartoon character. *Be done with this woman*, I thought. *Be done with her ... she has taken up too much of your energy already. Cut your losses, and move on.* The house in California could be sold just as easily as it was bought, since the money didn't matter one bit.

The thought of selling the house in California brought a fresh round of tears that lasted all the way to my room. It was stupid to have made such plans, but I realized now that I actually loved that house, if not just for the dreams I had when I bought it and the feeling of independence, which came with having something of my own. California would be more than just a failed invest-ment; it seemed now my second failed dream. When I got back to my room I was exhausted. I fell onto my bed fully clothed and covered in a salt mix of ocean spray and tears, and instantly fell deeply asleep.

I awoke suddenly from a sound I could not identify, and when I did, I was disoriented, still dressed, and the light was still on in my room. Was it morning? I glanced at the clock. It was two o'clock in the morning. I heard the sound again, and finally it registered as a soft knock at the door. Startled, I jumped up and stumbled for the door, still feeling half asleep.

It was Lorn.

"I saw your light was still on," was all she said as she entered the room. She had a light jacket thrown over her nightgown and she looked shaken.

"Are you all right?" I asked, shutting the door. A chilly puff of salty sea air followed her into the room. I tried to ignore the thought of tasting the salt on her skin.

"No," she said softly. "I'm so far from being all right." She turned towards me and stood so close I felt a surging heat in the small space that remained between us. My heart pounded in time with a more distracting area of my body. But I recalled that earlier that night, I had made a vow to be done with this, so I

169

asked, "What is it you want, Lorn? Why are you here?" And then added, a little cruelly, "Aren't you afraid someone might have seen you coming up to my room?"

She looked away from me. My comment had the desired effect, but the victory wasn't sweet, since I was fighting the urge to wrap my arms around her even now, to erase what I had just said.

"I couldn't stay away and I don't know what to do," she whispered in a ragged breath. "This has all happened so fast ..."

"No, Lorn, you're confused ... it's not happening at all."

Lorn turned away from me so I couldn't see her face. I had cried myself out last night, and now all that seemed to be left was anger. Mostly anger at myself, for doing all I had done before arriving in Jamaica; all to pursue a dream I had convinced myself was possible. And now that she was here, I was angry with myself for all I had done to get close to her since arriving here. Combine that with being ticked off at how helpless I felt in her presence, and that equaled a fair bit of anger.

She wouldn't look at me, so we stood in silence for long time. "Lorn," I said, finally, but she still kept her back to me, shoulders slightly shaking. I reached for her arm and turned her around to me. Her eyes were closed and she was crying, and soundless tears were slowly tumbling down her cheeks like a pitiful child who had lost her pet. All my anger vanished in that instant. I pulled her to me, and she instantly grasped onto the top of my shoulders with both hands and buried her face into my neck. I was in a strange state ... feeling sorrier for her than I had for myself last night, as well as thoroughly, painfully crazed to physically have her.

"It's all right ..." I said, trying to ignore the effect her body had on mine.

What would it be like to deny yourself the life you were meant to lead? I wondered how lonely she had been, forcing herself to take a different path, or maybe worse, no path at all, for all of these years. I held her tightly as her body shuddered with her tears. I felt my neck getting wet where she was pressing her face. *I'll hold her as long as she needs, for whatever she needs*, I thought, as I hurled my reservations aside to make more room for her to press against me. Her warmth was dizzying. She had a thin jacket over her nightgown, but it was wide open between us. I became aware of the unbearable softness of her body and I reacted with a shudder of my own; this seemed to be exactly when her crying stopped. She was taking long deep breaths now, and the heat of her seared my neck.

She moved her hands, so slowly at first, spreading her fingers wider to grasp more of my back. "I've wanted this," she said, softly.

Wanted what? I thought. A hot night with a card-carrying dyke? Sex? A week with a woman ... a month with a woman? There were too many possibilities. I tried to pull away then, knowing that it would be harder to let her go if we got any closer ... and we were getting closer. Before I could manage to pull away, her mouth opened against my neck with a flare of heat and the entire side of my body came alive, right down to my toes. If an entire side of your body could have an orgasm, I was having it ... or maybe a stroke, I thought, as the pleasure built to a level so intense, I felt madly numbed by it. My eyes rolled back as if she were draining my neck like a vampire. Wasn't that supposed to be my role?

No, I thought ... being with her to then be pushed away ... I didn't want to know that much pain. It would be so much worse than any pain I'd had before; somehow, I just knew this. "Please," I whispered, trying to extricate myself from her. But I said it with such a weak voice it ended up sounding like a sexual plea for more, and maybe it fucking was. My knees started to buckle and she surprised me by pushing me deftly against the door I'd planned to exit, to hold me up as she further devoured my neck. Her hands moved to both sides of my face, and just at the crest of her insanely hard sucking, she pulled away from my neck and covered my mouth with a hard kiss. I was drowning now, and nothing would stop the freight train pounding in my chest.

We kissed ferociously.

Lorn pulled away from me just long enough to speak. "I think I'm in trouble here ... please Marie, I have no idea what I'm doing ... I just can't stop." If she hadn't said my name, her exact words would have been my very own, if I had the strength to speak. By way of answering, I tore off her jacket. Next I pulled her nightgown from her, more roughly than I would have if I weren't in a race to take her before she changed her mind. If I was going to go down ... I was going to go down in a blaze of auburn hair.

Lorn pulled at my clothes too, but we didn't part from our kiss until I pulled her nightgown over her head. The view of her body entirely exposed stole the breath from my lungs, so instead of air, I drank in the sight of her as I led her to my bed; breathing was overrated, the sight of her was enough.

I left the nightstand light to shine brightly, not being able to give up the exquisite view of her skin, delicately freckled, evaporating into a smooth milky white and flushed pink in just the most perfect places. She was a most spectacular design ... and the thought struck me that she looked more like a painting of a woman, as if a master artist had planned every detail; and oh, how her exquisiteness contrasted with the bright green parrots in their pirate hats on the wall above her. I pulled away to finish undressing myself, as I watched her below me. It was only my knowledge of how important this moment was in both our lives that stopped me from mentioning the parrots ... that, and she was now pulling me down against the length of her.

Because I was feeling cocky, or maybe because I was Lisa's sister and shared some of the same DNA, I told her I was going to get inside her. I told her this for two reasons: first, because I thought she should know; and second, because I wanted to see that "How-With-No-Cock" look on her face; the gift with purchase of landing a newbie. Since I was feeling a very, very bad girl, I couldn't resist.

Lorn looked up at me with "The Look," but she opened for me just the same. My mind raced with ridiculous thoughts as I took her. Would she move into my house with me, or I with her? ... What on earth would my mother think? ... What would her mother think? ... Did her mother know? ... Did any mother really ever know unless they happen upon a stray letter or photo? My thoughts were halted, since she was moving wildly against my hand, and as I wrapped my mouth around a fair amount of her breast, she told me quite definitely that she was going to come.

She kept her word.

A moment later, I warned her I would need to spend the rest of my life with her.

"God help me, I think I'm in love with you ..." Lorn said, as she shuddered against me.

Now, as exciting as it was, I couldn't help registering the "God help me" portion of her declaration, over and over in my head. The "I love you" part was a confession I desperately needed to make myself, but it wouldn't have occurred to me to ask the higher powers for help. But as she clung to me, shaking, I soon forgot the weakness of her plea since although her breathing had slowed there still remained a great smoldering in her eyes, maybe a greater smoldering. We kissed deeply, and a moment later she rolled on top of me. "I want you now ... in my mouth ..."

Clearly, she was making up for lost time ...

She worked her way along my neck, breasts, and stomach, but did not linger. Within seconds she had buried her face into me, and the heat of her mouth almost finished the job on contact. Don't be such a man, I thought, trying to hold out. Maybe I should I think of baseball? It would be so convenient to be a sport-loving dyke right now. Instead, I tried to think of Martha Stewart baking holiday cookies; but that rarely worked, since I was always trying to get a peek down that denim shirt whenever she rolled out the dough ... and then of course the women's prison fantasies would begin. Lorn may have sensed my dilemma, since she delayed me by avoiding where I needed her most. Or at least I hoped it was intentional, as I'd never met a woman who didn't understand exactly what needed to be done. She moved around me making insane little circles and until I was desperate to get her where I needed to go.

It had been intentional. The only warning she gave that she was about to take a different tack was when she deftly grabbed both my hands and pinned them to the bed. A second later, she wrapped her lips around me, seizing the target and sending me into a frenzied orgasm.

God help me.

We awoke the next morning, naked and tangled in each other, with the lights still on, staring in silence at each other for a long time. I'm sure I had the "I can't believe this woman is in my bed" look, while she had the "I can't believe any woman is in my bed" look. Not knowing how to begin, I decided to cut to the chase; "I want a life with you," I said.

"So you mentioned," she said coyly, but I saw the fleeting flash of fear in her eyes before she masked it by kissing me again, sweetly at first, but only for a moment. We began again. This time I took her in my mouth, tasting the sweetness of her, obsessing over the thought that I would require a lifetime to please her, and nothing less, to satisfy me. I looked up as I feasted; at first her arms were outstretched, positioned as if on a crucifix, but as her expression changed from one of gentle surprise to near demented excitement, she twisted both her fists into the bed sheets as she came, pulling the white sheet down to the sides of her hips like folded angel's wings. I could have told her it would be heaven, but she may not have believed me. I instantly fast-forwarded to our Saturday morning rituals in bed ... and Sunday afternoons after brunch ... it's what happens in a dyke's mind. We start making lists and packing boxes ... after packing boxes.

It took a long time for us to pull apart from each other and get showered. There would be a lifetime of things to discover about her and I watched her shower in rapt attention as if I had never witnessed the act of a human using soap and water. Her skin shimmered and her freckles taunted me until I gave in and began an endless game of connecting the tiny heavenly bodies across a smooth Milky Way. I dried her off with a towel, and there were many interruptions for kissing. I let her borrow a pair of my shorts and a shirt so she could get back to her room without looking like a flasher in her jacket and nightgown and we lingered a long goodbye before I opened the door to let her leave.

There was no flash this time, since it was daylight, but we both heard the telltale sound of the camera firing from across the hall. I pulled back from the doorway so he wouldn't get us both in the picture and took a good look at him through the side window.

This time I was apologizing to Lorn. She didn't have time to respond, but instead hurried away down the hallway to the back stairwell without turning back. I didn't like how quickly she moved. There was definite panic in the way she took those stairs, and it made me wonder how much damage a photo of her leaving my hotel room could possibly do to her career; and to keeping her.

I needed to find Vince right away.

Chapter Sixteen

A Picture is Worth a Thousand Worms

I gave the man a head start, but peered out the window to see which direction he took. Since I couldn't risk losing the photographer to find Vince, I hurried to the end of the stairwell to first tail him to his room. It wasn't until I was across the pool that I noticed he was walking just several paces behind Lorn. When he stopped to take her picture again, I had to restrain myself from tackling him right there under a palm tree. He looked like the type to cry after a good bitch-slapping. While he continued to click the camera, I fantasized about throwing a rock at his head, but luckily for him, the grounds were well groomed. That, and there was a woman approaching from the other direction, who could get caught in the crossfire. He stopped taking pictures to speak to the approaching woman who had an oddly familiar look and walk ...

I realized with horror that the woman was Jessica. *What the fuck?*

I fought the urge to get closer to see them better, but I didn't need to; it was definitely her. She spoke with him briefly, before she hurried off to a room that was just one floor away from mine. That bitch ... She couldn't possibly think she could scare Lorn away from me by bringing a photographer here? Then I thought, maybe she had.

I waited until Jessica closed her door before continuing to tail him. He never once looked behind him, which, I thought, in his line of work was a sure sign of stupidity. I tailed him with more confidence, thinking my past stalking skills had paid off. I was sure he never got a look at me, but just in case, I pulled my hair back in a ponytail; and again cursed myself at not having a dark pair of sunglasses.

Lorn turned down into her stairwell but thankfully the man walked right past it, and turned down the second row of buildings where the non-water view rooms were. *Cheap bastard*, I thought, and then realized I was probably talking about Jessica, since he was probably on her payroll. I noted the number of the room he slithered into, before jogging off to find Vince.

Vince wanted details about my evening with Lorn, but all I could talk about was the man with the camera. He was furious when he found out it was the same photographer who had harassed Lorn before. Vince liked Lorn, and I knew that telling him the protection of her privacy could make or break our relationship would make him help me.

"I have to see Uncle Freddie," he said, standing to go.

"Vince, there's something else. It was Jessica."

"Jessica is the man taking the pictures?"

"No, I saw him with her, she's here. I think she must have hired him."

"Marie, are you sure it was her? That seems awfully paranoid since nobody even knew Lorn was here."

"Jessica called a few nights ago," I confessed, "she was pissed I was selling the condo and when she badgered me about Lorn, I threw it in her face that she was here ... with us."

"Well, that may not have been worth the joy it brought you."

"Seemed it was at the time," I said. "Jess thinks she can spook Lorn away with some bad press ... and Vince," I said, grabbing his arm, "the thing is, she may be right. Lorn is spooked, and I'm concerned about how much."

"Tell me which room he is in, and I'll get Uncle Freddie. He's dealt with guys worse than this in his day. He was a fucking Teamster!" Vince said.

"Yeah, and now he is pushing seventy. What the hell do you think he'll be able to do? He'll have a fucking heart attack!" I said.

"Not him, me. I just need his advice. Listen, don't confront Jessica; it will be easier if she doesn't know we're onto her. Don't worry—I'll be back!" he shouted as he ran off.

"You're not exactly a Soprano or Schwarzenegger, Vince—" I called out after him, "this ain't Hollywood, it's Jamaica—don't be an idiot!" I knew as I watched him tear off that his enthusiasm had already spun out of control.

Shortly after, Lisa and Mom came around the corner where Vince had disappeared, and spotted me at the café. "Where was Vince running off to in such a hurry?" Lisa asked, and I gave her the shut-up signal when Mom wasn't looking.

"He's heading to the gym. He's convinced all the margaritas are making him fat."

"Are you available for dinner tonight?" Mom asked. It was probably just my paranoia that detected a slight tone left over from blowing off her birthday dinner, but maybe not.

"I guess so," I said, not used to thinking of myself as half of a couple again ... or was I?

"Uncle Tony wants us all to have dinner. It seems to be very important to him, so I think we should all go."

"Will Katherine be going?" I asked, when I really wanted to ask if Lorn was going.

"Where the fuck have you been?" Lisa said, "They've been inseparable since the day they met. Like some other people, I'm guessing?"

Mom shot me a look. "What's happening, Marie? Have you been ... seeing ... Katherine's daughter. That actress?"

"Her name is Lorn, Mom." I said, surprised at the directness of the question. She didn't sound thrilled by it, but it was a start. Lisa was looking at our mother as if she had grown an extra head.

"And I have no idea if I'm seeing her, to be perfectly honest," I added.

"Maybe not, but I bet you've had her!" Lisa said, slapping my shoulder like she was my army buddy.

I growled at her, "Are you a friggin' man, Lisa? I mean really, are you? You're so crass!"

"Girls, please!" Mom said in The Voice. Lisa started laughing, and despite myself, I couldn't help but join her.

"I knew it," Lisa said, "you whore!"

"Girls!" Mom admonished again. We laughed even harder, after making a valiant attempt at stifling our giggling. Mom tried to hide her own smile with her coffee, but she lifted the cup just a moment too late and I spotted it.

After taking a sip, Mom said, "Well, she seems nice enough," and Lisa abruptly stopped laughing.

"Hmmm ..." Lisa said, "maybe I need to find a date for tonight too, since we're all getting so comfy with this."

"Don't steal your sister's big moment," Mom said.

Back at my room, I left a message for Lorn. I decided to give her some space, since I would see her tonight at Uncle Tony's family dinner. But the nagging thought that the photographer had rattled her again wouldn't go away. I restrained myself by only leaving the one message, although I spent the greater part of the day courting my phone and waiting for Vince, or for Lorn to call back.

At 5:00, Vince finally showed up at my room, but I still hadn't heard from Lorn. When I shut the door behind him, he said, "All set, how much do you want to know?"

I could tell he was dying to tell me everything. "All of it," I said, and he beamed.

"OK, but Uncle Freddie said the less people who know about these things, the better."

"Stop with the wop-drama and start talking ... I know you didn't ice the guy."

"Well, I waited for him to leave his room, which took a while, then I just broke in." He was trying to sound casual.

179

"Broke in? How? I assumed you'd just have a talk with him and maybe scare him a little." But I really hadn't thought that. Deep down, I guess I knew Vince would do whatever it took to stop further intrusion from the man; just short of hurting him ... I hoped.

"Uncle Freddie gave me a refresher course in credit-card lock picking, and it turns out it comes back to you pretty quickly, like riding a bicycle. Then I waited for him to leave, busted in and took all his photo stuff. And I do mean *all* of his stuff. You know, next time we should really pick a hotel with better security."

"Vince! If you get caught with his stuff they could arrest you!"

"I won't get caught with it. I weighted a small duffel bag and fed it to the fishes. Plus, I paid a local kid five hundred dollars to buy all the extra film from all the gift shops and nearby hotels and stores. I told him I'd give him an extra three hundred bucks if he brought it all back within two hours, which he did. If our photo hound has another camera stowed away somewhere, he won't have any supplies to use with it, or at least not nearby. It didn't look like he even knew how to use the safe. He had stuff in it, passport and some money, but the idiot didn't even lock it. I wonder if he is even a professional by the look of his crappy equipment. There was only the one big camera, and not much else. He may even be someone Jess knows who agreed to come here and play photographer. I hid his ID and passport just for fun; that will eat up at least another day of his life to get that straightened out, too."

All I could do was hug him. Then I hit him hard on the arm. "You idiot!" I said.

I knocked at her door. In a few minutes, I heard movement and the door opened.

"Hello Marie," Jess said, trying to hide her surprise. She was in a robe and looked as if she had come from the shower. The front of her robe fell partly open, but she made no move to close it. Her exposed body actually repelled me. Even in our darkest times I had found it hard to deny the aesthetic beauty of her. Now it was finally gone ... Lorn had washed the last of it away.

"What the fuck are you doing here?" I asked.

She stepped closer, just outside her door. She seemed mystified that her naked body had not rattled me. "I came to convince you that you made a big mistake."

"I've made many mistakes—I'm trying to correct them all, starting with you," I said.

"What if I told you I came here to win you back?"

"I would tell you that it was a wasted trip."

I saw her glance past me, over my shoulder as she let the robe open completely before me. She seemed pleased that anyone walking past her room could have seen her body in plain view.

"Close your robe before you make a fool out of yourself."

She reached for my arm, and I tried to pull away, but she held firm and gave a contrasting smile. "You used to have difficulty resisting my body ... even when we were fighting."

"The problem was you couldn't resist anyone else," I said. "I know you hired that reporter, Jess. What the fuck did you think that would accomplish?"

Jessica hid her surprise like the pro that she was. The game appeared fun to her.

"Exactly what it did. She'll never be with you, Marie. You might as well know that now rather than later. She has no idea you've been following her, does she?"

"I haven't been following her." But Jess knew me too well. "She came here on her own. I met her for the first time here," I said.

She glanced past me again and pulled my arm towards her. "Come inside," she said, smiling, opening her robe wider with her free hand to reveal her perfectly toned, nude body.

"What? Are you crazy?" I said.

I looked over my shoulder to see what Jessica was staring at.

Down the hallway, Lorn stood motionless on the stairwell leading to my room. I pulled my arm from Jessica's grip and turned back towards her as I spat, "Stay away from her, do you understand? I want you out of here by tonight!"

I turned around again to see Lorn had gone.

"I won't let you have her, Marie. Too bad, she's not bad looking ... for her age. I guess I could always try sharing you."

"Leave Jamaica tonight," I said, "or I'll spend every penny I have to make the rest of your life miserable. Trust me, money can buy a lot of things."

"It won't buy you that actress," she said.

After knocking at Lorn's door with no result, I was finally able to get her on the phone about an hour before we were to all meet for dinner. I could tell instantly from her tone that she was done with me, not to mention all the baggage that had followed me to Jamaica.

"Lorn, I am sorry you had to see that ... I wish you had let me explain. That was my ex ... Jessica, she showed up here completely uninvited. It's been over for a very long time and she only has interest in my inheritance. She's not interested in me at all; actually, she never really was."

Lorn was silent.

"I just found out she was here today ... she saw you coming and she wanted you to think ..." It was all starting to sound so Jerry Springer. "Nothing happened between us," I said.

"I believe you," Lorn said. She didn't finish the sentence, but I knew she wanted to say: It still doesn't matter.

"I'm sorry. I know she hired that photographer ... but you don't have to worry about any pictures. I took care of it ... well, Vince took care of it. All the film is gone, and you're not supposed to ask how. You know, it's an Italian thing ..." I forced a laugh.

"I don't want to know," she said.

"OK?" I asked when she grew silent again.

"OK," she answered.

"Lorn, Jess means nothing to me, and I only went to her door to tell her I knew what she was up to and to get her to leave the island. She knows it's over between us."

Lorn didn't say a word back and within the silence I realized in this case it was me who didn't know something was over.

"All I have been thinking about is you ... and last night," I said in an effort to fill the silence. "She'll be gone soon, and that photographer too, after he straightens out his missing passport situation ... I promise you. Will you tell me where you were today?"

"I stayed in my room most of the morning, and told my mother I drank too much last night so I could be alone to think. And then, I couldn't stand it anymore ..."

"You came to see me," I said. "I'm sorry you had to witness that. Lorn, I'll make sure she never bothers you again." I was embarrassed, in addition to fearing losing her. "Will I see you tonight at dinner?"

"Yes."

"Lorn, we took care of the problem. You can enjoy your time here without worrying about it."

"Maybe, but our time here will end. I appreciate what you and Vince did to try to protect me, and the chance he took to take care of it, but there'll always be another photographer looking for a story."

"Lorn, it's not a crime to be gay. Have you ever thought about just giving them the story they're looking for? What happened to 'any publicity is good publicity' in Hollywood?"

"I can't do that. I won't risk my career ... I already ex-plained that to you. I've worked too hard for too many years." She sounded cold and resolute.

I forced myself to ask the question I didn't want the answer to. "Are you saying we're over before we even had a chance?"

She didn't answer. Her silence did.

Finally she said, "Let's not talk about this on the phone. We can talk tonight, after dinner."

"Is there anything to talk about? You sound very sure you can't do this ... am I right?"

There was a long pause, and when she spoke, her voice sounded closed and distant. "I hope you know how much I wish it could be different."

"Oh, I do know it could be different. Goodbye Lorn." I gently hung up the phone, feeling my emotions begin to boil again. I had lost her, and worse, now I knew what I was missing. Better to have loved and lost? No fucking way.

Chapter Seventeen

Ellen-Shaped Ice Sculptures

I was with Vince and Lisa outside the restaurant when Lorn arrived with her mother and Uncle Tony. She looked perfect, as if she had dressed to torture me, and I was concentrating all my energy on not throwing up. She avoided eye contact with me and I felt my stomach shred further. When Vince saw the expression on my face, he slid his arm around me. "It'll be OK," he whispered. "You're my date this evening."

Even Lisa, not usually the touchy type, gave my hand a squeeze in a show of support as they approached. "I wonder who she got so fucking dressed up for," Lisa mumbled. I had wondered the same, but it felt more a cruel act than a hopeful one. The three of them joined the three of us, and Lisa and Vince kept me between them, as if we were dogs that may fight. I had told them earlier there was nothing left for me to talk about with Lorn, and any more contact would just make the recovery of my heart that much harder. If I could recover at all ... I might just decide to give up the whole love thing after this mess and beg for a permanent position as a contractor's assistant to Erica As In All My Children ... if I even bothered to go back to California.

Lorn could not avoid looking at me now, and when she did, I felt something I hadn't expected to. I felt her profound sadness. The fire in her eyes had been extinguished, and for the first time, I thought about how breaking it off might be harder for her, since she was inflicting the pain on herself. I couldn't fathom how difficult it must be to think you could not choose whom you could love. While I'd never been much of a parade marcher, I could never do anything except run like a maniac towards the person I wanted to be with. It never occurred to me this was a luxury some people didn't have. Granted, the luxury of it hadn't worked well for me thus far.

We took our seats at the table, and I was seated right across from Lorn. I childishly planned to be cold if this happened, but abandoned the plan as I watched her now. I attempted a smile towards her as Uncle Tony chatted on happily to the rest of the family. Lorn looked briefly at me before averting her eyes and excusing herself to go to the ladies' room. Before she left the table, I saw her eyes had begun to shimmer with the threat of tears. I fought the urge to follow her, and would have lost the battle if Lisa and Vince hadn't anticipated my move and both tightened their grips like vices under the table, one on each leg, to hold me in my seat.

Katherine sensed something about her daughter's abrupt exit and scanned Vince, Lisa and me for an answer, and finally fixed her gaze on me. I could tell she somehow knew what had transpired. Katherine excused herself to go to the ladies' room as well. They were away from the table for some time and, thankfully, Uncle Tony seemed oblivious to what was happening. He looked excited, nervous, and completely in love. He had been holding Katherine's hand as if it were a found treasure and now that she had left to follow Lorn, he didn't seem to know where to put his empty hand. It was impossible to not be happy for him, despite my own shattered heart.

Lisa leaned over and said, "You need to look strong right now. I'd like her to come back and not see you sitting there waiting for her like a fucking sap." A protective thought, illustrated in Lisa's own touching style.

I answered, "She's not intentionally being cruel. She's just not ready for this. To be fair, she hardly knows me ... how could I

186

possibly expect her to move so quickly or to trust that I won't screw with her livelihood?"

"It sounds to me like she'll never be ready," Lisa said.

To avoid staring at the door, I started a conversation with Dad about the differences between New England seafood and Caribbean seafood (even though I didn't eat either). I didn't have to look up when Lorn came back into the restaurant, as I could strangely feel her presence. Instead, I focused on my father, even though every fiber of my being wanted to look at her again, needing desperately to see if she was all right. I picked up my wine glass in a further effort to look casually engaged. Why was it that after only such a short time together, like my uncle Tony, I too didn't know what to do with my empty hand?

As soon as Katherine rejoined us, Uncle Tony stood with the champagne he'd poured and proudly announced, "Please let's raise our glasses in celebration of my complete joy; for Katherine has put an end to my relentless begging, which began the first day we met, and agreed to become my lovely wife! *Salute!*"

Cheers and applause erupted at our table, and for a blissful few seconds, I forgot my own problems. Although they had just met, there was not a soul at the table who'd fault them for impetuously following their hearts. Our uncle had lived long enough to twice meet the woman of his dreams. I looked around the table to share the moment with my siblings and parents, and when my eyes fell upon Lorn, she was staring at me; smiling for her mother's newfound joy. But this time when her eyes filled with tears she was unable to stop. I wondered if she too was thinking that while one couple had announced a new beginning, another was at its end. I looked away from her to compose myself. I wouldn't ruin this night for my uncle, just as I knew Lorn wouldn't for her mother. The tears came at an appropriate time, so when Lorn blotted her eyes gently with her napkin, there were only a few of us at the table who knew the tears were sadness mixed with joy.

Lorn forced a smile and was the first to raise her glass as she said, "My mother is a lucky lady to have met such a gentle man."

And she said it like that, gentle … man. With a multitude of clinks we toasted the new lovers and the sweet promise of a new life together. My stomach tightened as my glass touched Lorn's. Would this be as close as I would ever get to her again? I imagined sitting across from her at the family functions that would come over the years, wanting her and not being able to have her … having had a glimpse of what could have been.

I hadn't meant to follow her (isn't that what all stalkers say?), but when our party dispersed, cheerful from the happy announcement and from the good wine, I saw Lorn didn't take the stairwell back to her room. I felt a powerful need to protect her, or at least this is what I told myself, so I followed her down the stone walkway to the beach and instantly lost her in the darkness, hearing nothing but the gentle movement of the surf. I walked more quickly, trying to quell my absurd and rising panic. Scenarios instantly took shape in my head that perhaps the photographer had been following her as well … and maybe he was angry over his camera and passport misfortunes … In no time at all, I whipped the unlikely ingredients together and baked a panic cake. When I didn't find her in a few more minutes, it became a triple layer.

"Lorn!" I called out, startling myself with the sound of my own voice. Just as I didn't mean to follow her, I also hadn't decided to yell her name.

"I'm here," she answered softly, and her voice came low, towards the sand, and very close to me. I saw her then. She was sitting in the sand, her dress gathered around her, now completely colorless in the dark. I knelt down in the sand and reached for her. She fell into my arms and I tasted her tears in a steamy kiss, but she ended the kiss abruptly, taking hold of both my wrists, gentle, yet firm, as she pulled away from me.

She said, "What am I supposed to do? I can't be with you; and I can't stay away … what am I to do about that?"

"Trust me?" I said, weakly.

When she finally released my wrists, it was to let me go. I stood over her for a moment, but she wouldn't look at me when she whispered, "Please just go ... I can't be near you, Marie."

Jamaica was unexpectedly short two tourists today. As instructed, Jessica did leave (she was witnessed checking out and catching a taxi during Lisa's shopping spree in the lobby gift store). I didn't credit myself, since it probably wasn't due to any threat I had made. It was more likely due to the fact that Lorn had left as well. I saw a new family checking into her room, perhaps Jess had seen it too, and figured there was no more damage left to do. Game over: Evil Lesbian wins; Stupid Lesbian loses ... and Closeted Lesbian remains eternally the same.

I had felt a ridiculous spike of hope when a knock came at my door late in the afternoon when Katherine had come to tell me Lorn had left to go back home. She also came to deliver an envelope her daughter had left for me written on hotel stationery. The resort logo was emblazoned in the green, black, and yellow of the Jamaican flag and my name was written in small letters across the envelope.

Katherine said, "I've always made it a practice to let my daughter make her own decisions, even when she was a little girl. She was always so cautious and confident about her choices, I never thought I needed to worry about her." Katherine's voice trailed off.

"I don't know what she told you about us," I said.

"She said there was nothing for me to worry about. Whenever a mother hears this, it makes us worry."

"She's right, there isn't anything to worry about. Whatever happened between us is over now."

Katherine took hold of my hand as I reached for the envelope. "Is it because I'm an old lady that you both are under the mistaken belief that I would worry less about her decision to not fully live her life ... rather than be happy in a ... forgive me for not finding a better way to express this ... an unconventional relationship?"

I stood dumbly before her. Whether Lorn had told her or not, she seemed to know everything. "If I thought I could change her mind, I would go after her," I said, weakly.

"Are you sure about that, Marie? I don't know if I would, and I think the world of my daughter."

"Of course I would, Katherine ... I would give anything—"

"Except the freedom to be who you are. Isn't that the reason you're not running after her right now? My daughter doesn't have the right to ask that of anyone, and thankfully, for your sake, she knows that. I only hope that she can find the courage to love some day; even if it arrives in the most unlikely of circumstances."

"Like you and my uncle."

We both smiled. Her smile fractured my heart a little more, as she resembled Lorn more than a little, a living hint at how gently Lorn would glide into her later years. The mere mention of Uncle Tony's name brightened the woman's face.

Katherine politely turned to leave me with the letter, which I still held at arm's length as if it were a grenade recently stripped of its pin.

"What would you do?" I impulsively asked.

She turned back to me. "I wouldn't choose to make any promises I knew I couldn't live with. Forget about whatever you've read; people don't really change that much. You shouldn't go after her unless you can live with the way things would be, a life of secrets. And why should you live that way?"

Damned fine advice, but not what I wanted to hear.

I was alone with the letter a long time before I opened it. As long as it stayed sealed, the letter could contain anything. A list of desperately hopeful ideas immediately came to mind.

The top three:

"Dear Marie: Since I am shooting a movie about a closet-case woman who cannot come to terms with

190

her sexuality (can you imagine, in this day and age?), I thought it would be a helpful exercise to start acting in character right away. The truth is, I am actually a raging lesbo, and I have a whole entire closet filled with baseball hats and RYKA running shoes to prove it. When you get back to California, we'll immediately share that cute little house of yours in the hills. This way, when I have to leave for work each morning, you can continue to play that cute little stalking game that turns me on so."

"Marie, you glorious hunk of woman, you ... It was so hard to leave Jamaica after what we shared, but I should have never left the water running in my kitchen back in California. Thank goodness my neighbor discovered it so I could fly back home and turn the spigot off before my kitchen was completely submerged. Now, I know what you are thinking: Why can't my neighbor just call a locksmith to get in and turn the water off? Well, she is also an author and very busy helping me write my coming-out autobiography: *Lorn Elaine: A Dyke's Life*. She needed to stick to her deadline or I will not be able to autograph copies of the book in a 10 x 10 pop-up vinyl booth in front of the Womancraft store during Woman's Week in Provincetown, Massachusetts."

"Marie: Can you believe Mother actually bought the 'I'm-too-afraid-to-come-out-so-I-am-running-home' story I handed her! Good thing I cooked up that whopper of a lie, because I barely have enough time to get back to California to plan her surprise wedding shower. It has to be soon, 'cuz honey, let's face it, the old birds aren't getting any younger! It should take me about a week to do the prep work, including

191

getting the Ellen-shaped ice sculptures, just so our community is well represented at the party. After the prep work is done, I'll remain naked in my bed waiting for you to come back to California so we can start our lives together. Please Marie, don't make me wait too long ..."

The actual letter took a slightly different turn. When I opened it, I stared at the shape of the letters, thinking stupidly how much I'd loved getting a handwritten letter from her, before I remembered it was to kiss me off. The delicate script was graceful despite being written by a hotel pen that skipped dreadfully:

> Marie,
>
> I am sorry I am leaving like this, but it seemed the only way I could stop myself from seeing you. I wish I could be strong enough to simply stay away, but after last night, I know that I can't. You deserve to be with someone who can shout her love for you from the rooftops; and no matter how much I wish this could be me, I can't pretend that it is. Know instead, I'll be whispering my love for you every day, under my rooftop.
>
> I fear the time needed to pass for me to be simply your friend is not time I have left in this life, or quite possibly, my next. So I have to ask your forgiveness there as well.
>
> L

I thought, Hollywood people ... always assuming there would be another life. Was there anyone in Hollywood who could resist reading Shirley MacLaine's book? And, I might add, pretty presumptuous to think I would even have her as a friend. Where

I come from, friends don't fuck each other. Well, actually, they do, but that pretty much ends the friendship. They certainly don't make you want to hurl yourself off a balcony; nor do they make you want to hurl at all ... coincidentally, my stomach was insisting it was time. I got sick, felt better, then felt sick again. She had even been too afraid to sign the letter, I thought, as I began to fall into a sleep which lasted well past morning.

Chapter Eighteen

Thy Will Be Done

It was a face-off that was long overdue. All the piña coladas and elegant dinners in Jamaica couldn't hold these women at bay (even Montego Bay) forever, and now Mom and Aggie had the gloves on, and it was early evening, and the ring was poolside. It was the shouting that sent me running from hibernation in my room:

Aggie: "I'm tired of you reminding everyone you are a fucking accountant and this entitles you to be making all the money decisions in this family!"

Mom: "I'm tired of you reminding everyone what a bitch you are!"

Aggie: "Well I am tired of you making me be a bitch in order to get what's rightfully mine! It was my mother that died, not yours!"

Mom: "I saw your mother almost every fucking day, taking care of her in the evenings after work—"

Aggie: "I know, I know after your fucking accounting job! No one asked you to take care of my mother! She hated you, too!"

Mom: "She hated everyone, but someone had to take care of her, since you weren't about to!"

Dad: "OK now, let's calm down and go back to our drinks ..."

Mom: "Shut up Sal! This is between your sister and me
    and is none of your business!"
Aggie: "Don't talk to my brother that way! He's a better
    man than you deserve for all the grief he says you
    cause him!"
Dad (to Mom): "Now, I never said that exactly ..."

The shouting had gathered a small crowd around the perimeter of the pool, and Lisa speculated later that I had probably caused this blowout with my intense brooding over Lorn. She guessed Mom and Aggie had both feared I might pick up and leave them all there to follow the actress again, with no settlement decided on the distribution of cash. In a few days, Uncle Tony and Katherine would be leaving as well, so the ladies were getting restless. I had been surprised over their restraint over the last several days, but we could all feel their edginess building. For the sake of the other folks at the resort, I decided they had suffered enough family bonding (hadn't we all?) and maybe it was finally time to give them their share of the money and Dad and Aggie the news about sharing Grandma's house and land. When I heard the shouting, I grabbed the sack I had brought with me from home and ran to the pool.

I had brought along ceremonial bricks of three hundred one-dollar bills that Vince and I had prepared at home. Although they were only stacks of ones, the bills still looked impressive, and I had bound them together with a paper band that read "THREE MILLION $" across each brick.

I simply had not been quick enough on the delivery. It looked as if we were not going to avoid a similar atrocity that Vince had once dubbed "The Mother's Day Massacre of 1996." It was an event which left Mom and Aggie not speaking for two years. It had happened during a birthday party, not anywhere near Mother's Day, but Vince remembered it wrong, and by then, the Mother's Day Massacre name had stuck. Aggie had claimed ownership of a piece of Grandma's jewelry that had been given to

Mom, and had not made up until two long years later. The olive branch had been Aunt Aggie's invitation to one of her famous Frozen Turkey Dinners, but I never asked for the details on how that evening went, since my mother despises frozen food, so I knew it would be a painful memory for her to dredge up.

Since Lisa was sticking with the premise that money was the root of all evil, it was up to Vince and I to decide what would happen with the estate. I have no idea when this prejudice against money could have taken root in my sister, because all my memories of her as a kid centered on how she could make her next buck. Notice I said "make" her next buck, and not "earn" her next buck. Our mom once caught her at a neighbor's house reading a book under a tree with the lawn mower on, but parked in neutral. This may not seem so bad, except that not only was Lisa being paid to cut the lawn, but also the neighbor was blind. I gave her credit that she was caught with a stopwatch on her, because as she explained, "The time sure gets away from you when you're reading a good book, and I didn't want to waste Mr. Williams's gasoline."

There were other incidents as well. In high school she had sold her own panties to a group of boys at school, and would have gotten away with it if she hadn't started buying bulk packs from the department store and stashing them in her locker. (Later, she confessed to using various condiments to help them look "not so new.") She also got busted selling smooth river rocks to the neighborhood kids. Lisa told them that the stones were petrified dinosaur feces and that the Museum of Natural History would buy them for triple what the kids had paid (once they were old enough to go to New York to sell them). This would bring a net profit of two dollars to all eight kids she had convinced to hop on the opportunity. Even today, she was charging eight dollars a head to feed her guests Italian dinners in Maine, but I guessed she justified it by the incredibly fair price, for incredibly good food. As with selling her undies, it was hard to argue with Lisa's profit margin.

Vince and I decided to keep Lisa's cut of the cash in an account for her for the day she changed her mind or decided she wanted to open a legit restaurant or simply needed bail money. We had agreed if everyone behaved on the trip, we would give equal shares of three million dollars to each family. As Grandma's letter had requested, Aggie would get the house and Dad would get the land, but in what I thought was a creative loophole, their spouses would get the cash. The remaining cash would be held in three accounts: one for Lisa for the day she decides money is not evil, one for us three siblings to retire on, and the third account for any emergency family needs.

Mom twitched only a few times upon hearing they would all be getting equal shares, but ended up taking it like a trooper. Unlike Lisa's elementary school chums, the woman knew a good deal when she saw it. Meanwhile, Aunt Aggie was twitching like a flea-riddled dog as Dad and Uncle Tony watched her with their usual amusement.

"She was my mother, not hers," Aggie spat again, indicating Mom. She was using a thinly controlled voice as she said, "Don't you think out of consideration for that, I should be given a larger share than a daughter-in-law?"

Now, I didn't give a rodent's behind what Grandma wanted, but I planned to remind her, since I was not in the mood to hand over three million dollars to Aggie's husband while being made to feel as if I had slighted someone. I was about to indicate this point when Lisa interrupted with her impeccable timing.

"OK everyone, listen up. If Marie were doing exactly what Grandma wanted, you all would be getting precisely *jack shit* in regard to the cash, so I suggest everyone should be shutting the fuck up now." I had to hand it to Lisa, she was there when it counted, and that was the end of it ... or so I thought. There were some chuckles coming from the growing groups of people who had stopped to watch the commotion.

I hadn't intended to do this in front of an audience, but I just wanted it done and so I made the rounds and handed Uncle

Freddie his brick of bills (which Aggie promptly snatched away from him) and turned to give Mom the last brick. When I did, Aggie reached out to grab my arm to stop me. She surprised me, so I instinctively pulled my arm up to get out of her grip, and in that moment, Aggie gave a yelp and kicked her walker towards me as she fell backwards into the pool.

"HOLY SHIT!" I yelled, too entangled in the walker to be able to reach for her in time. She hit the water with a giant typhoon slap against her ample ass. It was the loudest water cannonball I had ever heard, and that, along with her shriek, had gotten the attention of several more guests. People gasped and shouted at the sight of an elderly person's walker tumbling away from the pool. In the water around Aggie bloomed a bright, floral island, her housecoat billowing wide, appearing as if a gay paratrooper had miscalculated a landing in the pool. My aunt unintentionally calmed the crowd by her somewhat graceful dogpaddling, despite the fact that she was blinded by her giant black helmet of hair. Her hair helmet had crested in a huge black wave, then collapsed, completely pasting over her face … underneath which came a soft giggle.

Uncle Freddie clasped his hands together in thunderous laughter as she continued to dogpaddle blindly, yet gracefully, to the edge of the pool as Dad pointlessly jumped in after her, while my mother reminded him too late about his good shoes. Uncle Freddie knew Aggie could swim quite well, and he was too busy wheezing his high-pitched belly laugh to be of any help.

Dad and Aggie reached the edge of the pool together, leaving a strange wake of green behind them. Floating dollars … Uncle Freddie's cash dispersed and filled the pool with giant monochrome confetti, blanketing the water around them. Aggie was blissfully unaware of the floating dollars since she was still entrapped under her helmet of hair when she muttered, "Shut the fuck up, Freddie, I can hear you laughing under here."

At that, Dad started laughing so hard he had to pinch his nose to stop himself from snotting into the pool. Vince was already secretly doubled over in a chair in the corner crying, and Lisa was leaning against a palm tree blatantly crossing her legs in an effort to not pee out her last margarita. "Christ!" she whimpered, turning away from the pool. "I can't look!"

I didn't allow myself to laugh until I saw that Aunt Aggie's giggling under her wet helmet had grown out of control, pausing only to slap my father across the back when he tried to help her. That's when the pinched-nose method failed Dad.

Aggie snapped at him though her collapsed helmet, "Just because you are going to own the land, doesn't mean you can plant trees that will drop leaves all over my house!"

Dad answered, "Actually, I was thinking of putting in a pool. I had no idea you were such a good swimmer!"

Then someone yelled, "The crazy Italians are throwing money in the pool!" and before we knew it, there were people, completely dressed, jumping and diving in from every side of the pool, grabbing at the cash, and screaming their heads off. Children seem to come from out of the woodwork, and a couple of parents even threw their kids in to grab a few bills in the shallow end so as not to wreck their own clothes. I watched Uncle Tony laughing as he unwrapped his stack and gave half to Katherine and without so much as a word, they held hands as they threw the bills, in perfect unison, up high into the air to flutter down and cascade into the pool as everyone cheered and splashed to grab at the money. Typical of the laid-back Jamaican attitude, several resort employees had gathered around the pool to watch or were jumping in to grab some floating cash, pool filter be damned. The remainder of the bricks were burst and thrown, with Vince unbinding his stack and adding a high cannonball jump to his delivery, sending an explosion of bills cresting on a monstrous wave. People swarmed in his wake from every side.

Mom waited until last, just as she does at Christmas time, opening her presents last so everyone can be a witness. The bulk of the bills had already been snatched from the water and everyone's eyes were on Mom, waiting for her to slowly unwrap her brick and even make a few fake throws before sending the bills fluttering over the pool as everyone cheered for her, Dad cheering the loudest. It struck me that he looked relieved about Mom's careless tossing of the money, and I wondered if he didn't care about the inheritance because he secretly worried if the money might come between them again, as it had so many years ago when we were kids.

When she had finished, she helped Dad get Aggie out of the pool as they both laughed at her drowned-rat appearance. Dad announced to the crowd that Jamaica had never seen a wet shirt contest quite like this one. I looked up into the sparkling Jamaican sky and whispered, "Well Grandma, who would have thought it would be you who would bring us all together?" Thy will is finally done.

The following day, I met Vince for our late-morning margarita, minus the snorkeling. The drink, I had to admit, tasted better when you felt you had earned it after pointing at hairy eels, but it was good just the same. Uncharacteristically for Vince, he was quiet as we sat watching small Sunfish boats chopping over the surf, occasionally toppling the drunken tourists into the ocean.

"I booked us on a trip this afternoon," he finally said. "Just you, me and Lisa. Don't tell anyone else where we're going."

"Easy. I don't *know* where we're going."

"Dunne's Falls. We're going to climb a waterfall. Be ready to leave from the lobby at one."

I didn't argue with him, but I felt I had already climbed one slippery slope and had promptly fallen down to the bottom, knocking my head on several rocks along the way. I thought better of it, since I knew I should stay busy and fill the rest of the days in Jamaica. The thought struck me: my family was all I had now. No relationship; no job. Just my family, a lot of money, and an adorable house in the hills across the country, in a state I feared I would never go back to.

"What are we telling everyone?"

"That we're going to a club called Margaritaville, right here in Montego Bay. And that the guidebooks warn it's very smoky and loud with a drunken college crowd."

"That should do it for most of them, but what do we say to Dad?"

Those last days went by fast in Jamaica, since Vince and Lisa kept me busy with every activity offered on the island. The down side consisted of the activities offered on the island. Jamaica has such a laid-back attitude that we had no idea when the tour guide tells you the bus trip to Dunne's Falls is about an hour and a half, it is safe to assume it will be three hours. More specifically, six total hours on the bus, due to stops along the way to hotels which had nobody waiting, but which we parked in front of anyway for about twenty minutes per stop. During this time, it seemed as if nothing at all was happening. None of the guides got off the bus for several minutes, and when they finally did, there was a lot of walkie-talkie usage and heavy consulting of charts with dirty, ripped, and what appeared to be blank papers clipped to them. I wondered if the paper was ripped where the key information was about cancellations, which would have allowed the bus to skip several unneeded stops.

"Air conditioned bus" meant that the windows were adjustable and "lunch provided" meant that the bus careened along at breakneck pace until it rattled to a stop at a roadside jerk stand so you could purchase a Red Stripe Beer and a bag of Fritos for eleven dollars. Good times. Vince was feeling too queasy from the ride to eat, and if he hadn't looked so green, I would have teased him about finally knowing what it was like to be in a car driven by him.

Oddly enough, once we reached our destination, and the long, drawn-out speeches came to an end, along with the Jamaica trivia games designed to keep the questions of when we would finally arrive to a minimum, our laid-back guides suddenly morphed into well-oiled machines that scurried you through your adventure as if you were late from having lunch at the jerk shack with the Fritos. The journey home was transformed as well. Suddenly, the female guide who wouldn't stop badgering us about all the fun we were having on the drive up now seemed vacant and bored on the ride home.

I think if someone had asked a question about Jamaica, she may have answered that she had punched a clock at the front of the bus and was off duty for the ride back. The part that was most odd was it was impossible not to like the local folks. They were friendly and the women called everyone "baby," and the men fawned over every female from 16 to 75 so you felt as if you were a supermodel visiting from the States. They were a warm and inviting people, and frankly, it was good to see our bus lady call it a day and kick up her flip flops after three full hours of cheer-leading Americans on how to have a good time on a hot bus. Especially since she probably made less money in a year then most of us made in a month.

My habit of developing lists in my head to keep my mind off Lorn had grown chronic. I made lists of everything. It helped to pass the time. Before we left Jamaica, on the only rainy day since our arrival, I had committed my observations to paper, hoping this would stop them from repeating in my head.

Straight men have no better ability to spot a lesbian in Jamaica than they do in America.

Buses in Jamaica all smell like pot—but not from the lingering residue of pot, from people actually lighting up on the bus.

White people sound really stupid when they say "Mon" during conversations with the locals.

People forget that while it may be unusual to see goats and half-starved cattle crossing the streets back home, it's quite rude to point it out in a loud, horrified tone of voice.

Fritos taste the same in Jamaica as they do in Connecticut and California: salty, greasy, and especially delicious when trapped for three hours on a bus.

My observations about family:

Even while away on an excursion all day, it is impossible to miss your family if you are all on the same island (and quite possibly even if they are on several islands, if there is a dependable ferry service).

You can take a stressful woman (Aunt Aggie) and put her in a stress-free environment (Jamaica) and eventually you will still have the same woman you have back home, but with more a higher number SPF.

Your family will never grow too old to stop surprising you (Uncle Tony), nor will they also stop remaining completely predictable (Lisa).

Even if there is a perfectly good explanation, siblings will almost never understand a family member who is also occasionally a stalker, especially when you don't tell them the truth.

When Dad tells you it is not safe to buy marijuana in Jamaica from the guy selling it though a hole in the resort fence, it just means you should buy it from the concierge or the bartender.

The amount of money you need to live comfortably is directly relative to the number of your relatives; if they don't get enough of your money, you won't live comfortably.

Chapter Nineteen

See What Happens When You Ignore Your Mother

I asked Vince to dare me to do it. He had, and so I did go back to my house in the hills of California. I didn't know how long it would last. Not the move, but the pact I made with myself on my last evening in Jamaica. Vince and I had gone for one last evening stroll on the beach, when I made the pact. I thought it would be more forceful of a promise if I made it treading on the very sand where Lorn and I first kissed, and so it was there that I made my vow for Vince and the Jamaican sand-raking crew to witness. I promised that at thirty-two years old, I would finally make a real effort to grow up and see something through. There. I actually felt better.

This could have become a Gym Promise, if it weren't for the strange love I had for the quirky little house in the hills of California. I'd only been there a few weeks, and only been away from it for a few more, but I when returned, I found I missed so much about it. I tried only to focus on the things I missed that had nothing to do with Lorn, so my list immediately got cut in half, even though she had never stepped foot in the place. But I was, however, impressed there existed a list at all.

I swept my hand inside my brand new mailbox, which still smelled of fresh paint and metal and the Home Depot store where I had bought it, readying myself to be disappointed until the very tip of my finger caught the edge of a postcard. I smiled, knowing it was from Vince before I even pulled it out. It was a picture postcard, with four horrifically boring scenes of Connecticut divided by a robin's egg blue border. "Connecticut Welcomes You!" it said in a computer's feeble attempt at handwritten letters.

Dear Marie,
Wish you were here; the weather is great,
Haven't seen much of you as of late.
I think of you often; but I'm not alone,
Both Mom and Aggie ask daily when you're due home.
Pay no attention to those money-hungry-fucks,
Oh, by the way, thanks a million for the bucks.
While in sunny LA, please think of me,
Sightseeing in Connecticut at the local A&P.
Love,
Vince

Vince had also noted on the card in a postscript a warning to the postman that he was delivering the mail to a known lesbian, and if it was "Take Your Daughter To Work Day," he had better leave the young lady in the truck while stopping at this address. Thanks Vince.

Since my sister Lisa had moved from Connecticut to Maine years ago, Vince was the only one I missed having daily contact with, so it was odd his communication was helping to give me the strength to stay. At first I had called him every other day, with Vince thankfully monopolizing most of the conversation with stories about Aggie and Mom, and firing questions at me about the particulars of the food in California. Since he was convinced that a state with no authentic culture couldn't have real cuisine, I made up stories. I almost had him convinced that California McDonalds only sold French fries made of tofu, and Pizza Hut had changed its name to Pizza House due to the politically incorrectness of the word "Hut" in this thoroughly liberal state.

Although speaking with Vince had been a thread of reality here in Hollywood, I started to feel foolish about replanting my life here, and whenever we talked, the craziness of it seemed much more glaring to me. Vince was careful to never say anything that would cause me to feel more embarrassed; but that was the problem, right there. For the first time in our lives, Vince was being careful about what he said to me ... he was clearly worried I was losing it. I could hear his concern over the phone manifesting itself in story after distracting story about home, so he wouldn't have ask if I was still okay about Lorn. It was a bit humiliating to have your baby brother worrying about you, especially when he was still young enough to wear his hair long and look good doing it.

Erica As In All My Children turned out to be good company so I asked if she would let me assist her since I had a lot of time on my hands and desperately needed a hobby. She paused to study me with both a puzzled and an amused look.

"Will you take orders even though you're paying me?" she asked.

I agreed, thinking that it sounded like a blissful distraction from my goal-absent days. Without the stalking and a screenplay to focus on, there wasn't much for me to do in a state where one of the two people I knew I needed to avoid, and the other worked for me.

When Erica worked, she didn't speak at all except to order me around. She would show up in the morning with a pile of materials she had bought the evening before, and I wondered how she had time to do any extra shopping since she seemed to be spending every waking hour at my house. As we ate lunch, her small talk included only what she planned to order me to do next. Sometimes she would head out in her Jeep to pick up more paint, wood or stone (but only if she deemed the pick-up job too difficult for me to do correctly, which was often) and return within the hour, barking orders to myself and her other laborers who magically appeared from what seemed like the neighbor's bushes. Before I got to the driveway to lend a hand, she was already shouting things like: "Get the lead out!" and "I'm not paying you to stand around looking like you own the place!" I actually liked this girl with the nicely cut biceps and valley girl voice.

This was the exact relationship I needed now with a woman, and we actually worked well together. I enjoyed learning from her, although she never explained what she was doing unless I was failing miserably at a task, like not holding the bag of nails properly. It was like learning from a TV do-it-yourself show on mute with no subtitles ... a do-it-yourself show starring a sexy little dyke with strong shoulders, to be more specific. Too bad I found her attractiveness annoying rather than titillating. Too bad I had now developed a prejudice against young, ridiculously attractive women.

Eight exhausting days into the job, when we were outside supervising the contractor and his team of four-less-than-good-smelling men working on the porch, I heard my cell phone ringing inside. I knew it was either Vince or Lisa, since they were the only ones who called the cell we dubbed the bat phone. It wasn't that I didn't share my number with my parents; they concluded that dialing a cell phone number was somehow more complicated than a regular phone number, and therefore never used it. Once, my mother asked if she had to dial the C-E-L-L first, since she noticed most people wrote "CELL" in front of their number. She was also convinced that if it rang while I was driving, I'd careen into a tree, even if the closest tree were several blocks away. Mom had once pressured Dad to find a new job when his boss required him to carry a pager. "Drug dealers and whores carry those things," she had said, carefully avoiding the offending gadget's name. "Mom, it's just a pager; even doctors carry them." I had tried to rescue Dad since he claimed that whenever he wore it, she glared at it like it was a parasite nesting on his waist. I thought he was making it up until I observed her glare for myself. She stared at it with the same horror as if he had accidentally left his penis flopped over his belt after a trip to the bathroom. "They make him wear that," Mom would say in a hushed voice to my Aunt Aggie, just to make sure she didn't get the wrong idea and tell the rest of the family. I wanted to enlighten her that you didn't need a pager to buy drugs. In Jamaica, Dad didn't even need a shirt or decent pair of shorts.

"What the hell have you been up to?" Vince asked, sounding a bit wounded that I hadn't called him in nearly a week.

"I am tearing apart my house, you know, just for something to do."

"Ah yes, the hobbies of the rich," he said. "I can't bust you about that one, since I bought an RV and have been dumping ridiculous amounts of money into it to try to make it look like my living room on wheels. It hasn't left my driveway except once when my car wouldn't start and I drove it to Target to pick up an ottoman. Unfortunately, the ottoman was on wheels and it rolled back and forth in my RV living room chipping the veneer cabinets as I drove it home. The fucking ottoman is going to end up costing me close a grand to repair the damage."

"You're a millionaire, Vince, don't sweat it. Any chance you would come out here? I need some company before I do something really dumb with this young decorator I hired."

"You hired a dyke to decorate your house? I hope she got you a good rate on the tractor tire coffee table." He laughed at his own joke, a laugh which I sorely missed hearing. "How about I take my RV? I could drive across country, see some sights and be there in a couple of weeks?" he asked.

"Perfect. My house will still be torn apart, but we can work around that."

"I actually called to see if you booked your flight back to Jamaica yet ... for Uncle Tony's wedding."

My heart lurched into my throat. Vince instantly guessed from my silence that I was clueless. I would have to go back to Jamaica ... and see Lorn ... that is, if I was invited.

"I just assumed Lorn had called you already. I got a call from her a couple of days ago; she's handling the arrangements for her mother. She asked Mom for your phone and address last week."

"I haven't heard from her."

"Sorry," he said, which felt even worse.

"Let's make it official. I'm coming out there to see you."

Vince to the rescue.

I was on a destructive kick lately of reviewing the women in my life. These reviews always took place whenever Erica As In All My Children left me to some insanely repetitive project, like pulling the nails out of what she called "antique wood," which was really just ridiculously expensive weathered boards with nails so old and rusted they turned to orange powder Kool-Aid when you grabbed them with a pair of pliers.

In my assessment of failed relationships, for which I was willing to take some responsibility, I wouldn't let myself count Juliet, the Maine variety. While I believed for many years that I let her go, she was in fact never mine. I couldn't count Barbara either, since she was straight, married, and totally fucked up in the head. Whenever I did my counting, I would handicap myself both Juliet and Barbara. My reasons were as follows: Juliet because of the not knowing I was gay thing, and Barbara because her dysfunction and my loneliness as a clueless twenty-year-old had led me into her lair. She also caused me to be a cheater for the first time in my life. It was a thought that still bothered me twelve years later. My affair with Barbara meant I couldn't claim I had never cheated, and I hated cheaters. *I are one*, I always thought whenever the subject came up. I hadn't cheated on Barbara; I had cheated *with* Barbara against her husband.

Barbara was a very sexy woman, and I was immediately attracted to her when I began my first job right out of college. She was sixteen years my senior, and so had a much clearer idea of my sexuality than I did ... probably still does. She was a brassy, married lady, with a feminine body and a contrasting masculine laugh. She told inappropriate jokes and didn't care who was in the room when she told them. She'd launch the C word in front of men, women, and teenagers alike, with irreverent glee. She scared me, preyed on me, and it was the best sex of my life, before Lorn.

Barbara worked in an office, but her real talents emerged at night, after her respectable job of account manager for a trophy company ended for the day. Barbara was a hairdresser. Oh, she was no Hair Stylist, she was a hairdresser. The hard and tough kind who, despite only being self-trained, slung around dyes and bleaches in jugs with thumbholes like they could have no ghastly consequence. Because she had no permit to run a shop from her house, her clients would park two streets away and sneak through the neighborhood under the cover of darkness, only to be charged full price as if they were styled at a luxury salon, instead of sitting in her plastic kitchen chair. She boasted being a beauty school drop-out. (But nothing like the girl from *Grease* who accidentally dyed her hair pink in a last cry for help before she quit ... really, she was Rizzo, the foul-mouthed older girl you fucked in the back seat of your car who had no respect for a person's personal space, and whose uniform was a small men's leather jacket that strained across her ample tits.)

Barbara would come upon me at work with incorrigible timing. Like a molester waiting in the bushes for the last kid on the playground, she would swoop into my office area whenever it emptied. I shared the office with three other people, so this was no easy feat, and I wondered if she had my office under surveillance so she could always catch me alone. If one of the three (or incredibly, two of the three) co-workers were out that day, Barbara would surround me more skillfully than a pack of dingoes throughout the day, testing the limits of getting caught with her skirt spinning around her ankles as she roughly guided my mouth to her suddenly exposed breast. The breast was a comfort to the pain of her pulling my hair.

The first time we connected was at a bar after work. There had been some drinking, and some jokes about lesbians, and shots and limes, and bobbing for limes in each other's mouths on dares from co-workers, the usual work party stuff for Barbara's crowd. Someone had shouted for Barbara to take a lime and choose someone to suck it from her lips, and without a moment's hesitation, her eyes landed on mine. Titillated, the men howled in applause, and, after I didn't move, one of them yelled, "Awe, she'll never do it!" It was the kind of doubting accusation that was designed to spur a grade-school child to meet the challenge, and I should have been unmoved by his moronic attempt. It wasn't my goal to be the source of hard-ons for a group of men, ages ranging from nineteen to fifty (although it may have been Barbara's), whom I would have to face next Monday morning. Although the quantity of booze made it seem logical for a moment, I would never have done something so dumb ...

Until Barbara said, "I picked her because I knew she wouldn't do it."

I leaned slowly across the table, thinking she would back off ... she was *married* for Christ sakes ... I was single. I would call her bluff this time ... so why isn't she backing away? The bar went to deafening silence as she lurched towards me to stuff the lime in my mouth with hers in an aggressive kiss. The room spun, we became the talk of the office, and if the kiss had been any hotter, I would have singed the wood floor with the bottoms of my shoes.

Barbara and I began a Bonnie and Claudette relationship that was red hot and dead wrong, where we stole from others to get what we wanted from each other. We met for steamy moments in her car after work, and in the woods in broad daylight just one path away from a public park. We met at work (before, during, and after), and planned group events in order to get her out of the house and away from her husband. We kept people waiting for us by showing up late because we met early to fuck in a car two streets from the restaurant. She easily stole my heart because I was young, but worse, she stole my soul. It was the first time I had ever been sneaking around and the guilt was getting to me ... but she always got to me first.

Barbara had taught me how to hit that often-unexplored area inside a woman by going inside with two fingers and hooking them around and up: "As if you decided to take a hard U-turn; like when you are going left and suddenly bang a hard right ... only you are actually going in and then suddenly going up ... oh, and you'll want to bang that U-turn several times, nice and hard, honey." Barbara had been my Mapquest in the bedroom and I had followed her directions well. The Kevin Costner movie *Field of Dreams* was one of her favorite movies, and Barbara had changed the quote during my training on how to please a women to, *"If you find it, they will come ..."* I was her best student, she had assured me, as I wondered how many others had attended the class.

When Barbara's husband found out, she instantly broke it off with me. I found out later they had an agreement. She could fuck around unless he found out; and the same went for him. Before she ended it, she explained a few details I later wished she hadn't. She said when her husband found out her affair had been with a woman, he actually didn't care at all. He said if she wanted to have a girlie relationship on the side, this would be fine with him; but Barbara had decided to stop anyway, out of respect for her marriage.

In a final humiliation, I attempted to change her mind and asked her to meet with me so I could have her just once more, but she refused. As with Lorn, my desire for her far outweighed my need to protect my own heart; and the simple fact was I was desperate to have her again. She had introduced me to an array of dildos, and the joy of trapping a vibrator between two women as we took turns straddling each other like wild animals. If Al Gore claimed to have invented the Internet, then Barbara should claim she had invented the best way to find the G spot. During our steamy affair, if I promised to suck her nipples very hard, as she had taught me, she would let me make her come that way; it was my reward, she had said. And it felt exactly that way.

I kidded myself that I wanted once more to feel her lose control of her body under my spell before we broke up. It was a great fantasy, except that she never once had lost control with me. She was always in the driver's seat, even if I was sitting on her; I was always playing the wind-up toy who had gone from lime sucking to another man's wife fucking at her command.

I burned myself for almost two years with that same candle, according to her whim and how she was getting along with her husband. If he ignored her, or if they had a petty fight over house-cleaning, I would be rewarded with her breast in my mouth when everyone left the office for lunch. It was a cruel game with her, yet I still licked my wounds for a whole year after we ended, only to meet Jessica. With Jess, I soon became the cheated-on half of the couple, and I thought this had a neat, ironic fit ... My Catholic upbringing made me wonder if God had designed it this way—the payback for my earlier sins. I had to agree that it really was genius if he did, and believed I had to pay back more than my share since I had not quite forgiven myself for what I had done, long after Barbara had left me.

I finally had forgiven myself for quitting on Jess. Maybe it was the one thing sacred that Barbara taught me; I had to leave Jessica out of respect for the institute of marriage. And now, I had lost Lorn. My relationships were getting shorter, I thought. Would it eventually shorten to the point where I would pass a woman on the street, glance at her, know I would screw it up, and just keep on walking? Maybe I would eventually hone my skills to learn to end the possibility of love before having to go through it all again? It sounded like a comfortable future.

After the crew had left for the day, Erica inspected their work. It looked good to me; although after receiving Vince's call about Uncle Tony and Katherine's wedding I couldn't have cared less, so I may not have been the best judge. Erica pointed out areas that looked rushed to her, and while I could scarcely see a difference, she said she would be calling them that evening to threaten withholding payment for the job. Who knew the girl with a valley girl voice could be such a hard-assed bitch? For the first time since we started working together, I stopped her at the door to thank her. In my fragile emotional state I entertained the thought of giving her a kiss ... not a sexual one, just a peck on the cheek. I decided this would be a mistake, especially since I was drowning in thoughts of Lorn and didn't trust my pecking abilities. There was that, plus, as I looked past Erica, Lorn was walking up my driveway.

Erica must have accurately assessed the look on my face, because she turned to see Lorn and in the next second, she was kissing me full on the lips. This was no peck, no sir. Next, she skipped down the steps like a schoolgirl, shouting, "See you tomorrow, hun!" That brilliant bitch, I thought, as I tried to focus on Lorn, who seemed to me an apparition. She had stopped midway up the walkway and her expression had the same shattered look she had on the stairwell in Jamaica after witnessing Jess's half-clothed antics. She recovered her expression as she approached, but still did not speak.

"Come in," I said, holding the door for her. I gave her plenty of room to pass by me, and she took every inch. I held my breath so I would not smell her perfume as she passed, but it didn't work. I was completely weakened by the presence of this woman.

"I'll only be a moment. You have a very beautiful home," she said coldly.

"Erica did it all," I said. "That was Erica ... she's my ..."

"You don't owe me any explanation," she said, but she looked as if she wanted one. I thought it best to take her up on her offer, and promptly shut my mouth.

Had I had purposely hesitated to explain who she was? Maybe my valley girl decorator with the soap opera name was adept at other things besides decorating ... like knowing how to handle a woman who cannot decide what the fuck she wants.

I noticed Lorn's hand tremble as she held out an envelope to me. It reminded me of her mother handing me her goodbye note, so I didn't reach for it, just on principle. "It's a wedding invitation," she said softly.

"You could have mailed it," I said.

"Strange that you never mentioned we lived in the same state. You led me to believe Connecticut was your home," she said.

"Connecticut was my home," I answered. "I came out here just before the trip."

She looked incredible. I was thankful she couldn't read my thoughts ... since I needed to be a little cruel. I was determined not to get sucked in again.

Erica's Jeep started in the driveway with its chainlike rumble. Lorn turned her head slightly to the sound. "I guess I came at a bad time."

"You didn't." I thought, she had come at the perfect time. She didn't need to know I had spent every waking hour since my return trying to forget her, or that I had occupied myself by working full time at a job I was paying Erica to do. She didn't need to know that heartbreak was costing me one hundred dollars a damned hour for the privilege of holding nails and fetching drill bits. Besides, since I was new to being rich, I still cringed at blowing wads of cash for distractions only meant to improve my mental health. However, I always ended the debate by deciding it was cheaper than hiring a shrink, and I would get a nicely decorated house out of the deal. I should think of the re-sale value as the conciliation prize for failing as a screenwriter.

"I hope you can attend the wedding," she said, turning to watch Erica inch the Jeep out of the driveway. Erica, who usually zoomed backwards from the house with alarming speed, was now dragging her exit from the driveway to a painfully slow crawl. I could see her trying to watch us through the window, and Lorn saw it too.

"Your uncle and my mother would like you there very much," she said.

"And you?" I asked. Lorn was trying hard not to watch the

Jeep, as Erica As In All My Children blasted a trio of defiant goodbye beeps.

"I think your new friend may want you to stay here. You've settled in pretty quickly for someone so new to town," she said, finally pushing the envelope into my hands. She turned to leave. "Well, I have to go," she said.

"If the thought of me being with someone else upsets you, maybe you shouldn't." The statement came out of my mouth before I could stop it.

She spun around, and for the first time, I saw what anger looked like in her eyes.

"I'm thinking you recover very quickly," she said.

I reached for her arm. She tried to pull away, but I held fast. "Lorn, I'm not with Erica ... well, other than for her to order me around and to hold an occasional piece of wood while she pounds a nail into it."

"I told you already," she said, her voice breaking, "you don't owe me an explanation ... or anything else for that matter. I know I was the one who stopped us from happening. Believe me, I've been thinking of nothing else since I left the island. You should be with her, Marie. She probably has nothing to worry about hiding in her line of work, and I'm sure she can give you everything you need. She looked quite capable, in fact ..." Her eyes filled, and I hated myself for enjoying it just a little, but my need to comfort her overtook the desire for revenge, which was suddenly not so sweet.

"That young woman is my decorator, who I hired to give me something to do so I don't waste away in this house thinking about you twenty-four/seven. She's smart, and apparently fig-ured out that you were the reason I was paying top dollar for the privilege of pounding nails just to keep busy. She thought she was doing me a favor by trying to make you jealous. I still love you, Lorn ... that hasn't changed."

Lorn said nothing, and wiped her eyes with the back of her hand.

216

I asked gently, "Well, did she do me a favor?"

"My mother said I shouldn't come see you when I can't offer you anything more than I could before."

"My mother would tell you I never listen to her. So, did you come to offer me what we had in Jamaica?" I asked. She trembled slightly, and when she did, I took this as a yes and pulled her to me in a hungry kiss. She surprised me by responding instantly, her mouth warm and open. She held me to her as a nagging thought fought its way though the delirious distraction of our kiss: Are we planning on coming together, or just planning on coming? I opted not to pose the question right then, although the distant fear that I was being sucked in again had begun to cloud my thoughts ... it just wasn't strong enough to pull me away from her.

Chapter Twenty

Even Naked Mole Rats Come Out Once In A While

I got sucked back in. Lorn was here, and I could feel life again, and really, how can you be expected to turn away from that? We didn't leave the house for three days. Erica As In All My Children was beside herself with the havoc it played with her schedule, until I told her she would be paid in full for her time if she left us alone for a few days. Lorn and I were entangled in each other for the entire three days, with short delays for bathroom and refrigerator breaks. We remained entangled even in the kitchen, as we ate raw food from the fridge ("*9 1/2 Weeks* style," I had told Lorn, and she replied that California had gotten to me) and then we finally resorted to cooking when everything that could be eaten raw ran out. When the last of the cook-able food was gone, we planned to emerge from the cocoon of my house, feeling starved, dazed and pale as naked mole rats.

While we prepared to head out for a bite to eat, Lorn picked a strange argument with me about how I had no idea how relentless the press could be, and so we should be careful where we went out together. She was declaring those very words as we left the house, when camera flashes lit up the front yard like an electrical storm.

"You stay, I'll just go," she said, and with that, she fled to her car as the photographer (a different slime ball than the one in Jamaica) kept shooting, as if photos of Lorn getting in her car would be enormously scandalous; at the speed she was moving, they just may be. I had no idea how right I was.

Knowing how Lorn felt about publicity, I figured it was best to give her some space. Okay, a total lie, I would have called, but the thought sadly struck me: She had never given me her number. That's how in love we were. From my past stalking days, I knew better than to think I could track down her phone number ... I would have to wait until she came back to me. If she ever did.

The next day, after waiting all morning for her to contact me, I drove down to the café at the bottom of my hill for some coffee and food. I made the mistake of glancing at the newsstand, where one of the daily rag papers had already used the photos, and how appropriate they were along with the story of an intriguing car accident involving Lorn and her mystery friend from Jamaica. It was complete with various photos of Lorn plastered on the front page. I couldn't prove it of course, but that story had Jessica's name written all over it.

I raced back to my house and called Vince, but remembered he had already left for L.A. so I was forced to call home.

"Mom, its me."

"What's wrong?" she yelled into the phone in a panic.

"Nothing, I'm fine."

"No you are not fine Marie, tell me what has happened? Is it Vince? A car accident? Dear GOD!"

"Mom—"

"I told him that RV would be a deathtrap!"

"Maybe, for everyone else on the road—Mom, Vince is fine. I just called for a phone number."

"A phone number?" Then she yelled to Dad, but mostly into my ear, "Sal, everything is fine! She just needs that Lorn woman's number!"

"But, I didn't say it was for ..."

"Oh Marie, please," she said, dismissing me. I could hear her rummaging through her phone desk drawer, cursing under her breath. "I want you to know this is all your father's fault."

"Mom, I'm not gay because of Dad."

"I mean that this fucking drawer is a mess."

"Oh."

"Marie, your father and I are not as focused on your sex life as you are, I promise you."

"Thank God," I said.

I was left to attempt explaining myself to Lorn over the phone.

"I wasn't being a stalker, I was being a screenplay writer ..."

Lorn remained silent, so I kept rambling.

"Remember the night we laughed about my friend's horrible idea for a screenplay? Well ... that horrible idea was mine. I just wanted you to read my screenplay. I would've told you, but ... well, I guess I hoped I could get away with not telling you."

Her voice came low and sounding far away, "Marie, *you staged a car accident?*"

It crossed my mind to lie, but there had been so many already.

I said, "And looking back on it, there may have been a better way to deliver the screenplay to you."

"This isn't a joke."

"Oh, I know that," I said. "None of this was supposed to happen ..."

"And Jamaica?" she asked.

"I don't expect you to believe this, but unless you were stalking me, that part was a total coincidence."

Although that wasn't a lie, I didn't expect her to buy that one either.

"Your family thinks you followed me there," she said. "I was just stupid enough to ignore that because I was so—"

"But I didn't follow you there," I said, but even I hardly believed me at this point.

Stalking and car accidents aside, could we really have survived the trials of a relationship with all the restrictions she would have insisted on, like never spending the night in case the paparazzi was waiting in the front yard? And how could she stay in a

220

relationship with a person she was convinced would eventually destroy her career? Not that I would intentionally of course, but I suppose she thought a woman who would stage a car accident was not the person you should trust with your livelihood ... and maybe she had a point. Now that the article about the accident had connected us in such a bizarre way, it was impossible to defend myself.

I would have hung up on me too. I should consider myself lucky she didn't file a restraining order.

Several papers had re-run the photo of Lorn leaving my house that day. The article blared, "Who is the mysterious friend Lorn Elaine has been seeing? Anonymous friends say it started as an accidental meeting during a fender bender, and blossomed into romance in Jamaica ..." I derived little satisfaction from the reporters assuming it had been a real accident. The papers were setting up the reader to stay tuned; yet there was nothing to stay tuned for.

Thankfully, Vince was about to arrive for his pity visit. Despite knowing it was out of a sense of duty, I was grateful just the same. I was probably more grateful because it was a pity visit. Erica As In All My Children was glad as well. She was tired of watching me mope around the house and informed me she would no longer be making it her number one priority to keep me busy; it was just too much responsibility to take on alone, and frankly the house could not possibly need that many nails. Up till now, she had been pretty patient with me, for someone like Erica.

Vince pulled into my driveway where I had hung a parking sign up for his RV: "Parking for Vince Santora—Spokesperson, Viagra." But when he walked to the side of his RV, I saw he was had a huge sign installed in the window with a bold political message that read: "I support my sister's choice to be a dyke." Outmatched yet again.

We greeted each other with our traditional slaps to the back. "How are you holding up?" he asked.

"I'm still paying somebody a lot of money to keep me busy," I said.

"How's the redecorating going?"

"Fine, I guess. You'll get to meet Erica, as in *All My Children*."

"Great. From what you tell me, it will be fun to butt heads with her a bit."

I hid my smirk from him. If he tried to butt heads with Erica, he would be toast. Despite my broken heart, having Vince home with me would make the time before the wedding bearable.

Vince was waiting out on the porch all dressed for a night on the town with his sister. He looked pretty handsome, but when Erica As In All My Children arrived back from the curtain store, she spotted him outside and scrunched her nose in his direction as if he were a fly that had landed on her cupcake.

"I don't want to alarm you, but there is a strange guy in a very shiny shirt standing on your deck. He appears to be checking out his reflection in the sliding glass door. I warned you that was one of the hazards of going with tinted glass."

"That's my brother," I said, giggling. The show was starting already.

"Oh," she said, trying to unscrunch her nose, but not quite succeeding. "Well, that's actually a relief, since only a sister could tell him he really should rethink that paisley shirt," she declared.

Vince came in from the deck, stroking the shiny sleeves of what he called his Retro Statement. "I'm so glad I packed this shirt," he said, smoothing his chest with his hands. Erica snorted from the kitchen and he turned around, surprised to see her.

"Whoa ..." he said.

I could see Erica was thinking the same thing as me: *Whoa? Who actually says "Whoa?"*

"Vince, this is Erica, my contractor and decorator," I said, and then kindly reminded my brother a fly could get in if he didn't close his mouth soon.

Erica came over and shook his hand as if she was a politician and was under a contractual obligation to be civil. "Hello," was all she said, before leaving the kitchen to carry the curtains down to the basement. Vince just stood dumbstruck.

"Don't even think about it," I said. "She's a little smart for you, and, details, details, she likes *girls*."

"Oh, I can be very understanding of that; I like them too. I'm going to see if Erica will join us for dinner," he said, marching off to the stairs. I could only pity a man willing to take on those kinds of odds, and I tried not to laugh at him as he scampered off after her.

To my surprise Vince did not come up for another hour, and when he did, he was grinning like an idiot. "Erica will be joining us," he said. I envisioned a cat agreeing to play with a mouse.

"I might go change my shirt," he said as if the idea had just struck him.

"No doubt that was the deal you agreed to," I said.

During dinner, Vince kept his arm across the back of my chair, but he was only interested in talking to Erica about her business. At first she only gave one-word answers designed to not encourage him to speak further; but her subtle curtness was wasted on him and Vince continued pressing her with questions.

"Erica was written up in *Home Trend* magazine for one of her houses," I interjected, and Vince acted as if he was surprised I was still sitting there.

He was impressed. "Wow, good for you. Don't take this the wrong way, but you're really young to be so successful in your own business," he said.

"Not so young." she said, as she eyed the baby-faced waitress vying for Vince's attention by hovering over his water glass with a pitcher that was dripping on my leg. Vince ignored her.

"Ever do a celebrity's house?" Vince asked.

"When I did Nicholson's house, the press followed me around for three months. I think the idiots thought I was dating him," Erica said, but only towards me.

"You mean Jack Nicholson?" Vince asked, taking his eyes off the waitress who had taken to leaning her breasts an inch from his face to top off his already filled water glass. He turned back to Erica.

The waitress asked him, "He's the guy who played Joker in *Batman*, right?" she said with pride.

Erica looked like she might fling a piece of zucchini at the girl as Vince patiently schooled her on Nicholson's résumé.

At Vince's request, I managed to score a couple of tickets to a charity event where there would be some celebrity sightings to satisfy his need to see the real Hollywood. Charity events are the one place where celebrities aren't allowed to refuse pictures, and Vince took full advantage. The only celebrity I wanted to meet was comedian Kathy Griffin, who pandered to a gay male audience and made a career out of stalking celebrities (I could relate). She would start out as a huge fan and then, depending on their response to her, she would be forced to expose any bit of Hollywood phoniness in her stand-up act. Quite ballsy for a straight girl. So ballsy that I wasn't surprised when she immediately sought me out as the reality TV story of the moment. Kathy's penchant for celebrities getting shoved out of the closet was renowned.

She made a beeline over to me with her TV camera crew in tow. "Hey, you're that chick who had an affair in Jamaica with Lorn Elaine from *Razor Falls* ... So, where's the new recruit?" she asked me. We of course were being taped on the likely chance Kathy got a real zinger in with the woman who she was betting would eventually kick the *Razor Falls* actress out of the closet.

"Hello Kathy, sorry, but she's not here. She's very busy you know. She is now under pressure to recruit two more women, or we kick her out of the club. Those are the rules, no exceptions."

Kathy was at an unusual loss for words, but only for a moment. She turned to the camera, "Like any good pyramid scheme, right?

Lesbians are the new Amway." She then froze for a second and said, "Cut. You guys got that, right?" The camera guy nodded his camera up and down.

She turned back to me. "Nothing I can add to that, you were perfect, darling, thanks for your time," Kathy said, giving my arm a reassuring pat. My anger and embarrassment about getting sucked in and dumped once again had gotten the better of me. But before Kathy had fluttered away, I had already begun to doubt my cockiness.

"We simply must do lunch," Kathy called over her shoulder.

Although I was new to this town, I had been around long enough to know this was the Hollywood way of saying, "I'm done with you now," since it was always said while one was walking away. In Kathy's case, it was said while she was running over to the next celebrity. Too bad ... I would have liked to have lunch with her, but alas, she was jetting towards her next conquest, and since it was Sharon Stone, I knew our friendship, however brief (and disappointing to Vince, who stood silently with his mouth open the entire time), had officially come to an end.

On one of the last days of his visit, Vince surprised me by having dinner waiting when I returned from a trip to the carpet store while Erica had been away at the lumberyard with her crew. I wondered if he might have been too distracted by his growing fascination with Erica to risk leaving the house in case she returned to the house to work.

I had smelled the sausage and meatballs from the driveway, and followed the scent into the house like a wild animal. That smell belonged on the east coast, I thought. It smelled as if someone had moved Federal Hill in Providence, Rhode Island to the Hollywood Hills ... during the Feast of St. Joseph's Day to be exact.

"Just like home, huh Mare?" he asked proudly.

"Damn, Vince, when the hell did you learn to cook?"

"Lisa taught me a few things when I last visited her in Maine.

I'll give you both a good deal and only charge you a five-spot, but you have to lie to Lisa if she asks. Apparently, it's an insult to her cooking skills if I ask for less than eight bucks a plate."

I noticed he'd set a table for three.

"What's this?" I asked.

"I asked Erica to join us. She said maybe. You think that means yes?"

"I think it means you're an idiot," I said, swatting him on the back.

As if on cue, Erica came though the front door, not bothering to knock of course. Her usual annoyed look was in place, but it contrasted fiercely with the cute little sundress she was wearing, with a deeply scooped neckline. I'd never seen her in a dress ... and she looked great ... and just a wee bit too comfortable in it. I was suspicious. While Vince opened the wine, I signaled to Erica for a private meeting in the living room. I looked her up and down with squinting eyes, and instantly, she cracked under the pressure.

In a careful whisper she confessed, "I never said I was a dyke. You just assumed."

My jaw dropped in amazement.

"It's not against the law to advertise in a gay magazine when you're not a lesbian," she said.

I just folded my arms and shook my head at her, as if I was seeing her for the first time.

"Besides, if you bought into my business as a partner, it would make it more legit. Unless you think the world really needs another lesbo prison movie."

"Stop going through my stuff!" I whispered harshly.

She stood defiantly before me, like a teenager caught after curfew.

I said, "So the plan would be the old 'I'm not gay, but my partner is'? Don't change the fucking subject ... you're a friggin' marketing guru who pulled a *Tootsie* ..."

"Screw you," Erica said. "And what the hell is a *Tootsie*?"

226

"You're a spy, an operative ... you're a closet-straight ... an acting lesbian ..." I held my hand over my mouth and gasped in mock horror, "You're a *Thesbian*!"

"SHHHHH!" she said.

"What the heck is going on in there?" Vince yelled from the kitchen.

Erica gripped my arm. "Keep your voice down, will you, and don't you dare tell your brother ... I'm having way too much fun teasing him. I keep turning down his dates, telling him he has one too many dykes in his life and he doesn't need another. This time the poor bastard's gaydar is actually working properly, so he just can't bring himself to give up the fight."

Returning to the kitchen, I watched with amusement as Vince followed her across the room with his eyes, and while Erica appeared oblivious, I noticed she even walked differently around him. Poser, I thought. Why hadn't I noticed before now? Imagine, all this time, a straight girl in our midst. I wondered if Vince had finally stumbled onto his match with this clever faux-dyke with the valley girl voice and tape measure whip. Maybe I could give him advice on how to win her over ... after all; I considered myself an expert at getting an actress to fall in love, even if they didn't stick around.

After Vince went back to Connecticut, I noticed it was Erica's turn to be downright mopey. I thought it might be helpful if I pointed that out, but she told me to mind my own fucking business by throwing a bag of nails at me. I wondered if I should try minding *our* own fucking business, because I had thought a great deal about Erica's offer to let me buy into her decorating company. Maybe it would be easier to generate respect from her as co-owner rather than a customer who works for no pay. Especially since I had no career idea of my own.

"So, do you really think I should pay you a sizable chunk of money to be your 'Homo Depot' runner?" I queried.

Erica was pounding a nail into a large piece of molding I was holding for her, so I made an effort to hold it more expertly to impress her. She stopped nailing for a moment.

"Eighty K for fifty percent; but I reserve the right to make you a silent partner at any time if you get more annoying than usual, or to replace you entirely for trained help. My lawyer will call you tomorrow," she said. "Now stop fucking around and bring that bag of nails where I can reach them."

Chapter Twenty-One

Even Bridesmaids Bring the Blues

It was strange to be back in paradise so soon, but since I was wealthy, this might be another thing I'd have to get used to. My family took the trip together again, requesting the same hotel rooms as we had before. Dad insisted, since he despised change of any kind. Ever since we were kids, he'd find a place for our family to spend the day or to go to for dinner, and this would be the place we'd always go back to, right down to the exact location to spread the blanket at the park or beach. "There," he would say proudly, "that looks just about right." He'd fuss with the corners of the blanket, tugging to make sure it was precisely parallel to the boardwalk, just like it was last time. If we were a few feet from where we had been, I think he believed it might ruin the day. He'd always ordered the same food at every restaurant or ice cream stand as well. "Last time I had the clam roll with ice cream for dessert," he would say, "I believe I'll stick with that." I realized this quirk was most likely the reason he couldn't make the divorce stick so many years ago. How could a guy who needed to order the same clam roll, at the same clam shack, and must eat it on the exact same blanket, in the exact same position, ever start a new life with another woman?

Uncle Tony had gone to Jamaica ahead of us to make sure all the wedding plans were in order, and I heard through Mom that Lorn would be traveling with her mother from the west coast. I joined my family in New England a few days earlier so we could all travel together. Unlike Lisa, any time I brought up the subject of Lorn, Vince would not automatically take my side, as I had wanted. "Not everyone can be a parade marcher," was all he would say before changing the subject. Deep down, I knew he was right. I'd expected Lorn to eventually pull a Rosie O'Donnell (whom I had loved since her closeted, mullet-wearing days, swinging flashlights and making safe jokes about aerobics instructors) and walk proudly down the street with me, hand in hand while the photographers swarmed.

However, that didn't stop me from arguing with him about it on the plane. "She wouldn't have to be a parade marcher ... she just shouldn't let fear rule her life. People are more accepting now."

"If that's true, why are so many more actors and actresses not out? I bet it limits the kinds of roles they're offered. Just look at how much attention the few that come out of the closet get ... it's because there are still so few ... that's why it's such big news."

"So instead, limit your life?" I argued, but I was talking to myself, since Vince had taken his usual Switzerland stance and jammed his iPod earphones in to end the debate. The truth was, when I wasn't pouting about his reaction, I had to admit his protectiveness of Lorn was endearing, however wasted it was. Lorn didn't need any help protecting herself, she was doing a fine job of it herself.

Jamaica had not grown less beautiful while I had been away, but the tropical theme looked a little forced through my present, more cynical eyes. I hadn't noticed before how the dotting of palm trees in their neat little rows along the beach looked a little contrived, and the tiki huts now appeared like props on a sandy stage. The ocean's expanse seemed empty rather than grand, and the two windsurfers on the horizon flew along the surf like two lost birds with no chance of ever crossing paths. I knew the change was all me, but that didn't affect my empty interpretation of the scenes. Like a spoiled rich brat, I followed glumly behind my family as the bellhop led us to our rooms. I swallowed hard when I saw the beach where Lorn and I first kissed, and delayed the misery of the memory for as long as I could. I waited until I was alone in my room to let the long version of the memory play again and again. I even added extra scenes, to punch up the drama. I was exhausted from the travel and my sadness and fell into the sweet escape of sleep; but even there Lorn led me, helpless, to that very same beach.

When I awoke, I wondered why the light in California seemed to have switched to the opposite window from where it always shone. Jamaica, I remembered. Paradise. It was almost four o'clock in the afternoon but we had all agreed upon our arrival to dine casually on our own. It took several moments to gather my wits and find my way down to the café to bribe a bartender to make me a fresh pot of coffee. I sat at the bar trying to ignore the pieces of the dream that were replaying in my head as I waited for my brew. Lorn wouldn't arrive until tomorrow; I reminded myself I could walk around looking like hell for one day.

"Here you arrrrre, my pretty lady," the bartender sang to me as I reached out both hands for the cup. "Rough night for you last night, mon? Too much Jamaican rum?"

"No, I just arrived," I said into my cup, hearing it echo as if I had spoken into a conch shell. *I can even hear the ocean*, I thought miserably.

I sipped the coffee and the bartender was perceptive enough to move on to the more jovial batch of young ladies at the end of the bar who were gang-admiring his biceps. They looked college age, although their giggling suggested they were much younger. They weren't dressed in the role at the moment, but I sensed the subtle yet nauseating odor of bridesmaids in the air. As the bartender leaned casually and elbow-walked closer, the giggles got louder and the hair fluffing was taking on the spirit of competition. I sat and observed with the interest of Dian Fossey after stumbling on a healthy pack of silverbacks.

They moved more like hyenas, working together with brazen

laughter to snare their prey, with an established hierarchy to determine who'd take the first bite at the man, and who would be left to pick at the bones. Ironically, the rules were opposite from those of the animal kingdom. It would be the thinnest and dumbest of the pack that stepped up for the first plate, while her more beefy associates were left in the dust, waiting their turn. She was a blond in a belly shirt, and I was lucky enough to actually witness a combo hair twirl, followed by a head toss and seamless landing into a perky giggle, in perfect succession. All this while she kept her shoulders pinched to show off her nearly B-cup breasts in their perkiest profile. There was a reason this dingo had risen to the top of her pack. She was the best at looking weak while she hunted like a pro.

"Fascinating, aren't they?" It was Vince, with his usual perfect timing.

"Awe-inspiring," I agreed.

"Come on, the blond leader is kinda hot," he said.

"You're joking."

"Look at her. You just know a girl like that will be like Gumby in bed. Easily excitable, bendable, and you can always expect a happy ending."

"And maybe an extra friend named Pokey will come along for the ride," I said. Vince had a drink already, so we clinked his beer with my coffee mug in an agreeable toast. "How are you doing, now that you're back here?"

He knew returning to Jamaica would be like going back to the self-pity mothership. "It feels like I should be happy for Uncle Tony," I said, "so I am."

Vince swatted me on the back to show his approval. It was as hard as usual, but I didn't flinch. He laughed at me anyway.

People always asked how Vince remained single so long, since he was sweet, gentle (except for the celebratory slugs to the arm) and more than a little handsome. I sometimes wondered if it had something to do with my sister and me. Had he been surrounded by too many strong females, including our mother of course, which formed ridiculously high expectations of what his mate should be? Is that why he didn't return the silly flirtations of the blond hyena bridesmaid when she noticed him at the bar? It was a nice egotistical thought, and I allowed myself to revel in it whenever I felt my baby brother's life slip into more reasonable territory than my own.

But he did expect too much from straight girls. For all the joking he did about wanting the beautiful dumb girl, he had more than his share of chances, and eventually passed—although usually not until morning (he was still a man, after all). He turned on a dime if he smelled, as he put it, "the desperation of bridal angst, safety-net seekers, and recently and most importantly, gold diggers." Consequently, this thinned the crowd of prospective girls substantially. Vince needed a smart girl who didn't need him; but I had to agree with him that only slim pickings seemed available.

While women lamented there were no good men, what many of them meant was there were no good men willing to take care of them. I'd seen it at my job, when the women talked candidly with each other, as if we had signed some sort of agreement on the subject. These women had their careers, but many of them had short-lived career plans, with the ultimate goal of meeting a successful guy to take over the financial burden. There were premature visions of vacation homes and babies, and yard parties and gardens, and television shows with helpful hints to conquer the stay-at-home woes. Although they would hate to give up their careers, they confessed, it would be better for the baby. And all of this was determined before they had even met the unsuspecting guy. This was the straight girl version of the dyke-driven U-Haul arriving right after the first date.

Men are suckers, I thought. They have no idea what they're up against. While the guys thought they were harmlessly shooting their weapons at every girl that allowed them entry, they had no concept of the behind-the-scenes war games some of these women were plotting. I wondered if my Benedict Arnold confessions to Vince about women had scared him away from their war maneuvers.

And now, Vince was wealthy, so this piled another layer of complexity onto the whole dating scene. He didn't say so, but I knew it had become a question in his mind. I suspected he might even be silly enough to blow a chunk of it on the first girl he liked since his windfall, because we were a lot alike. The money had burned a guilty hole in my pocket as well.

Meanwhile, Lisa had not taken a cent of it. However, she got Vince's attention with her cautionary advice: "Stow it away and pretend you don't have it. Some day, when you meet the right girl, you'll be glad you didn't do the stupid, newly rich kid thing and blow what should have been your children's college fund or your wife's vacation home. You don't want to face that kind of shit-storm for the rest of your life, now do you?" I had joined in with the less colorful remark, "Or, what if a family emergency came along, and you had given it all away?" This seemed to hold him for a while. The thought of rescuing one of his own appealed to him. He was Italian, after all. I'd have to watch for signs of weakening, to ensure his financial security didn't become an aphrodisiac to some bimbo. It reminded me of the antique metal sign my dad hung in the basement over his makeshift bar: "Beware of Pickpockets and Loose Women."

Lisa had helped finish our speech with: "If some day you fall for a roaring bitch with a hidden talent that could suck life out of the rigid cock of Satan, you wouldn't want her to dump you once she found out you had already spent the money that was rightfully hers, now would you?" His eyes widened and I felt sorry we resorted to scaring him like that, but was glad Lisa helped make my point. He nodded slowly like a kindergartener in the principal's office. As always, there was something very compelling about Lisa's Rigid Cock of Satan speech.

Vince stared over at the bridesmaids longingly, like a puppy dog standing at a back door leading out to a large garden filled with bunnies. They gazed back at him encouragingly, but he turned his head and sighed, resigned that he just couldn't deal with empty-headed girls anymore. The timing couldn't have been better if I had planned it ... except, I had planned it.

A woman grabbed him from behind and he stiffened (and not in a good way). I figured he was thinking the hyena leader might be attacking him.

"You take your eyes off of those bitches for one minute and they're all over you ... Surprise, Vince," I said to him. "Although our surprise guest is a little late," I said to her.

"I think I'm just in time to stop temptation," Erica As In All My Children whispered into Vince's ear. He stiffened again, in a good way.

Lisa, Vince, Erica and I had a late dinner once the older folks had turned in for the night. We started out safely enough with Red Stripe beer all around, but somehow the aluminum striped cans morphed into long gold bottles of tequila, and shots were flowing at an alarming rate. The bartender eventually gave up and left the bottle of José Cuervo on our table. Another unadvertised perk of the all-inclusive vacation that I'd have to share with Dad: exhaust the bartender and they will gladly leave you the whole damn bottle.

Lisa, who usually doesn't typically get "over-served" (she says it's a sign of weakness), was the first to sound stupid from the shots, although we had been feeling stupid for several hours now. She was telling a story I could only catch parts of because Vince, Erica and I were laughing like children every time she tripped up on a word. She would repeat the word over and over until she thought she got it right ... although it never was. We were so hysterical with fits of laughter that we didn't see Lorn until after she had already sat down at our table. Vince spotted her first and turned his head slowly as if under water, and I stupidly laughed and mimicked him, only to be nose to nose with Lorn. I was so drunk, I just kept laughing.

"Jesus, give me that," Lorn said, grabbing the bottle off the table. When she saw there were no shot glasses left, she glanced quickly around the emptied room before gulping her shot directly from the bottle. The table broke up laughing again, and I was too drunk to care how stupid we must have looked to her. When Vince asked for Lorn to pass the bottle, she refused and with her gorgeous smirk she said, "Fuck off, Vince, I have to catch up with you drunks."

We laughed as only a group of drunks can laugh, until our stomachs ached and all four of us were wiping tears away. Lorn was catching up quick. I finally choked out a reasonable sentence. "I thought you weren't coming until tomorrow?"

She waited a beat or two before answering. "I thought it might be too uncomfortable," she answered, and then joined our completely out-of-control laughter at absolutely nothing. We locked eyes during the laughter, both relieved to be all right in each other's company. My heart pounded as she leaned in close to me and whispered, "Drink all you want, Marie ... it's not like you're getting behind the wheel of a car; which is a good thing, with your fucking driving record." I almost spewed my drink all over her. When Lisa, Erica and Vince looked at us for an explanation, Lorn gave me an "I'll never tell" wink. My heart melted with the help of the warm alcohol, like hot syrup in my veins.

Lorn was not done teasing me. "Oh, and that really was some crappy idea for a movie you had," she whispered again, leaning even closer. "Tell me you didn't move to California to become a screenwriter."

"That would have been stupid," I said. "I moved to California because I thought I *was* a screenwriter. That was some crappy excuse for a driver you had ... stopping short like that. I could have gotten hurt. I would have been forced to bring a lawsuit ... No offense."

"I may not have even noticed if you did sue me. I've been so busy recruiting so I don't get kicked out of the club," she said raising an eyebrow at me.

"How's that going?" I asked her, fighting a giggle.

"No luck. Everyone in Hollywood is already gay ..."

"You could be cast out on a fucking technicality ... tragic," I said.

"Wait, what about her?" Lorn said, indicating Erica.

"No such luck. Straight as an arrow. Just another actress, I'm afraid."

Lorn's expression softened, "I've missed you terribly," she whispered to me as she reached across me for the bottle.

Vince and Erica missed our entire exchange since they were making eyes at each other, and Lisa was too busy eyeballing the remaining bridesmaid, who was teetering at the end of the bar. A wolf had sensed the prettiest dingo might be a lame drunk, and thus an easy target. But Vince managed to cuff Lisa by the wrist as she made a break for the bar.

We drank another shot as I wondered how this depressing day could have possibly evolved into a moment like this. *It's the tequila*, I thought ... *don't count on tomorrow being any different*. But right now, in this moment, Lorn was close to me and that seemed good enough for now, and remarkably, Jamaica turned beautiful again. As Vince teased Lisa about stalking the young bridesmaid, I took a deep breath of air at the Caribbean bar, which was laced with tequila, sweet pineapple and coconut syrup. If only it could stay just like this, I thought, as I wiped away another random tear of laughter, or maybe it was a tear of sadness, but the beautiful part was, I really couldn't tell, and really didn't care.

Tequila good, I thought.

Chapter Twenty-Two

Tequila Bad

When I awoke the next morning, my first thought was: *Tequila bad.* My second thought was: *Where did all the fucking sand come from?* There was beach sand in my bed and all over my floor, but it was my head and stomach that were getting my attention; thankfully, my head was out-hurting my raw stomach ... for now. The night came back to me in flashes. Had Lorn really been with us, or had it all been a dream?

I remembered her swigging out of the bottle as we all laughed. She had been there. I remembered she said she had arrived a day early fearing it would be too uncomfortable to come on the actual wedding day. I smiled at the way we had all laughed at her statement, despite my pounding head. After that, any details escaped me.

I took a quick shower, pulled my hair into a wet ponytail and threw on shorts and a T-shirt. While it was my head that hurt the most, I knew from past experience that I had to get some bread into my stomach before I missed the opportunity to block my stomach's attempt to take over top hangover position, with most dire results.

I was a little dizzy but the shower had helped and when I left the room, my damp skin felt good as the Caribbean heat steamed the water from my pores. Bread, then coffee, then a nap. The wedding ceremony didn't run the risk of going over sixty minutes since there was another wedding scheduled right after Uncle Tony's. I wondered if the bar bridesmaids would be at one of the other weddings that were sandwiching our family's. Our family ... after today, Lorn would become a part of our family. I was pleased the thought warmed instead of distressed me. As much as I wanted to protect my heart, the truth was, I felt like an attention-starved child, grateful to have whatever connection with her I could; and I tried not to think how difficult it would be to be near her again, especially sober.

I always woke up extra early after drinking, and it was barely six-thirty when I left my room on a bread-and-coffee mission. I reminded myself I should eat all the bread first before allowing myself even one sip of coffee. This was the only sequence of events that could guarantee a graceful exit from tequila hell. I had, through trial and toilet-hugging error during the course of my adult life, finally perfected the correct order I needed to treat a hangover.

I struggled to remember how the night had ended, but couldn't get past the table we had all sat around, laughing and drinking. I had a vague memory of opening the door to my room, since I dropped the room key and nearly kicked it under the locked door, in my drunken state. This hotel still had old-fashioned room keys instead of cards, and I remember thinking of this made me happy, until I struck my head on the doorknob as I stooped to pick it up. That was when I had kicked the key. It was slowly coming back to me, but the clearest thing I could remember was what I had been thinking, rather than what actually happened. I remembered finally managing to grab it with the very tip of my fingernail to coax the key back though the bottom of the door. I was happy with my accomplishment and made a ridiculous promise to myself that if some day Lorn agreed to be with me, we would only stay at a hotel with real keys. Real keys had to start a new life off better than a plastic credit card key.

Then, a hand touched the small of my back as I opened the

door. Oddly, I acted as if I had expected it. That was all I could remember as I arrived at the café in a daze; it was as if I was watching a beautiful scene in a movie playing in my head, like a perfect dream I wanted to escape back into. I wondered what else had happened ...

The bartender had the coffee ready, and was pouring me a mug before I even reached my table. The lovely man met me there with it. "Thanks," I said as images of Lorn began rapidly firing in my head, growing more clear until I gasped into my cup when I remembered her naked and swimming in the ocean with me ... pressing her body against the length of mine ... all the while being so careful not to make a sound, and to stay clear of the lights at the bases of the palms lining the beach. We had moved in complete silence, and I couldn't even remember the water making a sound; the complete silence of the memory made me doubt if it was real. I sipped my coffee in stunned slow motion as the recollection of the swim crystallized in detail; it had happened.

My stomach turned to acid from the coffee and I was reminded of the bread rule, but the memory of my hands sliding down the sides of her smooth and wet body made any thoughts of bagel-hunting vanish from my brain. We had made love ... no, I corrected myself, we had fucked. Fucked like two reckless teenagers, without regard to what it meant, or if it had meant anything at all. I remembered thinking we were probably kissing much too hard for people who would prefer having unswollen lips for wedding photos, but there had been no control then. When I lifted the heavy coffee mug to my lips, this explained the tender, mildly bruised feeling at my mouth. We had kissed very hard. She had only pulled away from me once, and at that moment, I thought: *That's it ... that's all she can give me ... it's over already.*

But it wasn't over. The memory came flooding back now, but in jumbled order ... on our walk back to our rooms she had clung to me, and I had reminded myself repeatedly that she was drunk … it meant nothing more, and it would be a mistake to think anything else. Then she kissed me again and I could think of nothing else. Crossing the beach, she had asked me to swim with her. Her clothes came off first and we briefly forgot about the swimming … then she playfully pulled from me and I chased her like a mad rapist into the water. We came at each other then, under the cover of the warm ocean. There she only pulled away to free her lips to tell me she loved me, and I quickly reeled her back in to me before she could say something counterproductive. We alternated between shallow and shallower water until we gave up all together on navigating raging passion and the bouncing tide, and sprawled out on the wet sand.

I had to be deeply in love, and more deeply drunk, to not think of crabs. (I must clarify: the ocean-dwelling kind.) We were also too drunk to come from touching gently; so thankfully, at that mind and pussy-numbing moment, she allowed me to act like a crazed animal and I plunged into her and hooked my fingers into that special spot deep inside and executed a perfect U-turn … thank you Barbara. And thank you Grandma, since, as well as your money, I inherited your very long fingers (in a lesbian world, this could mean I was a well-endowed catch). She pushed her body against me, begging for more in a raw and desperate voice. *Take that,* I thought … *just try to take that and then leave me again* … I made sure she was going nowhere but to the moon.

"I love you Marie," she cried out in my ear, and for a second I almost shushed her since she was so damned loud. "You know that, right?" she said, "You know how I feel about you?"

And the thing is, she was confessing all of this while coming again and again, just like a champion. Christ, I loved this woman.

Once, when Lisa and I watched a porno movie together, she commented on a woman who was servicing three men orally, simultaneously, and quite expertly. After the money shot she proclaimed with great admiration, "You gotta respect a woman who can take the chowder like a champion." Unfortunately, this saying always rattled in my head at the most inopportune times, and it rattled around plenty while Lorn devoured me on the beach that night.

That was the last thing I remembered. I didn't remember us going back to my room for the second time, although we must have, since half of the beach was all over my floor and in between my sheets—more damage than I could have done alone.

Bread, you fucking idiot, my stomach screamed as an attention-getting wave of nausea swept over me and I began to sweat profusely despite the breezy café. I spotted a tray of rolls near the entrance to the kitchen, and grabbed one with shaking hands, probably with only seconds to spare before I couldn't choke it down over the acid rising in my belly. I finished it before I reached my table, instantly feeling better. But I still could not suppress the uneasy memory I always dredged up whenever I felt I might be sick, or worse, when someone else might be sick in my presence.

It goes like this: Third grade. I noticed the school fat kid, Robert, waving his flabby arm in a panic at the back of the room with that unmistakable look on his face. He was clearly fighting the need to vomit. It was a look I was always on guard for. Please notice him, I silently begged the teacher, who was writing on the board. I hated that teacher for her obliviousness to what was happening. Robert was now stabbing his arm in the air repeatedly, and still she didn't see him. I looked away, not wanting to witness what I knew was going to occur at any moment. I decided I couldn't look, yet when he made the single, loud, very wet burping sound, my head spun around in unison with the rest of the class to look at him. The worse part of him getting sick all over his desk was that the teacher made us all stay in our seats, when, naturally, all we wanted to do was to run out of the room screaming. It had been a lot of puke, and the janitor had to use two school-issued notebooks as squeegees (with spiral bindings facing up, of course), to slide it all into a waste barrel with a heavy thud. So that was how they removed

242

puke in school, I remembered thinking. I had always assumed they had some sort of fancy machine in that janitor's closet, who would have guessed they used composition notebooks? While he scooped (and thus fanned the odor to higher levels), that fucking teacher only slightly cracked open one window while she continued to lecture us as if it was not her fault at all.

Early in the year, the teacher said that the one and only time we could leave our seats without permission was if we felt sick. Fat Robert probably hadn't believed her, since she made us raise our hands even to reach for a pencil that had strayed too far from our desks. Control freak. Fat Robert's nickname was changed to the shortened and more descriptive version, "Ro-Burp." Since the memory of a loud, wet burp prequel to a barfing incident is cutting-edge comedy to boys that age, and a lot more acceptable than being fat, Ro-Burp preferred the change in his name. All's well that ended well. While I had never connected two such unalike thoughts before, in my mind I could hear Lisa profess how that boy spewed his chowder like a champion.

As this memory always did, it re-ignited my waves of nausea, so I have no idea why my mind instantly dredged it up every time I felt sick. I took deep breaths, and while it took a while, gradually it appeared the bread had stopped me from sabotaging myself. I returned to the coffee again, in an effort to release more memories of Lorn, but none came. Naptime, my body was insisting. My head was spinning, I was sweating, and I was wet everywhere, especially where the memory of the nude swim had hit me hardest.

I decided I would be no good to anyone without a nap, so I started for my room, relieved I had not run into my family ... and wondering if Lorn was feeling as I was: dizzy and desperately drunk with the memories of her, and probably still some tequila as well.

Lorn was waiting, in broad daylight I might add, at my door. How could she look that good after all we had to drink last night? Unfair, I thought, as I slowly approached her.

"You're here," I said stupidly.

"I'm here," she answered with a small smile. "Can I come in?"

I led her to the door with my key pointing the way, as I tried to ignore the feeling that I might swoon right there in the damned stairwell. I opened the door and turned to see if she looked worried about who might see her come inside, but her eyes were on mine and signs of worry didn't seem to be what was in them. She was smoldering. I ignored every warning going off in my head to not let her in through the door, and instead with a gallant wave of my arm invited her in.

Apparently, the door clicking behind us had been the signal she was waiting for. She reached out and cupped her hands on either side of my face as if she were the old pro at this, and I was the fretful virgin, and she kissed me, but very, very gently. Her lips were no doubt sore as well. We began touching, I began undressing, and she began confessing.

"I'm sorry, I just can't stay away from you," she said.

"If you think back, I never asked you to, not even once," I said, and added, "... I should have ..."

"But if I can't get this right, you'll some day ask me to stay away," she said.

Not in this fucking lifetime, I thought, but I kept this secret to myself as I kissed along her neck. The smell of her unearthed more memories of how the sand got entrenched in my bed. While she had been out of my life, I had been starved for physical intimacy worse than ever before, and sex, which I could, in the past with Jess, give up for months on end, had now become a physical requirement with this woman ... like heroin, like chocolate ... like Howard Stern on satellite radio (after all, he talked dirty and worshipped lesbians, too).

This was the real deal. Even in the beginning of my relationship with Jess, there hadn't been this burning heat and desperate hunger. Maybe because there was never the discussion of IF we would be together, and IF what I wanted was what she wanted. Jess and I had simply begun, and our sex life, while satisfying, was a long way from red hot and desperate. It was more like luke-warm and cautious. I wished desperation could only be reserved for when you're not with the person you loved ... It didn't seem fair that I should always feel it with this woman, even *while* I was with her.

Lorn led me to the bed as if we were in her room instead of mine ... she was on a mission, and I was on a high that I didn't care to end. I illogically reasoned I needed to have her once more so when I had the faculties intact to remember tomorrow, and forever, I could; regardless of what happened, I wanted that. She had me lie down on the bed and lowered her body on top of me. Her softness astounded me yet again. This is what a real woman feels like, I thought, grateful that Lorn could not hear my tacky comparisons between her voluptuous curves and the sharper, more angular body of Jess. I had always been seeking flesh on Jess, trying to grab handfuls, but always ending up pinching bone or thin muscle. Lorn had enough flesh to feed my hungry hands, and I grabbed fistfuls of breast and hip and her glorious behind as she roughly straddled me. She seemed to be in a rush to have this ... was it before I could change *my* mind? She clearly had no idea of the impossibility of this.

I wanted to feel again what I was struggling to remember from last night; needing to see her come for me. But Lorn had latched on to my nipple like a starved kitten, and wasn't going to give me the inch I needed to slip my hand between us. I waited patiently for the moment, feeling the need building between my legs from her now frenzied sucking. She moved to straddle me higher, and this time, I was ready and slipped my hand between us, and into her body. This time she let out a deep groan before repeating my name, and I almost joined her with an orgasm of my own, simply from the sound and feel of her. She was the hangover drug I had been craving ... the morning-after pill to make last night's trans-gressions all right again. There would be plenty of time to worry about losing her tomorrow ... right now, I just wanted her to lose it.

She was pushing almost violently against my hand now, driving me deeper, and as she came, I thought: *How will you walk away this time, now that I've taken you like this?* I hooked my fingers into her to make her realize she hadn't really come very hard at all before, but she would now ... I had her like a marlin on my hook; she would not be getting away from me this time.

Chapter Twenty-Three

Wedding Gay

We awoke in a panic, but thankfully hadn't slept through the entire morning. As Lorn scurried to gather her things to get back to her room, I felt the too-familiar surge of panic at seeing her head for the door.

"Hey," I said nonchalantly, like maybe she simply forgot her lunch money. She turned and apologetically walked back to me. She stared at me for a moment before planting a warm kiss on my lips. This was enough to flip the switch again, and we kissed harder before we both realized there was no time to go down that road again. She smiled a small smile before we wrenched apart and she bolted out the door to go get ready in her room. Even though I knew why she needed to bolt, it did not stop me from feeling bolted from; but thankfully there was zero brooding time to think about this.

Erica As In All My Children greeted us on the way to the bar with her hands planted firmly on her hips. "Sorry, couples only at this bar," she said blocking our entrance. "By the way, I love your TV show," she said to Lorn. Lorn couldn't suppress a quiet laugh as Erica continued, "If you ever need someone to play a jealous lesbian on your show, I'm obviously up to the task. This decorator thing is just my day job. And you know I have no interest in Marie, here, no offense," she said to me. "Her brother ... maybe," she said as Vince approached and encircled his arms around her. Vince looked content for the first time in his life.

"What do you mean, decorating is just your day job?" I said, "I let you rip beams out from the underside of my house while it overhangs a cliff? Not to mention, I gave you a pile of money to buy into that expendable day job of yours!"

"Just because I can multi-task, doesn't mean I'm not great at my job," she snorted. "Just look at this haircut I gave your brother," she said, playfully tugging what was left of his hair. "Tell me I can't do anything I set my mind to?"

"I would never tell you that, Erica," I said.

"Nice haircut, Vince," Lisa called out from behind him, "I like how you left it a little longer in the back. Hey, I think they wrote a song about you on the Internet, it's called 'Mullet-Style Haircut,' you should check it out!" This sent Vince in a panic scurrying to the nearest reflective surface. She delighted in his panic, and her ability to push just the right buttons. Lisa laughed and slapped her own knee. "I kill me," she said, gleefully toddling after him to continue her game of torture.

Erica regained her focus on Lorn. "So what the hell is the deal with you two anyway? Are you a fucking couple, or what?"

Now it was my turn to take a step back. I had no idea how to answer the question, and since it was directed at Lorn, all I could do was wait to find out what the deal was.

Lisa walked by with impeccable timing as usual, "They're a fucking couple all right."

Erica stared back at Lorn, still waiting for her answer. Lorn found herself perched on yet another hook. "The deal?" Lorn asked.

Lorn looked at me for help, but I decided to sit this one out, since I really wanted to hear the answer too.

"Stop stalling," Erica said to her.

I said it before; this Erica girl was good. However, Lorn still looked hard pressed for an answer.

I finally took pity on Lorn. "Erica, it's complicated," I said. But

248

I thought it really wasn't complicated at all. Erica ignored me and honed in on Lorn again.

"Staaaaalling again," she said in a most annoying voice, making a big production of checking her watch.

I made a mental note to give her a nice bonus when the holidays rolled around, since Erica had recently decided I needed to take over the books for our business.

Lorn turned back to Erica. "The deal is ..." she had started, so strong, only to fall silent again. I waited patiently, but Erica was starting to grow bored with the dyke drama, and was now glancing over to the bar to see where Vince had strayed.

"The deal is," Lorn tried again, but her voice sounded less sure of what she was about to say.

"Marie and I ... are together," she finally said, but I noticed she exhaled a puff of air like she'd just delivered the bad news in a hospital waiting room. Hey, it was a start, I thought, as I winced a smile back at her.

"Nooooo," Erica said in mock horror, with both hands covering the sides of her face, *Home Alone* style. She had been bored into rudeness. I've seen this happen, even to polite people. Although I wouldn't categorize Erica as a polite person, she was by no means rude. But much like my sister, she only had a reserved amount of patience for people of the world who lacked balls. She looked like she wanted to give Lorn a little tap across the noggin and say, "Get over it!" and actually, I could relate to that. Erica raised her eyebrows and smiled at me in an "Aren't you lucky you got what you wanted" look before strutting off to bar to cheerlead Vince and Lisa into gulping a round of shots. Lisa was tugging hard at the back of Vince's hair, and teasing "You look like one of our people now!"

Well, Erica got her to answer, however weakly. Say what you would about Erica As In All My Children, she was a can-do gal. Lorn, on the other hand, continued to be my not-so-sure-she-could-do-a-girl girl.

❖ ❖ ❖

Everyone gathered around the wedding gazebo and, as if we had taken a silent pact, the younger people politely ignored the Celine Dion song which blared through the crackling Jamaican-made "Sound-Tech-Mon" boom box. I had made it just in time, and I spotted Lorn quickly crossing the other side of the lawn as I stood waiting in front of the gazebo like an expectant groom.

There were three photographers standing nearby, although the wedding party had hired only one. There were also several reporters with notebooks, and I recognized one of them as one of the blond anorexic women from *Entertainment Tonight*, but thankfully, there was no sign of our greasy reporter. Maybe between my antics and Vince's, he had thought better than come back to Jamaica.

To my surprise, Lorn crossed right past the clicking cameras, to take a place by my side. The cameras chattered among the crowd like crickets, and the photographers competed for the best angle, not of the wedding couple, but of us, the two women standing under a wedding gazebo. This photo just might make Lorn appear a bit suspect to the fans of *Razor Falls*. There was one young woman who joined our wedding party whom I couldn't identify, until I glanced at Lisa, who was standing next to her, giving the victory sign in close proximity to her lips, to slide her tongue in between her fingers, of course. It was the bridesmaid from the bar ... appropriately dressed in her bridesmaid outfit, pulling a double shift.

Katherine smiled at Lorn and me before giving her full attention to Uncle Tony, who was beaming. Mom and Dad looked over at us as well, and to my even greater surprise, I found them both looking with an approving stare, and I thought I even detected a nod from Mom, and was impressed, until I remembered that compared with Lisa and her hung-over-bridesmaid-one-night-stand, Lorn and I looked downright respectable. I turned to sneak a peek at Lorn and found that, while clearly she was nervous, she had grown the balls to smile and wink at me, and I melted in the sun like a pudding at a picnic.

The ceremony was simple and the imported white minister totally devoid of personality, but it was Uncle Tony's beaming smile that eventually transfixed our attention off the Hollywood cameras and on to the event at hand. The minister realized he was wasting precious wedding-business minutes waiting for the cameras to stop clicking, so he finally chose to speak louder to drown them out. Unfortunately, this gave the effect of the couple being shouted at, but with Uncle Tony's hearing, he didn't seem to notice, although I noticed his soon-to-be-wife recoiled from the shouting a couple of times. I could hear Vince and Dad's distinctive giggles in the crowd and then a discreet slap from Mom, which silenced them. Just for fun, I gave her back her nod of approval, and she lifted her chin with the prideful message: Don't fuck with the Momma.

Uncle Tony held Katherine's hands, and on this day, he appeared a man reborn from years of pain. When the newly married couple kissed for the first time, I felt the back of Lorn's hand pressed against the back of mine. Without actually clasping it, she was holding my hand the only way she felt she could, but the side of her body was close to mine, and even with a small distance between us, I thought I could feel her warmth; but more likely it was just our proximity to the equator.

Uncle Tony asked for everyone's attention, and although we were near the ocean, it seemed that everything went still and silent for him. Only the plentiful butterflies and one long-tailed bird silently passed above him as he spoke. He gave a gentlemanly clearing of his throat as we collectively held our breaths; and I noticed that Katherine did too. A reporter's camera broke the silence, but it made such a clatter that he only took one photograph before lowering it sheepishly to his side as we all admonished him with our stares.

"I won't keep you all standing in the hot sun for long, but I'd like to say something to my entire family ... and, thank the good Lord, this now includes my beautiful Katherine." He stopped for a moment before continuing, as if struck temporarily dumb by

251

her beauty once again. She was radiant, and for a brief moment I felt a pang of jealousy that Lorn would never stand by my side like that.

"I have no idea how I went from being the loneliest man alive to the luckiest, in a simple few months; but I have." It was probably the cracking of his voice that made tears burn in the corners of my eyes; or maybe it was Lorn's trembling hand that now smoothly entwined mine so naturally, that I hadn't even noticed she'd been clasping my hand for several seconds.

He continued, as I watched Vince, Lisa, Aggie, Dad and even my mother guiding the unexpected tears sprinkling from their lashes. We all knew Uncle Tony had been lonely; we all knew he'd felt more pain than he, or any of us, had experienced in our lifetimes ... but to hear him say it somehow made it real ... and to hear that it now had all passed made this perfect day even sweeter.

He turned to Katherine to speak to her directly, and her eyes filled as well. "I thought my life was over ... so I'll always cherish you, my Katherine ... I've learned if you're willing to take the chance, you may be lucky enough to experience the magic of love again ... and in my case, I'm the luckiest of everyone ... that you, a woman I couldn't possibly deserve, has agreed to take a place by my side ... thank you, Katherine, my love," he said, slightly raising both of her hands in his grasp, "for taking away the darkness and pain, and handing me heaven ... for however long we are meant to be on this earth. I can easily promise I will never disappoint you, or take our love for granted ... I'm blessed to know how rare it is, indeed."

Uncle Tony turned to his family and said in his grandest outdoor voice, "If an old man can teach his family one thing about life, I hope that it is this. That this is more important than anything else ... that this is what we are all here for. To know and share a great love."

My dad slipped his arm around Mom and gave a small squeeze, and I saw that Vince and Lisa had not missed that moment too.

Lorn squeezed my hand then, and let go as she encircled her arm around me. In an instant, the cameras started clicking, feeding on the moment in such a frenzy that I was afraid to turn to look at her. It was obvious the cameras were shooting past the wedding couple at us. I instinctively tried to step aside, but she held me hard, though I could feel her body trembling. The cameras shot faster.

I finally turned to look at her.

I whispered, "You realize they're shooting at us? You're giving them the story they came here for."

"I hope this doesn't sound too Hollywood, but I'm giving them the story I came here for," she moved closer to me and took hold of both sides of my face.

She has gone temporarily insane; what on earth is she thinking?

She kissed me full on the mouth. The cameras were now in a frenzy to capture the moment; but they needn't have hurried. Lorn lingered at my lips, trembling, but not weakly, kissing me. I heard Aggie gasp as everyone turned to see what directed the reporters' attention, and I peeked over to see my mother hold her head firmly up high, as if it was the most natural sight in the world. When Lorn finally pulled away, all eyes except Katherine and Uncle Tony's were on us. They were sharing a lovely kiss of their own, with only the one official wedding photographer bothering to capture it on film.

"Why?" I whispered to Lorn.

"Who am I to throw away a chance for love and a life with you?" she said. "Your uncle just explained how rare it is … weren't you even paying attention?"

"You may have doomed yourself to a life of cameras chasing you," I said.

"Actually, I've doomed you … think you'll mind?" she asked, in the same casual tone as you would ask to change the TV channel.

I didn't think I would.

I kissed her once more, briefly, so we wouldn't steal the show, but the cameras were poised and ready and whirred and clicked away as Uncle Tony and Katherine kissed on, not noticing the world outside their gazebo.

Later, when the wedding party had dispersed, Lorn went for a private walk with her mother and the ecstatic groom, who suddenly had the bounce in his step of a twenty-year-old. I took an equally enthusiastic walk with Vince, Erica and Lisa to the café bar. I had finally convinced Vince there were too many rolls of film for him to steal and "feed to the fishes" and he gave up trying to intimidate the paparazzi.

"To the groom," Vince said, raising his glass from the bar, and I slugged him in the arm because I knew from his smirk he had meant me. I raised my glass anyway.

"Aggie actually gasped," Lisa said, raising her glass as well. "Good for Lorn! For fuck's sake why would anyone want to be repressed in this day and age?" Lisa shouted towards the reporters milling about. "Go ahead and take your pictures! Repression sucks the life out of a society!" she ranted. "Didn't we fucking learn anything from *Footloose*?"

Vince tried to cover Lisa's shouting mouth with her hand while Erica encouraged her by laughing until she snorted. There's another girl who would have the courage to marry into this family, I thought.

"Let her yell, Vince," I said. "Who cares? We're rich." And for the first time, I actually felt like I was.

Epilogue

Don't Ask, Do Yell

The wedding photos made the front page of three out of the four major rag mags, and would have made the fourth, if it hadn't been for a drug overdose by a popular rock band's front man, which happened just before press time. Had the overdose happened just an hour later, the photo of Lorn "planting a kiss on independently wealthy female companion, Maria Santora" might not have been demoted to an inside page. Also, I happily noted, they spelled my first name wrong, however slightly. However, they got all of Lorn's information just perfectly.

Lorn handed me the clippings from the papers and sat on the couch next to me. "Sent by FedEx, courtesy of my management agency, just in case I didn't happen by a newsstand."

"Were they pissed?"

"Yes. But only because I didn't tell them, so they weren't able to 'spin the story in a way which would bring the most positive publicity.' This is a strange business I'm in," she said.

The photographers each had slightly different shots so all magazines could each claim they had exclusive photos, but it would have taken a forensic examiner to determine the difference. In each shot, Lorn was kissing me full on the mouth with varying panoramic shots of most of the wedding party not yet noticing us, but that didn't stop one of the papers from printing the ridiculously long headline: *"Relatives Stare in Shock as Lorn Elaine's Companion Exposes Secret During Family*

Wedding." Another one read: *"Aggressive Kiss by Companion Ends the Elaine Family's Don't Ask, Don't Tell Policy."*

"Fuckers!" I said.

"I knew the choice I was making when I did it," Lorn said, a bit smugly.

"Not that; they made me out to be the aggressive dyke! You were the one that kissed me!"

When I turned to her to say, "Now my reputation as a decorator's assistant will be in the toilet ..." she clocked me in the head with a sofa cushion before I could finish the sentence.

When I finally stopped laughing, I said to her, "Don't worry, they'll soon tire of covering our scandalous nights out to dinner and a movie." I patiently explained lesbians only make great press at the beginning and end of their relationships; as long as we stayed together, they'd surely get bored. It's the gay boys who really know to stay in the spotlight; photos of lesbians holding hands in the park eventually get to be as exciting news as watching paint dry.

I asked her, "So why the hell did you do it right then, when it was guaranteed that all the reporters would get the story?"

"Besides being inspired by Uncle Tony's words? ... I knew once I was exposed, there would be no point in trying to deny myself a life with you."

"So this is the lesbo-actress version of getting yourself knocked up to entrap yourself in a relationship?" I asked.

"Pretty romantic, isn't it?" she said.

It really kind of was.

Note from the Author

I like themes, and if I had to pick one for my biography it would be: Everybody is a frustrated-something-or-other, aren't they? When I was very young, I was frustrated I was not a boy—not because of the whole penis thing, although that has its points; it was simply because young Italian boys were not expected to wash dishes (I'm sure Mom wishes she could go back and change this, for all the post-childhood ribbing she has taken from my sister and me). To get out of doing housework I may have opted to go under the knife as a kid ... but, as they say in the medical books, "it's easier to dig a hole than build a pole" so I suppose I was lucky this was not to be. In the end, I decided to try never getting married to see if this might get me out of washing dishes ... it has not.

Next, I was a frustrated jock who was always trying to keep up with my sister in sports. I was better than your average girl but I could not hold a candle next to my sister and the boys in the neighborhood. I have a theory about that too. It involves my giant boobs ... the "girls" had not appeared yet, but judging by their eventual arrival, my body was probably too busy producing giant milk ducts to bother learning the nuances of field hockey. I will never forget when I broke my first heart. It was my sister's field hockey coach, who could not wait for me to get to high school to follow in my sister's footsteps. I knew I had destroyed all her hopes and dreams of having another All State athlete from the SanGiovanni family when she took me off the field to gently ask, "Are you her *biological* sister?" I was pretty sure I was ... but that Mexican boy who looked back from the photos always made me wonder. (See photo on my website.)

Later, I was frustrated in my desperate attempt to steal top honors as Top Drawer in our family. This is not the person who has access to the coveted top drawer for storing underwear (those of you who had to share a room with an older sister will laugh at that one). I was a frustrated artist ever since the portrait of *The Deer* was hung up in a place of honor in the hallway of my grandmother's house, right across from the bleeding Jesus with the sexy smile. *The Deer* was a pencil drawing by my sister of a deer jumping over a hand-shaped tree stump. I believe she actually drew that tree stump by tracing my brother's little hand, and so I threatened to expose her for the trickster that she was. (Okay, I didn't actually threaten to expose her ... she could have easily kicked my butt, hid the evidence, and scared me silent with a well-crafted threat, all before Mom could make it up the fourteen stairs to our bedroom ... but I sure thought about exposing her.) She had the gall to give *The Deer* to my grandmother, knowing that this would forever cement her as Top Drawer of the family. And oh boy, did it ever. Grandma lit candles on the table below it whenever she had guests. Thinking back, it may have been for Jesus, but at the time it looked to me like it was to highlight the underbelly of that jumping deer.

I did actually become a professional designer and attended college at Rhode Island School of Design, where all the young artists tried to look different by wearing the same spiked hair and paint-splattered black clothes and pierced eyebrows. (I escaped with both of my virgin eyebrows unscathed, but my closet is filled with tons of black clothes.) At RISD, I majored in illustration since my plan was to draw deer in children's books ... but while in college learning how to be an illustrator, I promptly became a frustrated sculptor. I would not let myself change majors since my decision to be a designer was risky enough. I didn't know a single soul who actually made a living as an artist, except for art teachers, so I thought pursuing a career in stone sculpting would be pushing it a bit. While in college, I got into acting and was in a short film which got picked up by the Playboy channel ... I hasten to add I played a fully clothed (not my choice) witch who places a spell on a cheating husband so that his dick falls off and runs away from him across several lanes of traffic. (My Mexican boy's influence?)

Toward the end of college, I became a frustrated writer and revealed my pursuit by re-writing episodes of *The Love Boat* to include my favorite actresses. After graduating, with student loans looming over my head, I took a job at a local chemical company, emptying huge barrels of blue dye powder (used to color Levi jeans) into large vats ... I would come home and sneeze blue snots into yellow Kleenexes and mourn the fact that blue and yellow really do make green, and I would probably never work as a professional artist ... alas, I had become a frustrated illustrator again.

I landed a design job three months after graduating school and stayed there for many years. During that time, I realized how commercial "commercial art" could become when you are drawing to pay the bills instead of drawing to provide Jesus a new roommate on Grandma's wall. I became a frustrated writer once again. I promptly wrote three silly books just to exercise my skills at writing sex scenes. It was the most fun I ever had in a creative pursuit; however, when I read the books it seemed as if a generic writer had written them instead of me. I ignored this nagging thought the whole time I was collecting rejection slips from publishing companies. I ended my writing career by locking the manuscripts in a closet for over ten years. That ought to teach them, I thought ... oddly, the world of publishing did not collapse due to my absence.

I became a frustrated stone sculptor and painter once again, until I spotted an ad on the Internet for a writing contest for which the submission requirements dictated you had to send a paper copy rather than a digital copy of a manuscript. (I saw this as a sign, as I did not have a digital copy of any of my three manuscripts, since the computer I wrote them on was an Amiga, and no longer exists except in the bowels of eBay listings.) I got a message back from Bywater Books: The good news was I had placed third in the contest, but the bad news was they were only interested in the first ten pages where I had attempted to be funny. If I could simply cut the last 250 pages and start over, they *might* be interested in publishing it since those first ten pages had shown potential. (Thinking back on it now, I believe this may have been my "Let Her Down Easy" call, but I was too stupid or stubborn to get it.)

I wrote like a madwoman and ditched all but about one paragraph of the original story. Kelly Smith at Bywater had told me to focus more on my wacky Italian family and less on the romantic drivel and the tons of sex ... oh, and she also told me I might try to move the story to a vacation destination where the family will be all trapped together while the plot unfolds. Since I am a Caribbean whore, I loved this idea and immediately imagined the meatball scene and was off and running. *Voilà!* The novel *Greetings from Jamaica* was born. I could be wrong, but I don't think Bywater really expected me to toss out all but ten pages and contact them with a new book, but I was at the height of a resurgence of my frustrated-writer phase, so the timing was good. (I had started buying leather-bound journals again, and this is always the first sign that my frustrations are mutating to a higher level ... the funny thing is, I never write in the journals ... I am a Mac laptop girl, but the smell of the dead deerskin always gets my creative and competitive juices flowing.)

Currently, I work full time for a large company in Boston as a Vice President of Product Development, which is a fancy way of saying that I lead a team of designers who design products for the tabletop, home décor, and giftware industries (... which is a fancy way of saying there is a good chance you have had one of my forks in your mouth ... I hope it was as good for you as it was for me). *Greetings From Jamaica, Wish You Were Queer* is my first published book, and my next manuscript, *Liddy-Jean, Marketing Queen,* took first place in Bywater's second annual writing contest (I am happy to report I have improved on my ten-page acceptance rate). Besides writing, I still like to carve stone ... it makes me feel so butch until I start weeping over breaking one of my fabulous fingernails.

I aspire to uphold in life my favorite phrase floating around the Internet: *Life should NOT be a journey to the grave with the intention of arriving safely in an attractive and well-preserved body, but rather to skid in sideways, chocolate in one hand, wine in the other, body thoroughly used up, totally worn out and screaming, "WOO HOO, what a ride!"* I have just skidded past my fortieth year and keep waiting for my taste in humor to grow up. No sign of it yet, as I am a slave to Howard Stern, *South Park*, and all humor inappropriate ... thanks, Dad.

Thanks for buying my book. For the latest news on upcoming novels (and some really embarrassing photos), please visit my website: www.greetingsfromjamaica.com or, after you read my email address out loud, drop me a note at: MariLaughs@cox.net.

Mari SanGiovanni
Lost in Rhode Island
January 2007